By Michael R. Davidson

Harry's Rules

Eye for an Eye

Incubus

The Incubus Vendetta

The Inquisitor and the Maiden

Retribution

Krystal

By Kseniya Kirillova

A Rehearsal of Life

(Репетиция Жизни)

IN THE SHADOW OF MORDOR
(Под сенью Мордора)

In the Shadow of Mordor

Copyright © 2016
Michael R. Davidson & Kseniya Kirillova

MRD Enterprises, Inc.
PO BOX 1000
Mount Jackson, VA 22842-1000
mrdenter@shentel.net

Library of Congress Control Number: 2016918565
ISBN 978-0-692-80520-6

Cover by Damonza
Russian-English Translation and editing by Michael R. Davidson

In the development of this novel the authors were inspired in part by actual events that have been amply reported in the press and literature.

Having made this clarification it is important to emphasize that this is a work of fiction and the situations described, as well as the characters and their actions are imaginary.

Michael R. Davidson is a former officer of the Central Intelligence Agency, and having reviewed the manuscript, as required by law, the CIA requires the following disclaimer:

"All statements of act, opinion, or analysis expressed are those of the author and do not reflect the official positions or views of the CIA or any other US Government agency. Nothing in the contents should be construed as asserting or implying US Government authentication of information or Agency endorsement of the author's views. This material has been reviewed by the CIA to prevent the disclosure of classified information."

FORWARD

Not being able to go home to your own country, to see your parents, to bury your loved ones or just visit their graves – these are probably the smallest of sacrifices today's dissident exiles must bear. This is especially true for those who actively come out against the war the Kremlin unleashed against Ukraine. Some people sacrificed their freedom simply for posting opposing views of the war in social media. The reality is that everyone, every day is forced to endure brutality, slander, persecution and more.

In this book we created a collective image of the Russian dissident. There is some exaggeration for dramatic effect - not every non-conforming journalist is murdered, although the journalistic profession in Russia has truly become dangerous. This is hardly a new situation. In Russia today, just as it has been in Russia throughout the centuries, particularly in the last century, the lives of the very best people are deliberately destroyed.

However, the purpose of our book is not simply to depict the inequities of life. Life is and always has been basically unfair. Fortunately, people who have "experienced Russia" are cynical enough to have a good laugh at quests for justice. Natives of the former USSR learned a long time ago to substitute the word "price" for the word "injustice."

All of these injustices are simply the price one pays to have a clear conscience. It's the fee you must pay for the moral right to consider yourself NOT a scoundrel. And the price is exactly as much as you have paid, and not a gram less. That's how it has to be; you can't accomplish anything otherwise.

This is the essence of the chronic age-old curse of Russia. The Kremlin's crimes impose on the most ordinary people – not the military or civil servants, but simply common people – a choice between extremes: between a feat of bravery and an act of depravity. The pathological demands of this criminal regime pull into its orbit as many ordinary people as possible, drawing them into mutually assured participation in terrible acts and leaving little opportunity to avoid the bad choice. For some categories of people – soldiers, officials, journalists, human rights activists, teachers, judges, etc., there is no choice at all.

In a country where a feat of bravery is required NOT to become an accomplice to a morally repugnant act, a third option is often unavailable. People are forced to perform brave and sacrificial acts, not to become heroes, but to avoid complicity in pervasive collective crimes, simply because "they couldn't do anything else."

How do you explain to a resident of a civilized western country that a government can drive ordinary people into the most inconceivable and unacceptable of situations, demanding that they approve of the most savage criminal acts, while stigmatizing disapproval and dissent itself as a crime, where you are deemed a criminal for simply clicking "like" on a social media page? And those people for whom a clear conscience outweighs fear or hypocritical conformity are forced to sacrifice everything – their security, their homeland, and their freedom–just to escape an overall "presumption of guilt," to rid themselves of their portion of the guilt that surrounds them and with which they find it impossible to live. Not because they dreamed of heroic deeds, but just to be able to keep living with a clear conscience. For this, they at times must pay an exorbitantly high price.

It is truly horrifying that from time immemorial Russia has forced her citizens (both her own and others) to pay too high a price for things that usually cost less in normal countries. The price of victory in World War II was a sea of soldiers' blood, ineptly used as cannon fodder, and then another sea of blood and sweat from those who managed to return from German captivity only to be sent to the GULAG - all to calm the paranoid fears of an arrogant "leader." And so invalids are sent to Valaam[1] so they won't be eyesores for the "leader." The price for the industrial surge: millions dead from hunger, tortured and exhausted from hard labor in the camps, where even children and teenagers were made to work. Stiffened corpses in the frozen tundra. The suffocating train cars filled with people of different nationalities, such as the Crimean Tatars, who died before reaching their place of deportation. That is the "price" paid for the Soviet Union whose collapse has been called "the greatest geopolitical catastrophe."

[1] ... disabled veterans, whose continuing need for more support was unwelcome evidence of the Soviet state's inability or unwillingness to adequately provide for all citizens' needs. During the late 1940s and 1950s disabled veterans were dispersed from Moscow and other large cities for forced resettlement in remote areas. According to Fieseler (2006:51), kolkhoz supervisors in rural areas, in order to shed inefficient disabled workers, sometimes turned them in as "parasites;" such workers were then deported, presumably to labor camps. Penal camps were established in the Soviet Union for disabled prisoners and disabled veterans of the Russian Civil War and the two World Wars. The most infamous of these is the Spasskaya labor colony near Karaganda, Kazakhstan, to which 15,000 disabled prisoners were sent in the late 1940s and early 1950s (Solzhenitsyn 1985). Similarly, disabled veterans of the Second World War were secretly exiled from Leningrad (now St. Petersburg) and Leningrad oblast' to the Valaam archipelago, in the Republic of Karelia (Russian Federation). Valaam and the fate of those veterans are still shrouded in mystery (Fefelov 1986:51-57).

And that's precisely the price that Russia is now making Ukraine pay. The price for freedom, for moving toward Europe, is war. Tanks, BUKs, grad missiles, mortars attacks on residential homes, destroyed Debaltseve, strikes on Mariupol, torture in the cellars of occupied Donetsk. That's the price people are paying for their desire to choose their own path, their own vector of development, their own identity. Not a gram less.

We are driven again and again into choosing between extremes: freedom or war, heroism or depravity. And the 10-15% of Russians who turn out not to have adapted to life in the swamp of ubiquitous depravity are involuntarily forced to become heroes. Although all they really wanted at the start was one thing: the opportunity to live a normal life. Yet, stubbornly, it turns out that not a single generation in Russia has been afforded such a luxury.

I've written before that Russians love to rebuke the West for being so "delicate," arguing with examples of the great heroism of the Russian people. Without disputing these examples, I want to remind our compatriots: this is not something to boast about. A normal society doesn't have to give birth to heroes. Heroism is born in conditions of trauma, repression, betrayal, and cowardice. It's tempered in persecution, crystallized in torture. It learns to love and to fight not by virtue of these conditions, but in resisting them. A feat of bravery is an indicator of an unhealthy society, the terrible conditions prevailing in it, the extremely high level of baseness. Heroism is the exceptional situation, and a true hero is not some superman fighter, but rather the hero starts out a traumatized, crippled individual. The personal example that he sets is one of pain and hardship, a sacrifice that is the fate of few.

Troubadours who get carried away with Romanticism forget that heroism is an extreme condition for the individual, and one does not survive without its scars.

There is a controversial saying that in some ways is very appropriate: "Heroes are needed in the moment of danger; the rest of the time, they are dangerous." To paraphrase it, we can say: "Heroes are needed in times of misfortune; the rest of the time, they are unfortunate." A feat is always a rupture, and often payment for someone else's baseness and wrongdoing. This is what destroys a person's ability to live a normal life.

And looking at the current state of Russian society, one can't help but pose the question: what sort of example will all this leave behind for future generations? After all, 85% [Putin's approval rating], that's an example of cowardice, conformity, a bizarre mixture of indifference, delusion, and in some cases, conscious depravity. And the remaining 15% – this is again an example of the maimed, the poisoned, the traumatized survivors of loss and actions for which they clearly were not prepared. They just could not do anything else. Once again we find ourselves unable to set the standard norm, the example of the golden mean, the model of the life of a normal person in a normal society. Again we have not been allowed to develop a normal life because exceedingly brutal conditions have been set before us, requiring an inevitable choice between extremes.

The same problem faced by Russian dissidents now confronts Ukraine: how to survive the loss, the pain, the tragedy of war and build a normal society, how to switch from a regime of constant struggle to one that builds a future. After all, this is where our long-term victory is: Not simply to survive, or to endure sacrifice, but to learn to live with this experience. To love, to create, not to forget about our own lives. And most importantly – to be happy. Otherwise, the exorbitant price we had to pay will have been in vain.

Kseniya Kirillova
2016

This book is dedicated to the brave Russian dissidents who face daily persecution, imprisonment, and even death. Their battle is freedom's battle, and they carry the torch for us all.

In The Shadow of Mordor

Michael R. Davidson
&
Kseniya Kirillova

©2016

The wood plank floor of the old house was rough against her cheek as she slowly, painfully regained consciousness. Her limbs were stiff with cold, and she remembered snow so heavy that even the old four-wheel drive truck struggled to climb the narrow road that wound upward to wherever she was now.

Her two captors were getting loud and probably drunk in an adjoining room. They spoke Russian, although with a distinct Kavkaz accent. Their choking laughter turned to howls, like ravaging wolves, and her heart rose to her throat. She recognized one word "девочка," girl.

Her wrists and ankles were bound. It was strange that she hadn't noticed at first, but the shock of coming to in such primitive surroundings and the raucous voices of the men who had snatched her from her apartment must have numbed her reactions – that and the cold. It must be near freezing in the room and several degrees colder where she lay on the floor.

The journey to this place had been a long one, both in terms of time and distance, and experience, too. She supposed it must have started that day so long ago in Moscow when they broke into Golovina's apartment.

"Once to every man and nation,
Comes the moment to decide,
In the strife of truth with falsehood,
for the good or evil side."

James Russel Lowell

CHAPTER 1

Frantic barking shattered the silence from somewhere in the semi-darkness ahead. Olga Vladimirovna Polyanskaya pasted herself against the wall with a half-desperate glance over her shoulder toward the brightly lit hallway and the raised voices behind her. Vovchik was arguing loudly with the people in the other room, and Pasha was jamming the video recorder in their faces as he peppered the American diplomat with questions.

She slipped farther down the dark corridor looking for any object she might use against the dog when a dirty little mongrel about the size of a cat sprang from the open door of the office. It regarded Olga with bulging eyes half hidden under shaggy hair with that mixture of stupidity and vulgarity common in lapdogs. Without warning it started bouncing and barking without moving toward her.

"Scat!" she hissed as she sidled into the room. It took only a moment to locate the switch, and bright light spilled over the narrow space of the office. The entire room was lined with metal racks with neat rows of shelves containing cardboard folders. The folders held decades-old, dog-eared documents with names, black and white photos and other excerpts from peoples' lives typed tersely into the spaces of forms.

Olga selected a file at random and began to untie the ribbon, but the shriveled cardboard crumbled under her fingers to reveal a stack of photocopies of court decisions and yellowed newspaper clippings. *"27 OCTOBER 1937, RED ARMY SOLDIERS VIKULOV AND GRIGORIEV WHILE SERVING IN THEIR UNIT CONDUCTED COUNTER-REVOLUTIONARY AND SLANDEROUS AGITATION DIRECTED AGAINST THE POLICIES OF THE PARTY AND GOVERNMENT CONCERNING WORKERS' LIVING CONDITIONS. THEY ATTEMPTED TO DISCREDIT THE STALINIST CONSTITUTION AND THE INVESTIGATIVE ORGANS OF THE RED ARMY. IN ADDITION, VIKULOV SPOKE OUT IN FAVOR OF ENEMIES OF THE PEOPLE WHO EARLIER WORKED AT KRASNOYARSK STATION ..."*

This wasn't what she was after.

She grabbed another clipping but it, too, concerned times long past. *"THE SUPREME COURT OF THE USSR PRONOUNCED ITS JUST VERDICT AGAINST A GANG OF HEINOUS CRIMINALS, TRAITORS TO THE MOTHERLAND. THE SENTENCE OF THE SOVIET COURT SERVES AS A WARNING TO THOSE WHO SHARPEN THEIR SWORDS AGAINST OUR MIGHTY SOCIALIST MOTHERLAND. THERE IS AND WILL NEVER BE MERCY FOR THE ENEMIES OF THE SOVIET PEOPLE AND THE ENEMIES OF SOCIALISM. MAY THIS NOW AND FOREVER BE A REMINDER FOR THE CAPITALIST BARBARIANS. LIKE AN ENDURING WALL, WE RALLY AROUND COMRADE STALIN AND HIS FAITHFUL COMPANIONS."*

She was wasting precious time. Olga withdrew a camera from her bag and snapped quick shots of the shelves, one after another, hoping the lens would pick out something overlooked in her rushed search. At the rear of the office she spotted a desk with a new computer. Beside it was a printer that still smelled of recent use. Like a hunter who spots his prey after a long pursuit, she rushed to the desk and rifled through the papers, her heart beating a tattoo. She couldn't believe her luck. *"REPORT TO THE AMERICAN FOUNDATION FOR THE CURRENT QUARTER"* was right there in her hands in black and white.

The barking from the hallway reached a crescendo, drowning out even the cries of the old woman. Olga turned from the report to the open office door suddenly wishing Pasha were there with his video recorder. Where was he? *Forget the damned American.*

She called out for him and tried to calm the dog, which at last fell silent. Instead of Pasha a tall, thin old lady with a wrinkled face appeared in the doorway. She affected an aristocratic bearing and spoke antiquated Russian in a high voice. The old fashioned clothing and manners seemed ridiculous, like an old Shapoklyak cartoon.

This was the granddaughter of hereditary Russian nobility, Marya Fedorovna Golovina. When her parents were sent to the camps to die, a great aunt took her in. But in 1968 while still a 20-year-old student she was arrested "for anti-Soviet propaganda and agitation." Ten years in the Gulag followed, and she returned to find herself in the midst of Soviet end of times stagnation, disgraced and needed by no one.

For the next ten years she worked as a janitor, living in a small set of rooms on the same street in *Maliy Karetniy Pereulok*, in the heart of old Moscow, not far from the Hermitage Gardens. When Perestroika began she devoted her life to the collection of information on victims of repression she hoped might be rehabilitated. She converted her old janitor's quarters into a sort of registry of victims of political repression and soon received the first foreign grants from an educational society with vague human rights inclinations. Despite this, Marya Fedorovna remained eccentric, like someone released from prison only yesterday.

Golovina's dramatic history didn't impress Olga. She didn't obsess about Stalinist repression. What bothered Olga was the way this old, overdressed hen drew parallels between Soviet totalitarianism and life in today's Russia. For that matter, Olga had nothing in particular against Stalin, but the subject was controversial, and comparisons with the current president could not be tolerated. As far as she was concerned the president had transformed a country devastated and impoverished during the Yeltsin years into a strong and prosperous state.

Golovina simply could not be appeased. She went from one institute or university after another spreading her poisonous opinions. Even worse, she did this for American money. It was as if the old lady was offended by the entire world and truly hated Russia. She wanted only one thing – to destroy her country and grind it to dust just like she and others like her destroyed the Soviet Union. And so, when the chief told her there would be a meeting today between Golovina and a representative of the American Embassy, Olga happily volunteered to participate in a provocation.

And now here was Golovina right in front of her staring at the report in Olga's hand. The old lady took a step toward her with a shriek. "Put that down immediately, and get out of here, all of you."

Olga was at once amused and frightened. What might a crazy old woman do?

"Where is Pasha?" she asked, "Let's see how

much money you spent on anti-Russian activities last month." She began turning the pages of the report. "So, showing a film about the political prisoner Sergey Litvinov at the Colosseum Theater. Well! Seven hundred dollars. Was that to rent the hall, or was it that Litvinov wouldn't take less?"

An amused voice sounded from behind the old woman. "And since when was Litvinov a political prisoner?"

Olga breathed a sigh of relief. It was Pasha.

He sauntered into the office, unceremoniously shoved Golovina aside and stuck the video recorder in her face.

"And how do you explain Litvinov's theft of ten million dollars when he worked for an oil company? The court confirmed this. And his speeches calling for revolution in Russia? Do you really think someone calling for the violent overthrow of the legally elected authorities is a political prisoner? Or did the guy in the next room from the American Embassy teach you to talk like that?"

Pasha was a big man and could be overpowering. The old lady reddened before turning on him with unexpected fury.

"You're just children, nothing but children. Someday you'll be ashamed of what you're doing here. You think your little camera gives you the right to interrupt a private meeting? Have you learned nothing from life, from suffering and loss? You're not worth even the little finger of the people you bully."

Olga felt a fleeting vestige of shame and pity. But the hysterical notes in the rights activist's voice had no such effect on Pasha. He took a determined step to Olga's side, snatched the report from her hands, and laid it out on the desk. He began photographing the document all the while cursing under his breath. With a yelp, Golovina threw herself at him and tried to grab the papers. With a guffaw, Pasha easily shoved her away and resumed taking pictures while the old lady circled him, trying to retrieve the report from behind his broad back.

Despite herself, Olga was embarrassed. "Pasha ..."

But the big man was ranting as he read parts of the document. "This is best of all. The organization and training of election observers. Elections! Just tell me where there is any repression. Now we can show how so-called human rights activists plan to interfere in politics with foreign money."

"It's nothing like that." Golovina's voice was thin and shrill as she continued to hop around Pasha like an animated scarecrow. "We don't participate in elections. Observers only monitor the integrity of the procedure."

"To hell with you and your Americans. Go to America and observe elections there."

He was interrupted by Vovchik's voice from the corridor. "Guys, let's get out of here. One of her friends arrived and called for reinforcements. They'll arrive any minute."

Pavel froze for a beat to assess the situation. He shot a hard look at Olga who was staring at the old woman. "What's the matter with you?"

She turned to him and thought she detected a hint of suspicion in his eyes. The very idea that her friends might suspect her of sympathizing with the enemy was unacceptable.

"You old witch," she yelled as she ran after Pasha to the exit. She almost tripped over the dog and stretched out a hand to one of the metal racks to regain her balance. The fragile structure swayed, but she didn't notice. She turned in the doorway in time to see the entire row of racks topple, bringing others down with it in a flurry of paper and crumbling cardboard.

The room was instantly obscured by a cloud of dust as yellowed photos and death sentences performed a macabre ballet in the air. Olga raced down the corridor and up the stairs, out of the dark basement back into the warm embrace of a late summer day in Moscow.

CHAPTER 2

Gleb Solntsev beamed at the small group gathered around him. Olga held her breath in anticipation. Even after three years she still reacted to his every utterance and gesture like a schoolgirl who wished for his approval more than anything in the world.

"This is wonderful," said Solntsev. "I offer praise rarely, but this time you outdid yourselves. The State Department report is especially significant. The day after tomorrow it will be the subject of an NTV exposé, and a fire will be lit under the old viper."

Everyone laughed, and Olga laughed with them, not because she shared the schadenfreude of her boss; she was simply thrilled to be included. An almost physical warmth united them in the camaraderie of their special mission.

The main office of the Kremlin youth organization known as "Svoĭ" («Свои» - "ours") in contrast to the cellar at *Maliy Karetniy Pereulok* was spacious and well lighted. Through the window, the sun lit a space on the wall where, in a place of honor under the bright stripes of the Russian flag hung a portrait of the president, on his face the steely gaze of the Chekist, the condescending irony of the eternal winner. Olga had been as close to the man as she now was from his portrait. Three years ago when he visited her youth camp he sat on a folding chair right next to her tent as he talked about the country and the vast prospects open to her youth.

Three years ago while still a high-school senior she accepted a classmate's invitation to her first "Svoĭ" meeting. The huge auditorium was filled with young people of all sorts, from schoolchildren to young adults, even some families. She was captivated.

On that occasion Gleb Solntsev entered her life – the creator and founder of the organization. He was still in his mid-40's, decisive and charming, and Olga thought he was incredibly handsome. He treated everyone informally but radiated such authority that no one thought of disobeying him.

He was passionate, and this helped him organize and inspire. He was like a magnet to young hearts, subduing them through strength of character and dedication. He could be tactless and rude, but no one held it against him because they all knew how much he cared about them. Olga was entranced by this mixture of fervor and cold calculation.

He was accessible to one and all but still inscrutable, and every personal conversation with him left her with vain worries about what Gleb really thought when he answered her naïve questions and heard her suggestions. She was still too distant from him, a newcomer to his exciting world. Gleb was a veteran of the FSB where he had distinguished himself in some secret operation. He was invited to join the presidential administration where he became involved in youth policy.

There was always somebody around him, beginning with recruits to the movement with whom Solnstev always spoke a long time one-on-one, and ending with officials and even the president. She learned not to be jealous of the crowds and to be satisfied to be on the edge of his immeasurably busy life.

They often talked on the run, during noisy meetings, or quick telephone conversations. For a long time Gleb did not include her among his most trusted people, those who undertook the most delicate tasks, such as the disruption of Golovina's meeting with the American diplomat. Solntsev discussed such operations with them privately, without witnesses. And now Olga was part of this privileged group.

"And I didn't get into the picture," she said in mock offense at the praise. "Even though it was I who found the report and began to read it, too. Pasha came in later. I was afraid that that crazy old woman would kill me on the spot."

"You did everything just right," said Gleb. "Don't worry about not being in the video. It may be for the best. We may reserve your charming little face for more peaceful appearances."

Turning to Pasha, he said, "In the future you must never allow anyone to be alone, not even for a short while. You saw that Olga was working alone and you should have backed her up immediately. You're a team. There is no place for solos. Work smoothly, but always together – that's our strength. Olga's idea to knock down the old lady's shelves is beyond praise. An excellent *ad lib.*"

Pasha's large face clouded at the rebuke, and Olga started to protest that knocking over the shelves was an accident, but she could almost believe she'd done it on purpose, and she remained silent.

Only a few years ago Olga Polyanskaya could not have imagined ransacking the belongings of an old gulag survivor. But the organization taught her that some situations demand one to choose the lesser of two evils. After all, Golovina would not be shot or even fined. Olga and her companions only uncovered the truth – the very real fact of a meeting between the "rights" activist and an American. The unanticipated acquisition of the report justified everything. Golovina was a willing traitor to the Motherland. Any suffering and shame would be fitting payback.

"Can you just imagine what would happen if there were to be a revolution?" Gleb would say. "People like Golovina could cause the collapse of everything – heat, electricity, children playing in the yard, the carousels in the parks, peace, and the tranquility of hundreds of thousands of people. You can see, for example, what happened with the Libyans and Syrians. Ruin, bombing cities, chaos, packs of looters in the streets, poverty, destruction, and death. People don't think about this because they can't imagine how possible it is if traitors like Golovina come to power or raise the zombie liberals to revolution. Yesterday you saw that she and others like her are getting money from our main enemies like Williams who want to destroy our lives."

He locked eyes with each of them in turn, judging their reaction.

"And our task is to demonstrate the horror of this western plague, to reveal all its rottenness, all the corruption, all the danger for our country. There should be no mercy for enemies and traitors."

The organization recruited volunteers for the Donbas and inspired them to mercilessly exterminate "unholy evil." He didn't speak of the Americans in this regard. But what did it matter as she was with people dedicated to the defense of their country and the lives of hundreds and thousands of their fellow citizens? What could compare with this?

Gleb continued, "I reward good work. Next week there is a meeting in the Kremlin Palace for the President and patriotic youth organizations. It will be a big deal with a lot of media, including foreign journalists. You are to conduct yourselves well. Remain polite with no radicalism, no mention of our secret actions, nothing about what we discuss here. Do you understand? There's an invitation for each of you."

Olga was outrageously pleased, but she wouldn't allow emotions to show. She'd learned to hide exultation behind mock coldness.

Mention of "the Motherland," "secret actions," or "meetings in the Kremlin" no longer elicited head-spinning passion or silly girlish delight. With each passing day the amorphous concept of "Motherland" coalesced within her. Only Gleb and his closest advisors understood such realities while ordinary people saw only what was in front of their noses.

The world was blind and existed in a flat, two-dimensional space. Olga sometimes imagined she was some sort of super human, aware of another reality. Without their organization quite a different reality might impose itself. She existed on a plane denied to ordinary Russians.

CHAPTER 3

Komsomolskaya Ploshchad', commonly known as the square of three train stations, grimy as usual and submerged in the clamor and unchanging rhythm of Moscow, was in sharp contrast to the quiet of the provincial streets of Ryazan. Streams of impatient people jostled one another as they rushed to the Metro resigned to spending an hour or so in the hustle and bustle with transfers to lines serving the outskirts of the great city. During these hours the transportation network is packed tight with grumpy passengers shoving one another and banging on the train doors. Yet, even amidst such chaos some of them managed to pull out a book to read while resting it on someone's back. This was Moscow.

Impervious to the evening bustle Sergey Illarionov squeezed into a car at *Komsomolskaya* Station. He was just back from a trip, on the trail of the most serious journalistic investigation of his career. The Dictaphone recording in his breast pocket contained danger as well as opportunity.

Illarionov didn't doubt that that the testimony of former FSB Colonel Viktor Tretyakov was true. The numerous stratagems employed by the regional administration and the management of the detention facility to prevent the meeting confirmed his suspicions. Sergey was grateful for the resourceful human rights activists of the Public Oversight Commission that monitored the condition of prisoners. They overcame many obstacles to secure his meeting. Alarmed by the prospect of publicity and complaints to the regional procurator, the prison authorities reluctantly allowed him to see Tretyakov. They confiscated his video-recorder and Dictaphone. But Tretyakov's lawyer had slipped him his own pocket recorder.

Such a complicated subject made recording the interview doubly important, but Sergey didn't think that only this meeting with the former Chekist would suffice. Additional evidence was vital, even if only hearsay. Rumors that the notorious bombings of apartment buildings in various Russian cities at the end of the 1990's had been organized by the FSB weren't new. The rumors gained credence when sacks of the explosive RDX, known as Hexogen, were discovered in the basements of several residential buildings in Ryazan. Hexogen was the same explosive used in the Buynaksk, Moscow, and Volgodonsk atrocities.

Men were discovered placing the explosives, and their arrest was underway when an order to stand down came from Moscow. Soon after, the Moscow FSB confiscated all the evidence and claimed that "training exercises" using "sacks of sugar" had been mistaken for a real terrorist act because the local Chekists had not been informed. Journalists discovered that the men on the verge of arrest were actually FSB operatives. The official investigation was quickly classified and all evidence, including the alleged RDX, disappeared into the labyrinth of Lubyanka.

Even after 15 years, individual dissidents and foreign journalists occasionally mentioned the episode, but no additional information came to light. But then word reached Illarionov that a former employee of the Ryazan FSB, now under investigation, wanted to meet him. There was no trust in Sergey's heart for the FSB, but professional instinct told him he should not refuse this request.

The case of Viktor Tretyakov was not unusual: he was ordered to establish contacts with the radical Islamist underground in Dagestan and conclude a deal with them. The purpose was to supply the *Vahabisti* with money and help them travel to Syria where they could join ISIL. In return they would carry out a series of tasks for the FSB. Not even Tretyakov knew the nature of these tasks. But the plan misfired when out-of-control Islamists nearly destroyed Tretyakov's entire operational group. There was a messy shoot-out in one of the most populated areas of Makhachkala, and it was impossible to avoid civilian casualties and the resulting publicity.

But this was not the entirety of Colonel Tretyakov's misfortune. The son of a local oligarch perished in the shoot-out, and his vengeful father with the help of his private security employees, discovered that Tretyakov's Special Services group from Ryazan knew the location of the terrorists at least a month before the shoot-out but for some reason had done nothing about it. Tretyakov chose to explain nothing. The enraged oligarch demanded retribution, and the leadership of the FSB resorted to the simplest means possible: they accused the Colonel of criminal misconduct leading to loss of life. They even raised the possibility that he had committed treason.

Unaccustomed to such betrayal, the battle hardened Tretyakov resolved not to make it easy for his former colleagues. At first, he sought justice from higher authorities but quickly realized that he should have known better. No help was forthcoming from that quarter. But if the authorities were going to take his life, it would cost them dearly.

Sergey had mixed feelings about Tretyakov. He

was face to face with a man who until recently had worked avidly against people like himself. This man had defended a regime whose crimes the journalist was determined to expose. Fortunately, Tretyakov was not after sympathy. This strong man knew what he wanted and admitted his wrongdoing in terse phrases devoid of sentimentality.

His question was straightforward. "You're the one who wrote an article about the Ryazan connection to the Moscow bombings fifteen years ago?"

Illarionov nodded. "Did it bother you at the time?"

"Not as much as it might have." Tretyakov was emotionless. "You didn't dig down to the most important thing – to the name of the man in charge of the bombings."

"And you know his name?" Illarionov prayed the pocket recorder was working.

"I planned the operation in Ryazan with this person. The explosions were supposed to be synchronized, but some insignificant little fucker found the sacks."

Sergey leaned back in his chair. The Chekist's *sangfroid* struck him: the hard eyes, cynical directness, and cold recitation of the facts. Across the table from him slouching in his chair was a man who had been prepared to blow sky-high several multi-story apartment buildings along with their occupants. Hundreds of lives snuffed out in a second by the spark of a detonator at the whim of a petty dictator.

Had the order from Moscow shocked Tretyakov? Or had he considered only how best to do the job and leave no trace? Was his response a banal, "Yes, sir?" Had he been proud to be one of the cogs in the wheel of a cruel system?

Illarionov forced himself into a semblance of concrete and steel incapable of terror or forgiveness. He asked only one question.

"The name?"

The arrival of his train at *Dobryninskaya* Station jarred him out of his reverie. He joined the stream of people headed for the connection with *Serpukhovskaya* on the Gray Line that would carry them south. He lived a couple of bus stops from Prague Station in a standard nine-story building. Like a gray soldier, it stood in a precise row with identical neighbors on *Krasniy Mayak* Street. A bit farther was the entrance to *Bittsevskiy* Park which stretched all the way to Yasenevo.

The long ride home provided ample time for thought. The name Tretyakov gave him was too well-known and influential to allow for mistakes. Of course, he could publish the material based on the recording, but in such form it could lose its significance, forever remaining only a rumor, the unique testimony of a lone individual rather than documented fact. There remained to Sergey only one other lead – the FSBnik had given him a telephone number.

"His name is Aleksandr Zhuravlev. Fifteen years ago he was the Chief of Staff of the Headquarters Expert Center for Civil Defense and Emergencies for Ryazan Oblast. He's retired now and lives in Moscow. He's the one who conducted the examination of the sacks of powder and established that it was RDX. He knows what happened, and I wouldn't be surprised if he kept a copy of the official report despite orders."

A call to Zhuravlev was first on the agenda for tomorrow. To judge from the distress of the prison staff, the FSB must already be aware of the conversation with Tretyakov, maybe even of its content. There was only one means of self-defense – make it public – that was the only thing that saved him whenever he discovered egregious cases of corruption in the FSB, torture in police stations, or official misconduct. And so, he must gather the missing information as soon as possible.

His son was already at home, and this pleased Sergey. He was proud of his only child. Vladislav Sergeyevich Illarionov had always been smart, inquisitive and impatient - the same qualities that had distinguished Sergey in his youth. Vlad was 25-years-old and a graduate of the journalism faculty. He had no desire for a "normal" life. While still a student Vlad had been asked to work at one of the big federal television channels but refused. He preferred to work at a dissident website which he moved from text-only to full-blown videos and won a fivefold increase in viewership. The authorities did all they could to block the site, which resulted in the loss of viewership and lowered salaries. These days most of Vlad's time was taken up helping people with internet anonymization software to get around government blocks.

"So what's new?" asked Sergey.

"Tomorrow I'm going to the Kremlin Palace to take pictures of the local Hitler Youth. They'll be with the President, and I managed to get myself accredited. Imagine, a week ago these freaks raided the office of Marya Fedorovna. Golovina's a classy old lady, a real human being, and these shitheels are so juvenile they can't even understand who they're barking at. They deny everything, of course, but I want to ask Solntsev a few questions to see how he reacts."

Sergey shuddered involuntarily at the mention of the man's name. "Be careful with Solntsev. He's very dangerous."

"Sure, papa. I know all about him. And how many times have you written about him? Yeah, he's a former Chekist who's managed to re-create the Nazi brown shirts. He's a rare breed. But where can he hide at a public event with a camera stuck in his face?"

Sergey considered whether he should share Tretyakov's information with his son? Why should he hide from Vlad something he intended to publish in a few days for everyone to see? He had only to visit the expert and find out what happened to the Ryazan report. Such a reliable source for his sensational article would be more than enough. In a low voice he said, "No, Vlad. You don't know everything about him. The man is a mass murderer. "

CHAPTER 4

The palace glittered throughout its broad corridors and richly decorated halls. The foyer boasted a well-stocked bookstore, its counters laden with colorful booklets, vividly illustrated calendars bearing the image of the President, and the eternal *matryoshkas* and models of the Kremlin cathedrals. Symbols, posters, books, pictures – all combined to lend to the scene the delight of a fairground with its various attractions connected by slow-moving escalators that stretched between floors.

Through a spacious window of the long, endless dining hall the lower portion of the Russian crest could be seen, as if the double-headed eagle had alighted on the windowsill. Olga gazed spellbound, reveling in the nearness of this symbol of Russian power. The eagle gazed into the distance as he spread his golden wings, separated from her only by thin glass. He made her proud.

She turned back into the hall and imagined the beating heart of the Motherland manifested in the crowd of "*Svoi*" members. A kinship of the spirit, never more powerful than at this moment, reigned in the hall, and she immersed herself in it as though sinking into a warm embrace. She would be with these people to the very end. To be among them was to experience the elation of victory.

Solntsev approached and took her by the hand. "Olga, will you speak?"

She was confused, not knowing what pleased her most – his unexpected enthusiasm or the proposal.

"When?"

"Right now, immediately following the break. That is, first the President will speak, then me, and right after that – you."

She nodded mutely, afraid she could not conceal her excitement. But why should she? She was nearly overwhelmed by emotion when Solntsev took her hand.

"What should I talk about?"

"Our educational and social activities. Talk about how we are positive and constructive, white as the driven snow. Remember, there are Yankees and other liberal scum in the hall. We must project a solid image. Understand?"

"Of course," she nodded vigorously. She was frightened, but she could not risk Gleb becoming disenchanted with her and never trusting her with anything important again. She could do no less than succeed.

She barely heard Solntsev's speech. She caught only his concluding remarks.

"Our history – a time of unprecedented Russian strength and power, the history of a great empire and untold misery, suffering, and inhuman ordeals. We have always stood in the way of the worst dangers that threatened the world ..."

Solntsev's amplified voice reverberated in the hall, and Olga feared that her lungs would burst with the incandescent air, the noise, the sound of *his* voice.

"We paid for the right of America to become a superpower. We paid for the right of Europe to live without concentration camps. The world turned away from us and fears us in the belief that we might hand them a bill for everything we have done for them, and then they would have to pay forever! The only way for the West to avoid paying their bill is to humiliate Russia ..."

There was a burst of applause. Pride filled the room to the ceiling, a sense of superiority over the miserable and cowardly West.

Gleb's voice boomed over them as if it descended from the sky. He continued in a lowered voice, businesslike and concise, the way he spoke at their internal meetings, "Our army was the most powerful in the world. We were the most heroic nation. It is unjust that a great country should have exited the world arena after all of this. It is unjust to live without pride. There is no one in the country besides you. Do this – for Russia for the sake of our history."

He spoke like a father in his own peculiar, convincing manner. Olga was seized with terror as he stepped from the stage. How could she speak following that?

She couldn't feel her own body as she stepped to the microphones under the gaze of thousands of eyes that suddenly seemed strange and demanding. She began to speak as if her entire life consisted of good deeds, as though she had never snatched the report from Golovina's printer, as though she hadn't overturned the shelves. This was for her country, her organization, and her leader, and should it be necessary she was prepared to lie about anything to anyone, even to God, if he existed.

The applause dissipated her fears like clouds carried away by a strong wind. She was a conqueror, a supremely strong being capable of anything, as she stepped from the stage into the crowd of enthusiastic supporters. From somewhere a video camera focused on her.

During the intermission, still euphoric from the attention and recognition, she walked out to the foyer to reap the benefits of her newfound fame. She was immediately surrounded by journalists, and one of them, a young and especially bold man, stepped toward her and said something completely unexpected.

"Olga. I would never have expected you to be with these fascists."

She belatedly recognized him. Vlad - her former schoolmate and first adolescent love. He stared at her with a mixture of pity, confusion, and disgust. She took an involuntary step back.

They became fast friends in the seventh or eighth grade because they had been so alike. Common interests and a disdain for stereotypes united them in spite of their youth. At a time when young men fell in love with girls but were too shy to express it, the class seemed divided into irreconcilable sides. The boys talked about rock and roll and cars, tried out smoking, and surreptitiously watched porn. The girls flirted with older boys and university students and wore too much make-up, ignoring boys of their own age. But Vlad Illarionov brought computer printouts of world news and clippings of his father's articles to school and shared them with Olga, eager for her opinion.

Vlad was fortunate in his bold and cheerful character. He was bright, lively, and interesting, and maybe because of this did not slack off in his studies like many of the other boys. He might unexpectedly demand that a teacher account for how money contributed by parents had been spent. Or instead of a movie he might suddenly invite Olga to visit the Cosmonaut Museum or go to an American jazz festival.

He was interested in the world in all its variety, and when asked about plans for the future, Vlad always answered, "I want to do something worthwhile in life."

Olga was one of the few who completely shared his dream of an uncommon, full, and meaningful life, full of challenges and successes. But had she not managed to realize those childhood dreams now when she occupied a solid position in the most advanced youth organization in the country, step by step changing the familiar world for the better?

Vlad's life progressed in quite a different direction. Olga had not seen him since their senior prom, but knew that even as a university student he had fallen in with those very enemies and traitors against whom she now fought. His articles sometimes appeared in hostile publications, and they were vicious, anti-Russian, filled with hate and sarcastic bile.

They were attracting attention. She was embarrassed even to know him. Fearing a public scandal, she said irritably, "Let's go somewhere we can talk. There are too many people here."

They took an escalator to the now empty dining hall, the same one protected by the outspread wings of the two-headed eagle, the mute witness of Olga's loyalty.

"What the hell?" she began, the sweet tone of her presentation forgotten. "What are you doing here?"

"I might ask you the same," he said. "How did you get mixed up in this? For a free lunch in the Kremlin dining room? For some cheap popularity? How long have you been involved in Solntsev's outrages to appear on the same stage with him?"

"Don't you dare judge me," she snapped, her

gorge rising. "Do you think everyone is like you, vilifying your own country hoping for a handout from the Pindos[2]? Do you think they'll invite you to a free jazz concert at the American Embassy or maybe give you a trip to the States? Are you jealous because you've not been able to curry enough favor with them? I love my country, and I'm helping create her future."

He snorted. "An interesting sort of love - you support a charlatan who turns young people into zombie thugs. They spew poison and slander, glorify Stalin and the new *"vozhd,*[3]*"* attack people about whom the country should be proud, bully old women and anyone else who thinks differently. Such people are cowards, mockers who rely on force and lies. They're rude, stupid street punks. This is degradation, Olga. This is the transformation of people into crude beasts. But you – you weren't always like this. I don't understand how Solntsev managed to brainwash you."

"You're the brainwashed one." Resentment bubbled in her chest. "Have you repeated pro-American banalities so often, hoping they'll give you table scraps, that you actually believe them? You never appreciated the Motherland; you can't imagine living for her, fighting for her. You're ready to drag it all out in the open: the foreign stuff, the hostile stuff, just like the kind of newspaper trash you dragged to school. You would betray the very best of what we are for a pack of chewing gum because you never cared for anything that's worthwhile to a normal Russian. You're ready to sell our history and culture for a pair

---

[2] Americans. From the ancient Greek Πίνδος

[3] Leader

of phony smiles from people who want to destroy us."

Her anger spread to him like fire in a forest. "History and culture? Don't tell me you didn't know that your 'Hitler Youth' ransacked Golovina's office. She's our history, our living history, the real thing with all its cruelty and its heroes. Our science – Sakharov exiled to Gorkiy, our culture – Tsvetaeva committing suicide in exile from hunger and isolation or tormented like Zoshchenko and Akhmatova. Russia has always destroyed her best people. But I hoped that in our time it all would be done with. "

"'*Svoi*' had nothing to do with that." Had she not only recently decided that she would lie to anyone for the sake of the cause? She was a woman and could not serve in the military. Unlike Gleb she had no experience working with the FSB. She had never held a weapon in her hands. But she was fighting here and now by word and deed. This corrupt populist didn't deserve to know the truth. He would never understand.

"You really don't know the truth?" His voice was filled with doubt. "They made a video and it's become a regular propaganda feature on NTV. The guy in the video was immediately identified. He's spoken at meetings of your organization. There can be no mistake. The whole country knows who did it. There's no way you don't know. Did that murderer Solntsev teach you to lie so well?"

Olga choked with anger and resentment. "Murderer? Do you know where he worked and with whom? He served in the FSB, fought terrorism, risked his life so that people like you can sleep peacefully. He defended everybody, Vlad. All people, all beliefs, including you. You hate the people in his profession, but they keep you safe. And you say this isn't honorable? Do you know anything about honor, about dangerous professions and real achievements?"

"Olga," Vlad spoke as though to a small child. "The FSB organized the bombing of apartment buildings in our city and others fifteen years ago. And it was Solntsev himself who was in charge of the bombings in Moscow - personally in charge. His subordinate from Ryazan has already confessed. Just wait a few days – my father will publish a lot of material about this with proof, eyewitness accounts, quotes. Your idol cold-bloodedly murdered people while they slept peacefully in their own beds. You or I might have been in one of those buildings. He might have killed us with no thought, not even knowing that we exist. How old were we then? Ten? Would you have wanted to die as a 10-year-old child at his hands?"

"This is nonsense!" *Was he insane?* "Do you even understand what you're saying? You've picked up rumors, gossip, slander ... You don't dare spread such abominations. You don't know Gleb. You don't know him, at all. He could never have done that. You can't even imagine the kind of man he is, the soul he has, his qualities, the way he relates to people. You just can't ... Vlad, promise me that you and your father will not spread such slander."

"You can't be convinced because you don't want to know the truth. But in the real world not everything is the way you wish it to be. Other people, the ones who lost loved ones in those bombings, deserve to know the truth. Everything will soon be out in the open. Get used to it. And think about who it is you're defending. I don't think you knew about the bombings, or even Golovina."

"Yes, I knew everything about Golovina." She

hadn't expected to feel such all-encompassing hatred for Vlad. This impudent boy had spoiled the happiest moment of her life and now threatened all she believed in, defended and loved more than anything on earth.

"I was there. Do you understand? With my own eyes I spotted the American funding report. That's what it costs to buy people like her. Forty thousand dollars a quarter. And for that kind of money she and others like her invent hundreds of falsehoods like the one you just told me. I held that report in my own hands, and she was jumping about like a chicken at the trough trying to keep us from seeing it. And I knocked over her shelves, and I don't regret anything. If it were possible I would have burned it all down because it blackens the history of our country. And you ... you're no better."

She turned on her heel and walked quickly to the escalator casting a final glance at the dark, indifferent contour of the double-headed bird that fell across the window. Surely what Vlad said was untrue.

CHAPTER 5

The empty square glistened wet from rain, indifferent to the fact that Dzerzhinsky's enemies no longer filled it. The end of August in Moscow was predictably damp, and already an autumn chill was in the air. Olga stopped on the opposite side of the square in the shadow of the yellow brick façade of Lubyanka.

Thanks to decisions taken behind these forbidding walls she could sleep peacefully at night. That orders to destroy entire buildings, knock them down like so many paper houses originated here was unthinkable.

Her sense of participation in the fate of the country and nearness to power connected her to this building and the people inside, especially Gleb Solntsev. This was the beating heart of the strong and unassailable mechanism that daily protected the future of Russia.

When she spoke with "regular" people, she used simple terms, with no ostentation, but with a special, slightly condescending dignity. She treated people correctly and with respect, almost on their level, but she spoke with authority. Sometimes she permitted herself some sincerity in the knowledge that these people would soak it up like a fur coat in the rain.

The slightest indication of approval from members of the organization, the smallest gesture or nod of the head, confirmed her personal value.

She rushed away from Vlad to find Solntsev to warn him about the filthy slander his enemies planned to publish. She found him surrounded by television cameras in the main hall giving an improvised press conference.

After fifteen minutes, he made his way to the exit with an apology to the press that he had an important meeting with someone from the Ministry.

She rushed after him. "Gleb, we have to talk. It's urgent."

"I can't right now, Olga. I'll be in the office this evening after seven. Come then."

Now, on Lubyanka Square, she had second thoughts about going to Solntsev's office. She was sure he had forgotten already about seeing her.

But this was important. In only a few days terrible and slanderous "revelations" would be made public naming the man she held dearest a murderer and terrorist. She couldn't live without telling him. It was impossible to explain to people like Vlad how her entire being was defined by the organization. She had no choice but to warn Solntsev.

She rushed along the sidewalk on *Bol'shaya Lubyanka* Street, past FSB Headquarters looming on the right. It was nearly three-quarters of a mile to the intersection with *Sretenka* Street, but she barely noticed the distance. "*Svoi*" maintained an office here hidden away from prying eyes inside a courtyard.

Gleb was waiting for her.

She spoke clearly and concisely, like a soldier reporting on an important mission. She told him how she knew Vlad, who his father was, and most importantly, the plan to slander Gleb in the press.

The act of doing her duty produced nearly a physical catharsis, as though her energy were being renewed.

Solntsev listened attentively. When she finished, he smiled and said, "I would never have believed that you knew the son of Sergey Illarionov. He's one of the most dangerous journalists in the country. I haven't figured out who he's working for, but for a long time now he's manufactured a wild and crazy campaign against key people. It's well known that his articles don't contain a grain of truth. But you know Goebbels' basic rule of propaganda: the more outrageous the lie, the easier it is to believe. Illarionov never bothers with evidence. He just makes a lot of noise and sows doubt in the hearts of our people."

"So what's to be done about it?" Olga was alarmed. "He will cause a lot of trouble this time. A lot of people might believe him ..."

"Don't worry." He was unperturbed. "We have only one weapon on our side – the truth, and it is we who must deliver it. Sooner or later the entire web of slanderers will collapse upon itself. But I'm very grateful to you. You acted correctly. Now we know what to expect."

Olga's alarm turned to pride. Gleb was strong and kind, as always, prepared to face any threat. "They should all be exiled," she said, surprising herself. "They are so arrogant."

He only smiled and led her to the door.

*****

Dark thoughts consumed Solntsev. The information in Illarionov's hands could be published at any time. He shuddered like a criminal about to be caught, and this incensed him. What had this upstart dug up after fifteen years? Who did he know in Ryazan that might have helped him?

He grabbed his jacket from a peg on the wall

and hurried out of the office. He had to take action before it was too late.

****

The day after the Kremlin affair, Vlad Illarionov was editing the video he had shot there, adding commentary where needed. He also spliced in scenes of "*Svoi*" activities not intended for public exposure.

It was the end of the day by the time he turned to his computer to dredge up the news. "AT ILOVAYSKIY, THE DONBAS MILITIA DEALT A RESOUNDING BLOW TO THE KIEV JUNTA ..." *Propaganda.*

"THE PRICE OF OIL REACHED A TEN-YEAR LOW."

"IN CHELYABINSK A CHILD FELL FROM A TENTH STORY WINDOW OF A MULTI-STORY BUILDING."

A tautology right in the title, he thought, and then mentally chastised himself for being so accustomed to deaths in the news that the life even of a child had not affected him.

The next headline jerked him upright in his chair" "LAST NIGHT IN THE RYAZAN PRISON FORMER FSB OFFICER VIKTOR TRETYAKOV COMMITTED SUICIDE ..."

His father had just returned from Ryazan. Vlad could not know for certain that it had been Tretyakov his father had met there – Sergey Illarionov never mentioned the names of his sources before publishing an article. But on the flickering screen of his monitor, the news about Tretyakov glowed like an omen.

Someone in Ryazan told his father about Solntsev's crimes, someone who had worked with Solntsev in the past. So it could only be an FSB officer. Why would he have revealed such information to an opposition journalist?

Vlad was seized by a quiet panic and paced the

room trying to decide what to do. Call his father's cell phone? But what to say? *"Papa, did you meet with a Viktor Tretyakov from the FSB?"* But such things were not discussed on the phone. Besides, his father had likely already seen the news. He would know what to do. Maybe he could just call and ask when his father would be coming home. But this seemed childish. It was still light outside, and his father often was out until dark. He might be conducting an important interview.

Vlad went to the window overlooking the courtyard. A thin line of trees between the building and the sidewalk lent some coziness to the two-room apartment. The leaves of an overgrown poplar brushed against the window sill.

Vlad squinted through the leaves. From the fourth floor he had a good view of the iron frame of the toy rocket with its peeling paint, a relic of Soviet times. He had played in the courtyard as a child. Beyond the rocket was a new playground with a tall slide and large sandbox. There was a bench near-by, shaded by birches, where two mothers were smoking and drinking beer. They shouted occasionally at their children playing in the sand.

He could hear the screech of the swings with their long metal beams and worn wooden seats. The swings, too, had been in the courtyard as long as Vlad could remember, and not once had they been lubricated. Now, as a child swung in vigorous arcs, they complained, clanging and screeching as though about to break apart.

Vlad resumed editing his video in a vain attempt to quiet his fears. The last pre-twilight rays of the sun, filtered through a lacework of clouds, penetrated the room, and traversed the wallpaper, moving closer to Vlad's desk, but failed to reach it before disappearing into the carpet.

After two more hours Vlad finally punched his father's number into his cell phone and listened to the far off ringing.

"Papa, where are you?"

"On my way home." Sergey Illarionov sounded in a good mood. "I was in Yasenevo, and you know how long it takes to get there. I took the subway this morning because it was quicker than the car. Now I'm taking a shortcut through the park. I'll be there in a half-hour."

"It's not the best idea to be strolling through the park in the dark. Remember, there was a murder there not long ago. They're still writing about the 'Bittsevskiy Maniac.'"

"He's long gone," replied Sergey. "There's little to fear in the woods while the biggest maniac of all is sitting in the Kremlin."

Vlad chuckled with relief at his father's playful tone. He was abashed that he had become so agitated, like a frightened child. He went back to work and did not notice the passing time.

After a half-hour passed he hesitated to call his father again, not wanting to play the fool. Perhaps Sergey had miscalculated the time it would take to get home. It normally took no more than an hour to walk the whole way through Bittsevskiy Park to *Krasniy Mayok* Street.

His mother poked her head into the doorway. "Did you call papa? When will he get home?"

"In a half-hour," Vlad lied, not wishing to alarm her.

He decided to send a text message: *Mama wants to know when you'll get here.*

There was no reply. After ten minutes he tried calling again. There was no answer.

Car horns pierced the night-time silence, constant and unrelenting like alarums. *Papa, where are you?*

Vlad stepped onto the balcony and lit a cigarette, something he did only when he needed to calm his nerves. The darkness on the street was relieved by weak cones of light from streetlamps, surrounded by gloom. Someone began to use the swing in the courtyard again, and from the deep, viscous darkness the scrape of the metal sounded like a cry for help.

The night was deepening, and his father might well have fallen or turned his ankle – but if so, why didn't he call? Vlad would have gladly grabbed a flashlight and headed for the woods, but he knew full well that in the huge park he would be lucky to find anything by himself.

After another half-hour his mother became seriously concerned. "When did you speak with him last?"

"Two hours ago. He was in Bittsevskiy Park."

"My God! And you said nothing all this time?"

They called the police but were informed that people were not considered missing before three days had passed. "Are you sure he doesn't have a sweetheart on the side?" was the only comment of the indifferent police duty officer.

Vlad would remember events of this night for the rest of his life. The scenes would repeat themselves minute by minute, over and over, indelibly imprinting the inevitability and helplessness of it all. His mother called her father and brother. Along with a good-hearted neighbor they armed themselves with flashlights and spread out among the many pathways of the woods. In some spots they crossed depressions full of mud from recent showers with the ends of fallen branches protruding from them. The night enveloped them in cold desperation, abetted by another shower driven by a wind that whined through the trees.

It was Vlad who spotted the shapeless form lying face down at the foot of an old, cracked birch. He rushed to turn it over. In the flashlight's beam he recognized his father, beaten nearly beyond recognition. Viscous blood that had not yet been washed away by the rain fell in rivulets over his disfigured face.

Vlad grabbed the lapels of the gore-covered jacket and tried to lift his father's body. One arm bent unnaturally as though instead of bones it was filled with straw.

He cried out, not from terror, not from pain, but rather from an impotent wish to break through the hopeless wall of death, to reach his father, to call him out of this broken shell.

His mother screamed behind him, and he heard his grandfather wail. From the corner of his eye he saw the quick gesture of his neighbor who pressed his hand to Sergey's throat to find a pulse, but Sergey's heart had stopped beating.

Vlad knelt on the muddy earth and grasped his father's cold, muddy hand. From behind him, as though through a fog came his grandfather's words. "He was beaten ... beaten to death ... Dear God! Who could have done this?"

Vlad stood unsteadily and embraced his mother. She needed his comfort now. His father's careless words echoed more loudly in his ears than his mother's sobs: *"The biggest maniac of all is sitting in the Kremlin."*

That very maniac was behind every cruel blow that had beaten the life out of Sergey, behind the scum who gave the order and those who carried it out.

He forced himself to look again at the battered body and resolved to find every one of his father's murderers if it took the rest of his life.

Chapter 6

Gorlovka, Ukraine

The Ministry of State Security of the unrecognized Donetsk Peoples Republic (МГБ ДНР) (MGB DNR) was located in an unremarkable, Soviet-style gray building. It was the former quarters of the Ukrainian Security Service, the SBU (СБУ). Mihailo Korzh was challenged immediately by a guard, a sergeant of short stature with small, mean eyes.

He held out his passport. "Mikhail Korzh. I'm expected." Best to use the Russian version of his name in this building. It might get him farther.

The guard examined his documents and reluctantly wrote out a pass. "Go straight ahead then left to reception," he growled. "But first, empty your pockets and pass through the metal detector.

One wall of the faceless lobby was decorated with the black-blue-red flag of the DNR. The entrance to the basement was guarded by two rough men who might be Serbs.

Mihailo was long accustomed to the presence of Chechens and Serbs in his home town. Since February, thousands of Russian citizens, the majority of whom clearly belonged to the criminal classes, had flooded into his city with the braggadocio of an occupation force. Arrogant skinheads with swastika tattoos swaggered through the streets as though they owned everything and had come to oversee the conquered. They took over workers' quarters on the outskirts of town and came out in force to every pro-Ukrainian rally in the Donbas to start fights. Armed with knives and rebars from construction sites, intoxicated by their anonymity, inflamed by herd instinct, these gangs of bandits attacked unarmed groups of protesters and pitilessly beat them.

On their heels arrived the new "leadership" - officers and workers of the Main Intelligence Directorate of the Russian Army, the GRU (ГРУ), in khaki uniforms, unshaven and with a strange gleam in their eyes – a mixture of idealistic fanaticism and greed. Upon arrival they took over the city with predatory and ruthless force. They confiscated transport, businesses, money, kidnapped people and demanded ransom, cracking down on anyone foolish enough to try to escape their indiscriminate plunder. They dealt in the same way with anyone who disagreed with them.

Soon it was the Serbs' turn – wide shouldered, no longer young, veterans of the Yugoslavian wars, taciturn and cruel; without a word they got busy with arrests, torture, and firing squads. Chechens appeared at guard posts and on patrol with the terrifying appearance of merciless fighters with AK-47's at the ready.

It seemed as if the very earth had opened and hell itself had sown terror and death throughout the city. Hunger was one of the results – empty store shelves, astronomical prices and the absence of salaries. The battle over water and electricity would come later.

The local inhabitants watched with resignation as the familiar elements of civilization disappeared to be replaced by a monstrous amalgam of chaos and military drill. The once peaceful city became sluggish as it awaited its turn to become a battlefield ...

"Why do you need a pass?" The officer studied Mihailo from under lowered brows.

"My son urgently needs an operation on his eyes. This was arranged in Kharkov before the war, but his turn came only now," replied Mihailo. The office was a normal room, impersonal and maybe too sparsely furnished for its size. The only thing to distinguish it was a map on the wall with red rectangles for houses and green patches for parks. Mihailo made an effort to memorize as much of the map as possible.

"On his eyes?" the MGB officer asked again.

Everything was upside down in this bizarre new world as though they had drifted into another dimension: criminals were soldiers, former civilians were on patrol, regular soldiers were in charge of security, and intelligence officers headed the city administration. And here was this well-fed *MGBnik*, clearly a bored and annoyed junior army staff officer, speaking to him in a sing-song voice. "There are children here of real patriots who can't leave. With heart disease, by the way, who've waited years for surgery. But eyes? You must be kidding. Get him some glasses."

Heart disease, in truth, was the first idea that had occurred when devising possible reasons for leaving. He didn't know any heart doctors, but he did have a friend who was an eye doctor.

From a cupboard behind him the officer withdrew a bowl filled to the top with sugar and set it on the desk. He unceremoniously intended to drink some tea right in front of his guest. Mihailo swallowed the saliva that started in his mouth. There was no longer any sugar in the stores, and when some did appear at a market it was outrageously expensive. Mihailo barely restrained himself from dipping into the white crystals to stuff some in his mouth and more into his pocket to take home.

Instead, he spoke, making an effort to inject some pathos into his words. "This is not to improve his sight. This is a special operation to prevent his getting worse. He suffers from terrible myopia, and if it gets worse, he could go completely blind."

The officer reluctantly turned away from his recently charged cup to Mihailo. "What was your job at the Defense Ministry?"

"I'm an artist. I designed all the decorations for military parades and the Victory Day celebrations. May 9," he specified, hoping to imply that the one day the Soviets had proclaimed for the celebration of the end of WWII was somehow sacred to him. "I don't know any secrets," he added. "I only painted pictures, wall decorations, devised ways to decorate parade routes."

"You saw all our weapons," cut in the officer. "You saw the weapons selected for parades, what was there and what was not, where weapons are stored, the types and quantities of heavy weaponry."

"But I know nothing about that. And anyone who saw the parade saw those weapons."

The officer gave him a dubious stare as he sipped his tea. "No," he said, not wanting to accept the responsibility. "I can't make such a decision. Permit you to travel to territory occupied by the Kiev junta? In time of war? I can't. You must go to the head office in Donetsk. Let them decide."

"Donetsk? But I have a child, don't you understand? I'm guilty of what? Painting a few damned pictures? I only want to help my family. I just need to go to Kharkov and back. It's the same New Russia we live in. I'm sure that soon we will liberate Kharkov."

"Well, then, when we liberate it, then you can go there."

Mihailo would recognize that significant and feigned unconcern from miles away. He'd encountered this unfortunate fact of life in Ukraine many times even before the war.

The officer was fishing for a bribe.

Mihailo sighed. Professionial intelligence operatives in such situations always have a handy bag of money near-by, but the Ukrainian "Donbas" volunteer battalion in which he served lacked such resources. People from Ukrainian villages provided food, medicines, clothing, even uniforms, handed over old binoculars, night vision equipment, army boots, and once they had even come up with an armored transport vehicle, a "BMP." Any money they came up with went for equipment or assistance to refugees from the occupied cities. There was nothing for bribing the occupying forces.

Mihailo pulled his last paper money out of his pocket and held it out awkwardly to the Chekist who peered at it from the corner of his eye as he calculated whether he should take it or pretend to be insulted. After a slight hesitation he took the crumpled *hryvna* and said, "I simply can't help. You don't have much ... justification here. But I can write a letter of recommendation to Donetsk. And one of our boys can take you there. Maybe you can get it all taken care of today."

One had to be philosophical. Something was better than nothing.

The car was a standard "UAZ" with its doors bearing a hastily painted DNR flag. The reason for the art work was most likely not the particularly zealous separatist patriotism of the driver, but rather a precaution against being shot at a road block. He knew of at least two instances of fighters confiscating cars from staunch Russian sympathizers. In one, when the driver protested, they beat him and then killed his younger brother to prevent them going over to the other side. And there was the danger of falling under "friendly fire." Not a single separatist had been punished.

Behind the wheel was a friendly young man, clearly a local. He grinned broadly at Mihailo and nodded toward the seat next to him. Mihailo got in without a word. He couldn't be sure whether this fellow, who appeared not at all threatening, might be an enemy. They might have played together as children at one of the schools in the Old Quarter, as the *Solnechniy* area was known. They might have watched movies on the big screen in the square at the city center. How could it be that this young man worked for the worst of the occupiers?

The driver navigated the checkpoint without a problem with neither of them speaking. Mihailo couldn't think of anything appropriate to say.

"Why are you going to Donetsk?" asked the driver.

"I need an exit pass." His companion wanted to talk, and it would be necessary to gather his strength and get to work. "My son needs an operation on his eyes in Kharkov."

"Why didn't they give you a pass here?" The driver was suspicious. "My name's Vasiliy, by the way."

"Because, Vasya, I worked in the DNR Ministry of Defense, and they just don't give passes to such people." He said nothing about being an artist.

"OK," said Vasiliy, now with the camaraderie

due a colleague. "I won't ask what your job was, but I hope they give you a pass," he added with unexpected sympathy.

"Why is that?"

"Because soon enough everything here will be blown sky high."

"Really?"

"Didn't you hear that yesterday they blew up the bridge? The day before yesterday it was the reservoir."

"Of course, I heard," sighed Mihailo, doing his best to act cold blooded. "It's because the 'ukropi' (dill pickles) are attacking."

He was accustomed to calling his fellow Ukrainians 'ukropi,' all in all a relatively inoffensive term from the rich arsenal of curses with which the separatists were so generous.

"Well, yes!" Vasiliy replied. "But that's small potatoes. I'm not talking about the chemical plant that our guys mined. I'm talking about the munitions factory. Do you know it?"

Mihailo went cold.

"Wait a minute ... there are a lot of defective explosives stored there. They could all be detonated by an explosion and there will be nothing left of Gorlovka. The whole city will go up."

"Yeah," Vasiliy agreed sullenly. "And the results will be worse than Chernobyl. They've even mined the conduit for contaminated water. If it goes, there will be no water fit to drink here."

"And no one knows about this?" Mihailo couldn't believe it.

"What do you mean, 'no one?'" snorted Vasya. "Do you think I'm revealing something top secret? Of course, they know. We in the MGB know practically everything. And the *khokhly* (Ukrainians) know it, too. We mined it so we could blackmail them. 'Bes' told them all about it yesterday. If they try to take the city, there'll be nothing left. We'll blow everything up along with them. So even the enemy knows. The locals are the only ones who've not been told."

"Bes" (demon) was what they called the new governor of Gorlovka, a former (or formally former) GRU officer. The nickname was well-deserved. Blow up the city! His native city, every corner of which he knew. A city with rooftop pavilions known locally as "Athens," the dilapidated façades of old houses that somehow conjured up images, not of ruins, but of comfort, parks full of frolicking children, and stores filled with tired women. And they so easily plan to murder these people if the lawful powers of this country should try to take back the city.

"Are you from around here," Vasiliy asked carefully.

Mihailo shrugged.

Vasiliy continued speaking with such vehemence that Mihailo feared he would lose control of the car. "What else can we do? *Himself* ordered this, understand? A direct order from the Kremlin. And he's right. It's unacceptable that Kiev's fascists re-take the city. During the Great Patriotic War they permitted the Germans to occupy Kiev, and what happened? The *khokly* and Banderites loved working for the occupiers so much that even after all these years they are returning to Nazism. All these concentration camps, genocide, torchlight parades with portraits of Bandera, all of it ... If it comes to it, it's better to destroy the city than surrender it ... There would be nothing to it. This fascist plague should be burnt to the roots. At any cost!" Vasiliy finished, and turned the wheel so hard that the car nearly careened off the pockmarked road.

Mihailo didn't reply. This wasn't his first experience with fanatics reciting Russian propaganda. Still, every time it happened the words shook his soul. What concentration camps? What genocide? This was all lies from the first to the last word. And thanks to these lies a bunch of dimwitted fanatics wanted to erase a city from the face of the earth. It was impossible to come to terms with this.

"Are you sure all that is true? That they've already laid the mines?" he asked, hoping for a negative response.

"I'm sure," growled Vasiliy. I planted the explosives myself."

Maybe his trip to Kharkov and the meeting with the battalion command should be postponed. He couldn't leave Gorlovka without discovering the precise locations of the explosives.

Chapter 7

Moscow, Russia

"Like I said, this is all I have." Vitaliy Tolmachev repeated himself in a dry voice. "Just the recording of the conversation with Tretyakov that your father copied onto the editorial computer. I don't know who he met with before his death."

"But you said it was the man who wrote the report on what was in the sacks they found in Ryazan. According to my father, the report was prepared by the research center at the Headquarters for Civil Defense and Emergency Situations of Ryazan Oblast. Someone has to know who wrote it."

Vlad wasn't backing down from the chief editor of his father's newspaper. He had to follow the Sergey's trail.

"There's no way you'll find it. The report was classified, and the names of the authors will never be made public. No one will give you this information. It was fifteen years ago, and most of those people are by now retired and long gone. Whoever it is you're looking for must have moved to Moscow. This is a big city, and you have no idea where he might be."

"My father was returning from somewhere in Yasenevo."

"What of it? You're still looking for a nameless person."

"Wait a minute," said Vlad, "Did you listen to the recording of father's conversation with Tretyakov? If he named this second witness it must be in the recording."

"Listen to me," said Tolmachev. "I already said I'd give you the recording, and you can do with it whatever you like. But don't count on us for help. With due respect to your father, don't come here again. It'll be better for you and for us."

"But I hoped that if I can find the rest of the evidence, we would still publish the material. He died for this." Vlad was almost shouting. "We have to at least finish what he was working on so that his death wasn't in vain!"

"You're such an idealist." Tolmachev heaved a sigh. "Vlad, my boy, we can't print this stuff. Do you want to know the truth? Good. We got a call from a very influential organization that told us that under no circumstances may we write anything on this subject. Otherwise ... well, you can guess. Otherwise, we'll end up like your father. I have a family." He had the grace to hang his head before saying, "I understand that you have a family, too, but ... Everyone chooses his own poison, my boy. I have no right to demand this of others."

The editor was right. After all that had happened, he could demand nothing from these people.

"But if the material is published there would be no reason to kill anyone." This was his last hope. "Their goal is to prevent publication. If we tell the readers everything we know we would no longer represent a danger."

Tolmachev greeted this with a short, bitter laugh. "And you don't think they would put an end to us out of spite? You don't understand the kind of people your father tangled with. And you don't seem to understand what it is to be a journalist in Russia – if you're talking about real, honest journalism."

"Then why do you even try if all you can do is compromise. Just for the money?"

"No," Tolmachev was not in the least insulted. "Money is a problem for us, yes, but I persist so that I can provide the people with just a small piece of the truth, a tiny bit. And in order to do this, you're right - we make compromises. So take your recording if you want it so badly, but take my advice, too – it's not worth your life. They're much more powerful than we, and you'll never get the better of them."

In the depths of his soul he understood the truth of Tomachev's words. But he could not give up, not just for the sake of his father, but for his own self-respect. It was time for perseverance. He could not hesitate, not even for a moment, or he would have no meaning, and would be alone with the horror of his loss and the bitter realization that death had triumphed.

He feared despair and emptiness even more than death. The investigation gave his life some meaning, a way to resist, even if he was alone.

Arriving home to an apartment even emptier than his soul, Vlad went to his computer to listen to the conversation that had cost his father's life. An unfamiliar voice filled the room, cold and cynical, speaking of how the murder of hundreds of people had been prepared, as usual, carefully and professionally. When Tretyakov came to the moment when an alert resident discovered the sacks of explosive in the basement, his voice even now betrayed irritation.

Evidently, Sergey Illarionov noticed this, as well, and asked sharply, "And who was in charge of this operation in Moscow? What is his name?"

"Gleb Solntsev."

The words crackled in the air, dry and hot, as if

they would scorch Tretyakov's lungs.

This is how hatred enters the world: the heart pounds against the ribs as though trying to escape while blood hot as lava surges through every capillary and permeates vessels. This name, pronounced clearly in a stranger's voice was the essence of universal evil – if one excluded the main evil-doer, the one behind Solntsev without whose direct order neither the innocent residents of Moscow apartments nor Vlad's father would have perished. The murderer was the person who ran the country – a hardened and bloodless killer.

Vlad listened to the end of the recording with the alertness of a hunter, and he finally came to what he had been waiting for.

"His name is Aleksandr Zhuravlev. Fifteen years ago he was the Chief of Staff of the Headquarters Expert Center for Civil Defense and Emergencies for Ryazan Oblast."

Vlad could imagine his father hearing the same words just a few days ago. He continued listening.

"He's retired now and lives in Moscow. He wrote the report on the powder found in the sacks and concluded that it was RDX. He knows what happened to that report – and I wouldn't be surprised if he kept a copy in spite of orders."

Vladislav Illarionov collapsed against the back of his chair. It shouldn't be hard to find an Aleksandr Zhuravlev who lived in Yasenevo. He could use the hacker's directory of Moscow telephones and addresses that a friend had given him years ago – illegal, but very useful. And he must do it now, before it was too late.

Chapter 8

An early autumn crept into Moscow, wrapping her in gold and crimson, almost stealthily replacing outgoing summer, but preserving its warmth and adding its own special tints. The temperature remained pleasant, in no hurry to give way to rain-induced depression. But this time of year that inspired Russian poets had little effect on Olga.

She was aware of Sergey Illarionov's death. According to the official reports, the dissident writer was attacked and robbed while walking through Bittsevskiy Park at night. He had been unfortunate, perhaps even foolish in his choice of routes.

Vlad would be shattered by his father's untimely end in so violent a manner, but Olga could not bring herself to go to her old school friend's apartment to offer condolences. The unpleasant conversation at the Kremlin Palace, especially his disparaging remarks about Gleb Solntsev terminated their friendship so far as she was concerned.

In fact, she had to admit to herself, the sudden absence of Sergey Illarionov meant that the odious man's lies about Gleb were now silenced forever.

That gave her comfort even though Gleb would easily have weathered such obvious slanders. Hadn't he told her not to worry about it? *"We have a powerful weapon on our side – the truth, and we have to spread it. Sooner or later the slanderers' house of cards will collapse on itself."*

His words were those of a man absolutely certain of his own verity.

The world was unambiguous, clear-cut, black

and white - divided between true friends and obvious enemies. There could be no middle ground in the struggle for the Motherland's soul.

Pasha, Kostya, and Volodya (whom they simply called "Vovchik") were recent acquaintances. She had rarely seen them at meetings and was surprised when she when Gleb took her into his "inner circle" that these previously barely noticed men were there.

Her first serious act with them was the provocation at Golovina's office when she won her spurs and Gleb Solntsev's respect, perhaps even admiration. She would be making more speeches at public rallies, and she had even appeared on television, standing on the stage next to Solntsev. She could imagine no higher honor.

Chapter 9

Aleksandr Zhuravlev opened the door without a word, as if he had been expecting the visit. He was no longer young, but nevertheless physically imposing with a full head of iron gray hair and wildly tangled eyebrows that lent him a stern appearance.

Vlad introduced himself, offering his I.D. for Zhuravlev's inspection. "My father came to see you a few days ago."'

The old man gave the document a cursory examination and smiled thinly. "That's not necessary. Such things are meaningless. But you resemble your father a great deal. I thought you would be coming to see me. And ... I'm very sorry for your loss," the last words spoken in an undertone.

Vlad expected to be invited inside, but Zhuravlev stood in the doorway a few beats longer before saying, "I have the document ready for you, the one your father asked about. I didn't have it here when he came because I don't keep such things in the house. Given what happened, maybe it was fate. Wait here."

He disappeared into the apartment leaving Vlad standing awkwardly at the door, his entire being tingling with anticipation. It was happening so fast - too easily, too fast, and this did not fill him with joy but with worry and a sense of desolation. He was moving from one task to another, losing himself in work to escape his pain. He had no idea what to do next.

Even his father's old newspaper refused to print the material. What would happen if the website on which he worked did the same? He could publish the revelations on his blog, but that would be a waste of the information and get him bogged down in the back and forth of social networks and ever present internet trolls. The material must be used in a way that did not permit the criminals to escape punishment. Should he hand everything over to the Western media? This was probably best, but he had to find the right contacts. This would take time, and Vlad didn't have much of that.

Zhuravlev reappeared at the door with a timeworn file folder. "Perhaps it's best that you have this now. It can bring nothing but trouble to me. Use it as you wish, but forget where you got it, understand? Forget my name, my address. Forget that I even exist."

"I understand. That's why I didn't call before coming. The last thing I want is to bring you trouble."

"I know." Zhuravlev for the first time looked like a tired old man. "Your father did the same, and that's the only reason I gave him the time of day. I'll give you one bit of advice – leave the country. I don't think you realize who you're dealing with, and by the time you do, it'll be too late. Under no circumstances can you leave this document in your apartment. Find a safe place for it."

Chapter 10

He sat for a long time behind the wheel of his father's car before the idea struck him. There was only one place in the city where he was always welcome, where he would find a reliable and brave person, and where he could easily conceal a document among hundreds of identical dog-eared folders – the modest basement apartment in *Maliy Karetniy*.

As soon as he crossed the threshold and stepped onto the steep stairs leading to the basement, Marya Fedorovna Golovina rushed to meet him.

"Vlad, my dear, dear boy," she cried. "Please come on in. I know. I know everything ... My God! You poor boy."

Vlad was normally irritated when women made over him as though he were a little boy, but it was impossible to resent Golovina.

"I'll make tea," she said.

This was no time for tea, but he accepted the invitation.

She conducted him to the room that served as an office, the same office that the tough guys from "*Svoi*" had invaded. There was a small electric burner on a counter along one wall, and she busied herself with the kettle.

"I can't stay long, Marya Fedorovna. I have work to do." He was now feeling guilty for what he was about to ask her. "I want to leave something with you for safekeeping, if it's OK," he said as Golovina poured the tea and set a plate of waffles on the table.

His words tumbled over one another, sounding jumbled and confused to his own ears, "It's the recording my father made with the former *FSBnik*, the one who directly accused Solntsev of having managed the bombings in Moscow on orders from the Kremlin. This was why they killed him. And I have the official report on explosives in Ryazan, the original, and it confirms that the sacks contained RDX – hexogen."

Golovina's face turned hard.

Vlad realized at that moment how much he and other Russians owed to this old woman who had been beaten but not broken by the Soviets and now was persecuted by their successors. It was remarkable to see how this fragile old lady transformed suddenly into the fearless dissident of the past, molded by decades of caution.

"And what are your plans?" She transfixed him with a stare.

"I don't know. Even father's old editor refuses to print it. I'm thinking of giving it to someone in the West."

"Correct," nodded Golovina. "But it's not enough simply to hand the proof over to western journalists. You have to go to the West yourself, as soon as possible, preferably to America. Get any kind of visa you can, even a tourist visa. Tourist visas can be valid for a long time. You might be able to take advantage of some sort of study grant. I'll get word to Williams at the American Embassy to see if he can do anything. And as soon as you get to the States, ask for political asylum. Only then should you take this material to a serious media outlet."

Vlad was discouraged. He had not expected to encounter such a serious and uncompromising tone from her.

"Wait a minute, Marya Fedorovna, I don't plan to leave Russia. This is my country, after all. I was born and raised here. Let *them* leave. We could get an article published that would rid the country of this bunch of thieves and murderers."

"Vlad!" Golovina was so agitated that she half rose from her chair. "Don't you understand who you're dealing with? This isn't just a gang of common criminals. By now you should know how pitiless and powerful they are."

Vlad barked a humorless laugh. "You're the third person in the past two days who's told me I don't know what I'm mixed up in. I know what you're talking about. But if all of us run away, hide, give up without a fight, these maniacs will slit our throats one by one. I can't just surrender the country to them because I'm scared. My father was no coward." His throat constricted as he forced out the last words.

"Your father was a great man, and someday he'll be honored as a hero in Russia, but leaving doesn't mean giving up the fight. Your greatest weapon is the truth, but here no one is allowed to speak it. Sometimes from abroad it's possible to do much more than you can here."

No, my father will never be thought of as a hero in this country, no more than you are considered a hero. Even now, after so many years, after all the truth that was revealed about Soviet times, they smear you with mud. Russia has always destroyed her best people.

"I must identify the people who killed my father. I can't leave without doing that. And my mother is all alone now. May I leave these papers in your files? And I'll be grateful if you could ask Williams about getting them published."

"Of course," said the old dissident, resigned to the young man's stubbornness. She'd seen it before in others, had been in their place as her friends disappeared one by one into the Gulag. "You may leave whatever you wish. I'll contact Williams today. And don't worry about me. They'll never take me alive."

Vlad couldn't contain a smile at Golovina's stab at black humor. "Take care of yourself, Marya Fedorovna. If any of those bastards show up here again, call me."

She surrendered a haggard smile and a final warning. "Agreed. But please think about getting out. If you can't do it for yourself, do it for the sake of your father's legacy. There are too many people who need you to stay alive."

Vlad returned home full of gratitude for this sturdy old lady who had endured so much.

Chapter 11

Derrick Williams was the cultural attaché at the American Embassy in Moscow and was frequently in contact with Russian citizens who had beefs with their government. His favorite was Marya Fedorovna Golovina, whom he considered a woman of great courage. He'd learned to trust the iron-willed old lady and respect her opinion. Thus, when one of her people delivered a sealed envelope to him at the Embassy, a rare occurrence, he took it seriously.

Five minutes after reading the note, Williams entered the office of Vance Johnson.

"Erm, Van. Could we have a word in the S.C.I.F.?"[4] He referred to the Plexiglas "room within a room" that was impervious to eavesdropping. This was a standard precaution for sensitive conversations.

Construction on the new embassy building on *Bol'shoy Devyatinskiy Pereulok* began in 1979 at the height of the Cold War with some of its structural components built by the Soviets. Six years later, American inspectors discovered that the building was literally riddled with listening devices and strange apparatuses for which no purpose could be determined, and the site could not be occupied for years.

In retaliation, the State Department refused to permit the Soviets to occupy their new embassy high up on Washington's Wisconsin Avenue. Too late, the feckless State Department realized they had given the Russians a site ideal for the collection of signals

---

[4] Secure Compartmented Information Facility – pronounced "skiff."

intelligence. In the meantime, of course, the FBI tunneled under the Soviet structure in order to tap into phone and telecommunications lines. In due time, this was discovered by Soviet technicians.

Finally, in 1991 following the fall of the USSR, KGB Chairman Bakatin supplied the Americans with diagrams showing all the listening device emplacements. Nevertheless, the Americans took the structure apart and re-built it at enormous expense.

The recidivism demonstrated by the current Russian government dictated that security precautions still be taken seriously.

Vance Johnson was the CIA Chief of Station. His friendship with Derrick Williams might seem odd to many, but the two shared a common love of Russian poetry and single malt whiskey, as well as growing horror at the kleptocratic Russian regime. They seldom were seen together outside the Embassy for the very good reason that it would do Williams no good to be associated in even the most innocent way with anyone from the CIA.

Johnson looked up from his desk with raised eyebrows. Williams, whose tall gangly figure and wire rimmed glasses reminded Johnson of Ichabod Crane, was a good source of information on what was happening in this increasingly Machiavellian country.

The two found the S.C.I.F. unoccupied and settled at a corner of the conference table that took up most of the space inside.

"What's up, Derrick?"

Williams handed him the note from Golovina. "I just received this, and I think it's dynamite." He could not conceal the excitement in his voice.

Johnson read the handwritten note, then read it again before speaking. "I know about Illarionov's death. It's the latest in a series. The *siloviki* have a knack for getting rid of troublesome journalists like Anna Politkovskaya. We suspect they even killed an American, Paul Klebnikov, some years ago. Unfortunately, there's little we can do about it."

"Did you see what she says Illarionov's son has – a recording naming Gleb Solntsev as the mastermind of those apartment bombings fifteen years ago? And maybe something even more important – the original investigation report from Ryazan, the one they suppressed."

"I'm not surprised about Solntsev. He's former KGB and then FSB, and he's a real bastard. I call him Putin's Goebbels. But it's just an accusation from a man convicted of crimes and now in prison in Ryazan. Written reports can be forged. The Kremlin will just dismiss it."

"The Kremlin might, but outside of Russia it will be taken seriously. It could do real harm to Solntsev and that means harm to his bosses in the Kremlin. Why else would they resort to murder?"

"That may be, but it won't matter much what western journalists say. The Russians will just dismiss it as propaganda."

"What if we could get Illarionov's son to the West? What if he published the material there? He has the actual recording."

"That might work." Johnson chewed his lower lip. "What are you getting at?"

"Couldn't you guys help him out of the country?"

Johnson's lopsided smile was bitter. "Derrick, as much as we might like to, exfiltrations are complicated and risky. We don't undertake such things lightly, and then only for our most valuable sources when they get in trouble."

"I'd say that Vlad Illarionov is in pretty deep trouble."

"Maybe, but he's not one of ours. And there's another consideration. You know our policy is to remain at arms' length from the dissident movement. It's bad enough that the Kremlin claims to see our hand behind everything they don't like. If we start actually getting involved with dissidents and the Russians were able to confirm it, it could well destroy the legitimacy of the opposition. I'm sure you wouldn't want that."

"So you won't help?" Williams' disappointment was palpable.

"Not 'won't;' can't. And you'll agree once you think about it."

Williams slumped in the chair. "They'll kill this kid next, you know."

"I wish I could do something, Derrick, I really do, but my hands are tied. You know that everyone at the Embassy is under surveillance by our friends at the FSB. It's back to Cold War days here, except the new bosses in the Kremlin are fascists rather than communists."

"Fuck," said Williams.

"My sentiments exactly."

After he returned to his office, Johnson sank heavily behind his desk. The importance of the documents was unquestionable regardless of what he'd said to Williams. But without a living, breathing witness, a Russian witness, nothing would come of them.

Langley, he was certain, would dismiss any suggestion of an exfiltration out of hand. There were more important things going on in Moscow, and the care and feeding of dissidents was not one of them. The value of dissidents was here in their own country where cases such as Magnitskiy's could be seen by the entire world. The persecution of such people meant that some realization of the sly brutality of the Kremlin would leach into the consciousness of the world and bolster resistance to Russian aggression.

If the Illarionov boy could only get out on his own, maybe something could be done. Even then, the long, toxic arm of Russian vengeance could snuff him out.

Johnson resolved to follow this case, discretely, of course, and Langley had no need to know about it for the time being.

Chapter 12

Gleb Solntsev gathered his inner circle at the small office on *Sretenka* Street. Olga was not among them because she was the subject of discussion.

Pasha, Kostya, and Volodya, Solntsev's most trusted enforcers were there, and they all wore expressions of concern.

"Gleb," said Pasha, "we don't know enough about her, and she would have noticed our absence from the organization meeting the night of Illarionov's death. What if she starts putting two and two together?"

Their anxiety surprised him. "Boys, do you really think she is so stupid as not to have known what she was doing when she told me about Illarionov's plans? She's a smart girl, and she's been with us now for over three years. She's never shied away from any task I've given her, and her behavior at Golovina's was near to spectacular."

"But she's not really one of us," insisted Volodya. What he meant was that she was not an FSB operative in mufti. "We still have to be careful of her."

Solntsev drummed his fingers on the desk. The only light came from the lamp at his side, and the corners of the room were cast in appropriately conspiratorial darkness. The group resembled hunters gathered around a campfire discussing their next prey.

After a thoughtful pause, Gleb said, "I understand what you're saying, but I've seen no signs of unreliability in the girl. Quite the opposite. She's dedicated and loyal."

"Nevertheless ..." ventured Pasha.

Solntsev studied the three men with their hard, feral eyes that glowed yellow in the lamplight. *My pack of wolves*, he thought. *They will not be satisfied with inaction.*

"Pasha," he said, "you're one of my best men, maybe the best, and I respect your opinion." He waved a hand at the group. "I can personally guarantee that you all have bright futures. Now go and leave this to me. I think I have a solution."

Pasha brightened visibly as he considered the possible permutations of Gleb's solution. It was easy, and not a little frightening to read in the big man's square face that he was willing to take care of anyone for the sake of the organization, even his own mother. Kostya was reliable, but stupid. He would obey any order without question. Volodya also was basically just muscle without Pasha's sly intelligence.

Solntsev remained in the dark office for a long time after they left.

The tenacious Sergey Illarionov's investigation and his collaboration with the traitor Tretyakov had required too many deaths. Olga Polyanskaya's acquaintance with Illarionov's son was the reason he had been able to nip the problem in the bud. The question Pasha now raised was whether the girl might see the Illarionov boy again and start to put it all together.

But Solntsev did not agree with Pasha's suspicions about her. She had demonstrated her value. Surely she had known what she was doing when she told him about Illarionov's plans.

But new complications arose daily, and Pasha might well decide to take matters into his own hands. Something would have to be done quickly if he were to avoid a serious problem. Without further thought, he picked up the telephone and dialed a number he knew by heart.

"Nikolay Davydovich? It's Gleb," he said, "Something's come up here that might be problem. I need to see you now."

Listening to the response, he hung up the phone, once again pleased at the handy location of his office. In a half hour he was on his way to the building with which he had been connected for most of his adult life and which, if the truth be told, was still his home. He could walk there, a few blocks along *Sretenka,* then south along *Bol'shaya Lubyanka,* then left onto *Furkosovskiy Pereulok,* past the small parking area and through the metal gates of the discreet "working entrance" of FSB Headquarters.

Prudence dictated that visits be rare over the past few years. The familiar beige carpeted corridors enveloped him in a kind of sweet nostalgia. These walls had molded him into the ruthless, shrewd and invincible professional he considered himself today. This was the only place capable of arousing sentimentality in him, and *"Davydych,"* as today's Chekists called him, was the only person toward whom Gleb Solntsev evinced any human emotion.

General Nikolay Davydovich Lisitsyn was known as "God's operative." He'd served in KGB Counterintelligence and played a role in the capture of famous traitors, such as Dmitriy Polyakov and Adolf Tolkachev. The old man was a living legend, the personification of a heroic past. In a word, *Davydych* represented continuity.

Chapter 13

1987

Dzerzhinsky Higher School of the KGB
Michurinskiy Prospekt, 70
Moscow, Russia

The man's eyes were wide, and he was screaming, the veins in his neck distended. His shrieks echoed through the empty foundry. There was no other sound.

The terrified man was naked and bound to a heavy wooden plank with what appeared to be thin piano wire, wrapped round and round his body in tight, painful coils, rendering him completely immobile except for his head. It required four stout men to carry him toward the open, flaming maw of one of the foundry's furnaces. The men wore heavy, heat resistant suits and gloves, their faces grotesquely masked by hoods with a rectangular slit of thick glass for eyes that made them even more hideous. The flames were so intense that the two men at the foot of the plank raised their hands to protect their faces from the heat despite their hoods.

The man bound to the plank, knowing what was to come, continued to scream.

With a heave the men dropped the foot of the plank onto the lip of the open furnace. The ones nearest the furnace retreated quickly to the other end to help their comrades feed the plank ever so slowly into the flames.

As his feet were consumed, the shrieks of the bound man took on an unearthly quality, warbling almost to the edge of audibility and renewing with each breath. His mouth was so far open that he might have dislocated his jaw.

The men continued to shove the plank into the flames. The bound man's legs were now completely engulfed as the white hot furnace, hot enough to melt metal, greedily ate away his flesh and then turned the bones black and brittle until they too were so much smoke up the flue.

The screaming continued until the flames reached the bound man's chest. By that time, the face was no longer human. His gut exploded in a riot of wet entrails that lasted but a few seconds, sizzling in the flames. When the screaming stopped, the men heaved what remained all the way into the furnace in a single motion.

In the back of the auditorium someone was vomiting.

Simultaneously horrified and fascinated, Lieutenant Gleb Solntsev did not dare turn his head from the screen or close his eyes like a child at a horror movie lest his fellow graduates notice his discomfort, and he choked back his own rising gorge. The film had been in color, and the sound track, while scratchy, had been amped up to ear splitting levels.

General Nikolay Davydovich Lisitsyn, accompanied by Colonel-General Rstislav Kromarkin, head of the Dzerzhinsky Higher School of the KGB, stalked to the middle of the stage. The only sounds in the auditorium were their footsteps.

Kromarkin, his slightly corpulent figure held stiffly erect so that the buttons of his uniform jacket strained to hold in his gut, stood in the middle of the stage and gazed out over the audience of new graduates. His voice, when he spoke, filled a nervous silence. "To be worthy of the title of *Chekist* you must remember always that ours is a mission of love and devotion - love of the Fatherland, devotion to the Russian people, the *narod*. This was the philosophy of our founder, Feliks Dzherzinski. And we, you, are the beneficiaries and guardians of his legacy. We do our duty in the true *Chekist* tradition."

Kromarkin glanced over his shoulder at the now blank movie screen, then back at the audience. "I want to introduce General Lisitsyn of the Second Chief Directorate, who will now address you."

He surrendered the dais to the Colonel, who in contrast to Kromarkin was lean and broad-shouldered and still with a full head of jet black hair.

Lisitsyn stared silently at them for long moments, seeming to engage each of them directly in the eyes until the young officers fairly squirmed in their seats. At last, he spoke.

"The film you have just seen would be shocking were it not for the truth behind it. The man was a traitor, one of the worst traitors in our history who betrayed the trust of the KGB and the Motherland. You are too young to remember his name, but he betrayed our most precious military secrets to the Americans. You are privileged to be the first graduates to see the film since 1965. It is a reminder of the fate that awaits all traitors to the Motherland, and it is a warning."

Lisitsyn glared at the audience to underscore the import of his words, before concluding, "From now on, as in the past, the film you have just seen will be a part of every graduation from the Academy. True *Chekist* tradition will be restored and honored."

Gleb Solntsev took those words to heart.

Chapter 14

The continuity with a glorious past that Lisitsyn represented inspired Solntsev as much today as thirty years ago. The general had generously shared his skills with the young KGB officer and others as he molded them into his own image. His legacy was to pass to the orphaned children of *perestroika* the iron spirit of the true Chekist.

"If you don't know what to do, talk to a veteran." Gleb followed this rule from the beginning. *Davydych* was just such a *starik*, having formally retired long ago he remained vigorous and worked in the Lubyanka archives where he planned to die on the job. He simply could not live without these walls.

It did him no harm when a former student was named to head the newly formed FSB, and even less when that same person became President of Russia. Certain tasks were entrusted to the FSB that would never have been shared with the SVR. One these assignments fell on the general's shoulders.

"Nikolay Davydovich, how're things," said Gleb, still in the doorway.

Davydych greeted Gleb with a warm smile, but spotted the concern on his protégé's face.

"So far, so good. But there's still a loose end. We had a chat with Illarionov's editor. At first he professed complete innocence, but finally admitted that Illarionov's son has the prison recording. He also said the little bastard was going to look up Zhuravlev, one of the people who wrote the original Ryazan report. That rat Tretyakov gave the name to Illarionov."

"Surely this Zhuravlev doesn't have any proof."

"We can't know for certain. He's dead," was the General's dry response. "Our boys went to his apartment for a chat, but the idiot threw himself from an eleventh floor balcony. No one expected that. It was all very unpleasant. They searched his apartment and found nothing. The possibility that he passed something to Illarionov's son seems small, but ..."

"Illarionov's son will have to be taken care of," said Solntsev, his voice low, as though he feared someone might overhear. "Otherwise, we'll never hear the end of it, especially now that he has that recording."

Lisitsyn shook his head, "I don't like it. Imagine the suspicions the boy's death on the heels of his father's would raise. We need to find out what materials he has before deciding. For time being, the public won't make a connection between the deaths of Illarionov, Tretyakov, and Zhuravlev. But you're right. We can't wait too long.

"Now why don't you tell me what brings you here?"

Solntsev told him about the conversation with Pasha and the boys.

"And what do you think?" asked Lisitsyn.

"She's too smart not to have understood the consequences of telling me about Illarionov. I think we can trust her discretion. But Pasha does have a point. She knows the son."

Lisitsyn folded his arms and waited like a patient uncle listening to a nephew's problems.

Solntsev shook his head. "I don't want anything to happen to her. She's truly talented and has served us well."

The general pulled at his chin as if arriving at a decision. "I may have a way out," he said softly. "At the beginning of this year the Ministry of Foreign Affairs requested a secret meeting with us that resulted in an interesting decision. They want to strengthen our disinformation and influence operations in the West. They finally realized that more needs to be done than buying politicians. The idea is to create organizations to attract the children of Russian emigrants and their American friends. In the old days we got them right out of the cradle, *Oktyabryata,* Pioneers, *Komsomol.*" He closed his eyes in nostalgic recollection, but caught himself quickly.

"It's not a bad idea, but we didn't show much enthusiasm. What intelligence officer wants to spend resources and send highly qualified professionals for youth propaganda work? Of course, there are some elements of espionage involved, such as spotting candidates for recruitment or keeping an eye on what dissidents and other traitors are up to – simple surveillance operations."

Gleb perked up as he caught Lisitsyn's drift. "Of course. Such work would not appeal to ambitious young officers. They wouldn't see it as a winning career track. It would take years to produce results. They all see themselves recruiting a brilliant source after a couple of years and getting some more stars on their epaulets."

Lisitsyn agreed. "This would have been an ideal assignment for the *Komsomol,* but there no longer is a *Komsomol.* I've been thinking about your kids and planned to call you. It's a job more for external intelligence than us, but you know who the Kremlin trusts more."

"So what you're saying is that we could give Olga a few months' training and send her abroad, maybe to the States?" Solntsev saw a double benefit.

Olga would be far away from Moscow and more importantly, far away from Illarionov's son, and she would be doing a job for which she was ideally suited.

Lisitsyn cocked his head and grimaced slightly at Gleb's enthusiasm. "You don't think sending her to the States entails a risk?"

"Her handlers will pay careful attention to her. On the plus side, Olga already has three years' experience with "*Svoi*," speaks excellent English and works well with young people. She's good at public speaking. It doesn't hurt that she's attractive, either. She's proven she can handle the tough jobs. And she'll get better with proper training."

Chapter 15

Vlad stared blankly at his computer screen. The hundreds and thousands of words were beginning to run together. The web was replete with obscure rumors, heated arguments that spread like wildfire and disappeared just as suddenly. There were pictures, faces, absurd clips from movies and cartoons designed to hide the true identities of their originators. He was a patient and methodical reader, shifting from one on-line forum to another like a machine, a cold mechanism incapable of human emotion, forever trapped in a virtual universe, a search engine like Google.

He was afflicted by the unthinkable suspicion that he was responsible for his father's death. The realization washed over his body like an icy shower. He had told one person and one person only about his father's plans. It had been irresponsible, a childish desire to win an argument.

Could Olga Polyanskaya have informed on him, pointed the murderers to his father?

Of one thing he was certain: the murder was no coincidence. There was Tretyakov's death, and now Zhuravlev's suicide. Could little Olga really have been the spark that ignited this horror, just as the FSB ignited those bombs so many years ago?

Olga was deeply involved in "*Svoi*," and he did not doubt that people from "*Svoi*" were responsible for his father's death. It was the only thing that made sense. It was far from the first time that "Solntsev's bully boys had beaten a journalist.

Vlad refused to spare himself the guilt. It would

weigh upon him forever and perhaps eventually bring him down. But before that happened, he would have his revenge on the ravening beasts that were devouring his country.

He needed more information, more evidence, and so he began with an internet search for anything related to "*Svoi.*" Many considered the organization an excellent starting point for an administrative career. But Vlad paid special attention to the critics in the hope that someone knew the organization's darker secrets.

It took several hours, but at last his efforts were rewarded. An anonymous writer using the pseudonym "Darth Vader" responded to a long, laudatory post about the Kremlin's useful work with young people. "This guy Solntsev trains 'socially active citizens? In truth he turns them into banal murderers. Compared to the things that take place in this sect the Soviet *Komsomol* was kindergarten."

Navigation of the Internet is a survival skill for Russian dissidents, and Vlad was no exception. Like a bloodhound on the scent, he teased out everything he could about "Darth Vader." The representative of "the Dark Side" was 29 years-old, lived in Moscow, liked to play the electric guitar, and his old instrument was up for sale. Vlad didn't need a guitar, but this was a way to contact "Vader." He posted a message indicating interest in the guitar.

He was rewarded by a return post the same evening proposing to meet the next day. The movie villain's real name was Nikolay, and he lived in the *Cheremushki* area in south-western Moscow.

Vlad spent a restless night disturbed by visions of a world on fire while he stood by and watched as houses, trees, and tiny human figures lost their form and color until they were shapeless mounds of ash. Then came a strong, cold wind that blew across the gray landscape to sweep away the remains of the charred universe and leave an empty black plane as the wind dispersed the brittle flakes.

The rendezvous in *Cheremushki* turned out to be a garage used by a rock band for rehearsals. He was met by a long-haired fellow whose indifferent manner did not promise a long conversation. As soon as Vlad asked about "*Svoi*," Kolya (Nikolay) refused to talk.

"You don't understand," he said with a nervous glance over his shoulder, "They're murderers. If I say even a word about them and they find out, I'm a dead man. Forget about them, and forget about me."

"I'll forget," said Vlad, "but will they? You've already written about them on the Internet and publicly called them murderers. It's foolish the think they didn't see it. If it was easy for me to find you, how hard would it be for a former Chekist like Solntsev?"

"But what can I do?" Kolya was terrified.

"Hiding for the rest of your life isn't the answer," replied Vlad. Then he remembered Golovina's advice. "Maybe you should go to the West, maybe to the US. Get any kind of visa you can and then ask for political asylum. Tell them all you know. Maybe after a while you'll get into some American rock group."

"Do they grant asylum so quickly?"

"Not right away. But tell me what you know before you leave. I'll not publish anything until you're safe. After that, no one will believe you could ever come back."

He had no right to say such things to Kolya, but his father's death drove him to extremes. He was fighting his father's war as best he could, like a wounded wolf cub snapping at every opportunity to strike a blow against powerful and ruthless enemies. He didn't intend to deceive Kolya, and would not, of course, publish his information so long as he was in Russia. He knew nothing about political asylum, but he was certain of one thing: he would never seek it himself so long as his father's murderers remained unpunished.

"OK," sighed Kolya, who was not as realistic as Vlad. "But don't judge me too harshly. I was there myself. I was young and stupid. I wanted to serve my country, understand? I wanted to be a part of something important. You probably don't understand."

"I understand perfectly."

"I was very active," continued Kolya. "I was dedicated. After a couple of years, Solntsev took an interest and invited me into what he calls his "inner circle." He uses these people for special tasks. There were ten of us, and they used us for all sorts of dirty work: beatings, blackmail, slander – I literally picked up shit and throw it at people. Sometimes we went to opposition gatherings and broke them up. Once we even released noxious gas. Solntsev said we were defending our country. Then some young liberal managed to infiltrate our group. He found out a lot and was going to make it public. Gleb ordered us to beat him to death."

Vlad struggled to keep his voice even. "And what did you do?"

"Me? What about *them*?" Kolya's words were heated. "I didn't sign up for 'wet work.' I left and didn't go back. I never found out what happened, and I didn't want to. It's better not to know. You don't just walk away from Gleb Solntsev. It makes you a traitor and a potential danger. So I hid and didn't say anything until I wrote that bit on the Internet. I wish I hadn't done it."

The former "*Svoi*" thug lived like a rat in a hole afraid for his life and stirred a vestige of sympathy in Vlad. "OK. Thank you, Kolya, man to man, if only because you didn't kill anyone ... You should try to get out of the country. Don't waste any time, and let me know. Agreed?"

"Agreed," glumly replied Kolya. "I want to make music in America."

Vlad shrugged. "Good luck."

Chapter 16

On the way home Vlad regretted the additional stain on his already overburdened conscience. He'd held out a false hope to Nikolay and secretly recorded their conversation. He would come clean about the recording once Nikolay was safe and unlikely to do anything rash, but this thought did little to lighten the mounting burden of guilt. It seemed to flow through his veins like poison that would infect everyone he touched.

The street in front of his apartment building was blocked by emergency vehicles and a fire truck. The smell of smoke became stronger as he approached the entrance, and the premonition of last night's dream hollowed his stomach.

Men in protective gear descended the stairs toward the landing below his apartment. The blue paint on the walls bore smudges of soot scored with rivulets of water. The smell became oppressive. Vlad rushed up the stairs.

"What are you doing?" One of the firemen restrained him.

"I live here!" he cried, shoving the fireman aside. "What happened?"

"A gas leak." Was the laconic reply, as though such things were an everyday occurrence. It apparently led to the fire. Unfortunately, a woman died – the only casualty." He attempted without much success to appear sympathetic. "Could you identify her? Who was she to you? Mother?"

Maybe the smell of smoke was too strong – he was suddenly faint, his will paralyzed to the point that he could no longer think. He stood there unable to move at the threshold staring into the scorched apartment that was now stained in the black and ash gray tones of death, like an old movie drained of color. In a breeze from a broken window brittle flakes of ash circled in a macabre ballet.

*****

Marya Fedorovna Golovina intuited that something terrible had happened. The look on Vlad's face expressed something inexplicably horrific – profound emptiness and despair infected his soul.

"My dear boy, what has happened?" She stepped aside to allow him to pass.

His voice was cold, mechanical. "Do you have the material I left with you yesterday?"

She detected the fevered light in his eyes and the barely perceptible shaking of his fingers. Her own tragic experience signaled that the young man was on the verge of collapse.

"Come in." She spoke calmly, willing her strength to him. "I have it. What's happened?"

"They were looking for them." He sank heavily onto a chair at the table in the big room. "They tried to find them in my apartment. Then to conceal the search, they organized a small gas explosion."

"My God!" Horrified, Golovina took his hand. "Was anyone hurt?"

"Mother is dead."

Golovina saw the tears start in his eyes.

"We've got to go."

She unexpectedly grabbed his arm, surprising him with her strength. She pulled him to the tiny office with the archived documents. Not a trace of her former worry remained. A remarkable inner strength showed through her wrinkles and frail frame.

"Forget everything I said to you before." She spoke rapidly as she closed the door behind them. Forget about a visa. You'll never get one. Any attempt to leave legally will be detected. But there is a way out. Before the war with Ukraine I managed to get some dissidents across the border, people with no other way out. We worked out a reliable route near Belgorod, not far from Kharkov."

She opened a drawer and produced an old, torn map.

"We saved about ten people, but these days it's more difficult to get into Ukraine. When the war began my friend Bogdan volunteered for the Donbas Battalion. As far as I know, he's on rotation right now in his home town, Kharkov. So I propose that you travel to Belgorod on the electric train. This is safer than by car. I'll write the name and address of the man you need to contact in Belgorod."

She reached across the battered wooden table and took his hand. "You'll stay here tonight, and tomorrow morning we'll send you on your way. I'll give you whatever money you'll need for the trip."

He started to object, but she shook her head vigorously. "Don't worry about it. You've got to get that information out of the country now. There's no other way."

He wanted to object, but in reality there was nothing left in Russia for him. To remain meant death. The uncompromising truth was that he could not stand up to an organized group of murderers. The gang of bandits in charge of his country would never permit the publication of the material if they had to kill half of Moscow.

Golovina's voice penetrated his thoughts. "You can do so much for Russia," she was saying, "but you won't survive here. You must live even if only so that your parents' deaths were not in vain. They were murdered, and so was Tretyakov and God alone knows how many more or where it will stop."

Guilt again engulfed him. People were dead because they had agreed to help him or had even a single contact with him, just because they had been seen with him.

I've got to get out of the country. Not for myself, but for them. So that no one else suffers.

He suddenly thought about "Darth Vader."

"I've got to make a phone call," he said, surprising Golovina.

He dialed Nikolay's number on his cell phone. He planned to arrange to meet him so they could escape together. After several rings, a female voice answered, and it sounded like she was in distress.

"Excuse me," he said, "but may I speak with Nikolay? I'm a friend."

"No." There was a catch in the voice now. "You can't."

"But what's happened?" His stomach plunged into a dark pit.

"He was in an automobile accident. He's dead." These last words sounded as though they were wrenched forcibly from her throat before she closed the connection.

Vlad slumped against the wall and closed his eyes, now more convinced than ever that he rather than Solntsev was an accomplice to murder. *I can't save anyone. I only destroy lives.* This terrible thought saturated his mind, and it frightened him more than the possibility of his own death.

Irresponsible, naïve boy! What have I done?

"I'll go," he covered his face with his hands and sobbed like a lost child.

Chapter 17

Gorlovka, Ukraine

Alena Melnichenko dreamed she was in a parched field searching for her son. He must be near-by, but she couldn't find him. There was a rumble in the air that grew louder and louder, until it was a roar of explosions and she awoke. From the edge of town came the sound of gunfire and the familiar echoes of artillery, though not as loud as in her dream.

Only half awake, she could almost imagine she was happy, but this lasted only a few seconds before she was brought back down by the realities of her existence. At such moments, she could barely gather the strength to get out of bed.

But she had to if only for the sake of going yet again to her mother-in-law's to try to see her son. It was already mid-day, but she felt exhausted. After a night of unending dances at the strip club where she worked, a few hours' rest in the morning just was not enough.

She stretched, wincing at the pain in her right shoulder, a reminder of Artem's anger the night before. *I must decide about Artem.*

Sometimes it might be better not to wake up, at all.

Seized by self-pity, she sank deeper into the pillow and tried to wipe the painful thoughts from her mind. Her husband and his mother would not return her child, and Artem would do nothing. This was especially clear after last night. In fact, the man she was living with seemed pleased not to have a young child underfoot.

It was the first time he had struck her, and that was a bad sign. She would have to find another place to live because the problems here would only get worse. But if she left Artem he would stop giving her money. Without money how could she pay for an apartment? If she took a second job to pay for an apartment, who would care for her son?

The autumn weather was chilly, but there was no city heat in Gorlovka. She tiptoed to the tiny kitchen with its bare shelves. Alena simply could not find the time to clean the stains or the scum from the gas stove or the oilcloth that covered the small table by the window. The fridge was almost empty, not counting the half-empty bottle of vodka that Artem had uncharacteristically left unfinished. There were some mushrooms she'd gathered in August. It would not be a simple thing to get more food.

She started at a knock at the door. Could it be Artem? But he always left early and got home late, if he even came home. She went to the door and fearfully put an eye to the peephole. With a sigh of relief, she opened the door to a welcome visitor.

"Misha!"

Mihailo Korzh smiled broadly as he stepped inside. "Shall we have a bite to eat?" he strode into the kitchen and set a large, cloth bag on the table then began pulling groceries out of it as he announced each delicacy with the aplomb of a TV announcer.

"Imported cheese. A forbidden product that must be eaten quickly. Real Ukrainian *salo*[5], bananas and sugared pineapple, but that's for dessert. A few cans of corned beef for reserves. Fresh milk and

---

[5] Fatback

yoghurt for your son. Chicken legs – you can find some vegetables and cook up some borscht. And finally, we have some oil, sausage, and fresh apples."

"Misha," she could barely speak, "where did you find all this?"

"My aunt was in Mariopol. Don't worry. She brought back enough for everybody."

"Your aunt?" Alena was dubious. "You're an orphan."

"A man is an orphan if he has no family, and an aunt is family. So, take a seat and eat something."

Mihailo was lying. There was no aunt. He'd bought the food with the last of his money from re-sellers from Mariopol. He hadn't worried about money since he'd sent his wife and son to Kharkov under the pretext of an operation on the boy's eyes.

"So, how are things with you?" he asked, taking a seat at the small table. He spread some *salo* on a slice of bread.

"It's not good, Misha."

He could see that she wanted to talk.

"You know," she said, "I told you already. Life was normal with my husband before the war, and then he lost his job. He fell apart. I'd come home and find him passed out on the floor with a broken vodka bottle beside him, and my son was crawling through it and playing with the shards of glass. I had to get my son, Vitya, out and at first found a small apartment. But the prices have gone through the roof, as you know. They don't pay much at the club, not enough to keep the apartment. I got into debt and then met Artem, just like I met you, in the club. I've lived here with him ever since. I took Vitya to my mother-in-law and tried to convince Artem to bring him here. But my mother-in-law gave me an ultimatum – return to my husband, or never see my son again."

She began to sob softly.

"And Artem? Couldn't he help you get the boy back? He's in the militia and has a lot of pull in the city."

"He doesn't want to, Misha." She finally broke out in tears. "He doesn't want my son. We argued about it again last night and he hit me. I want to leave him, to find an apartment of my own, but what would I live on then? Artem sometimes brings food home. He helps with my debts. I live here for free. Sometimes he gives me some money and I can go a few days without working." She rolled her eyes.

"Did you do what I asked?"

"Yes," she sighed. "No problem. He thought he must have lost his credentials somewhere in the city."

Alena rose from the table and retrieved the small, leather wallet from a drawer where she'd hidden it under some dish towels.

"But, Misha, you're not going to do anything bad, are you, something that would create a problem?" She was nervous.

"Alena, I already told you. No problems. I just have to get out of town. It's a stupid situation. My son needs an operation on his eyes, but they won't let me travel because I was an artist at the DNR Ministry of Defense. An artist! I made the decorations for the Victory Day celebration. But once you've worked for the military on DNR territory, they won't let you leave. I'm going to put my photo on this ID and go to Kharkov with my boy. That's all. I'm an artist, after all, so I can surely falsify an ID."

"I understand." She shrugged almost indifferently. "That's the way things are. I suppose it's necessary in wartime. The Junta won't leave us in peace."

Her words were painful for Mihailo, but he ignored it. He said, "Alena, if I can get out for a week or two you and your son could use my apartment. For free. Here are the keys."

"Misha." She leapt from her chair and wrapped her arms around him. "I thought Artem loved me, you know? But he's just like the rest. I know things are tough on him, too. He's in the militia. But that doesn't mean he can slap women around. War makes such pigs of men. Or maybe I'm just unlucky. But you're not a pig. You're a good man, but you're married ..."

"I understand why you hooked up with him ..." Mihailo stopped talking and gently extracted himself from her embrace.

He choked back a silent scream, keeping his face calm so as not to betray the storm that raged in his heart. *But he's a terrorist, a murderer, a tool of the occupiers, and you sleep with him and still wonder why life is so unpleasant?*

"He's a militiaman." She finished his sentence. "They always have money."

She said this so simply, so naïvely, that Mihailo didn't know how to react. He'd never figured out exactly how to act with Alena. She supported his enemies, she slept with murderers for a handful of *hryvnia* and a basket of food. But she was so unhappy and weak that he could not think of her as an enemy. She was another casualty of war, like many others – ignorant and deceived, maybe lacking some scruples, but still a casualty. Whatever her conduct, he was fighting for her.

Mihailo did not know Alena by chance. He'd gone to the strip club because fighters frequented the place.   He wanted to see if they had particular girlfriends that might be susceptible to providing military secrets they learned from pillow talk.   Artem and Alena were easy to spot.

A short investigation showed that Artem Volkov held fairly senior rank among the separatists and that meant he could pass through checkpoints without inspection and enter nearly any military site.   All of this power lay in his credentials.   The groceries were the price for Alena's cooperation.

He was ready to hate her for some of the things she said, incapable of coming to terms with her omnivorous naïveté. And still he cared for her the way one might care for a wayward child.   He wondered how she would react if he told her that her so-called Junta were fighting to protect the city's residents, risking their lives for her, while the man with whom she shared a bed was ready to blow up entire cities along with their residents.

It was strange, but the more he lied to Alena, the more responsible he became for her; the more he took advantage of her blindness, the more grateful he became for her involuntary help.   The more she became entangled in his net, the greater the need to protect her from danger.

This remarkable coincidence of cynicism and humanity was new to him.   It was strange that these contradictory emotions should so easily fit together, like pieces of a huge jigsaw puzzle.   So now he freely offered his apartment to her knowing that if he got out of Gorlovka alive he could not return before the war was over.

"Alena," he said, striking his palm against his forehead, "I'm an idiot. I brought food, but nothing to drink.   Could you run out to a store, even if they only have juice or water? I'll give you the money. Don't spend it on wine. You probably don't even have tea or real coffee here. I'll wait for you."

She was more than happy to take the *hrynia*. "Sure, it'll just take a few minutes. There's a kiosk not far from here."

"Don't buy the junk they sell from kiosks," he said. "Find a real store and bring back some imported coffee."

He waited for the door to close behind her and then went to the living room where a high cabinet stood against the wall. He started pulling out the drawers one after another. There were maps, documents, lists, and a diagram of command duties. Types of weapons, battle plans.

Good Lord! He was almost overwhelmed. His blood churned, threatening to burst through thin veins. This was more than he could have hoped - an invaluable discovery.

Using his smartphone, he photographed everything. The Ukrainian intelligence operative spread out every page, checked the focus, and pressed the button to capture every secret on the small screen and store it safely away in the phone's memory. He determined to copy every document regardless of what might happen.

He left Alena after an hour. The cell phone seemed heavy in his pocket. Now came the second part of the operation: alter the credentials and pay a visit to Vasya of the MGB – and then get out of town as fast as possible.

A talk with Vasya could not be more appropriate. Following the full-scale invasion by Russian forces at the end of August, local fighters in many occupied Donbas cities faced serious difficulties.

Professional Russian troops entered Gorlovka almost immediately, accompanied by GRU *Spetsnaz*. The GRU was ruthlessly efficient. Some separatist field commanders simply disappeared, some were dismissed, and others arrested.

"Bes" and his closest advisors had left the city a few days earlier for an undisclosed location, and those who remained behind occupied themselves with "cleansing."

The Russian "stewards" did not forgive their Ukrainian satellites the slightest initiative or disobedience. Amid the confusion, Gorlovka officials became so concerned for their own fates that they neglected to deal with the dissent among the common people.

The lower ranks did not know who their commander might be the next day and thought of only one thing: guess who it might be and do anything to please him. Some groups resisted the "cleansings" and engaged in armed skirmishes with the invaders. To be on the street after curfew could be fatal. In other words, it was hard to take advantage of the dark in Gorlovka.

Chapter 18

Mihailo found Vasya the next day at a table in a small café near MGB Headquarters and headed straight for him.

"Greetings," he said with abroad smile. "Remember me? You gave me a ride to Donetsk the other day."

Vasya leaned away. "Yeah, I remember." His voice was not particularly friendly. Maybe things were not all well with the MGB.

"They promoted me." Mihailo sat without an invitation and pulled out the altered identification. "You probably heard that the command has changed, there's a new Chief of Staff, and he knows me."

"Congratulations." Vasya had no desire to get on the bad side of anyone of rank.

"I have an almost official request for you," Mihailo began. "The new command is looking things over, and they want to know what we have in the old Gorlovka munitions plant. They need to know exactly where the mines have been placed so that our boys don't accidentally blow themselves up."

"I can't help you," sighed Vasya. "You need to send an official request to Command. That's the only way."

Mihailo gave Vasya a stare usually reserved for the mentally disabled, and then spoke slowly and carefully. "Vasya, What Command do you have in mind? Yesterday they found the head of the Gorlovka militia on his own doorstep with a cracked skull. The assistant prosecutor was shot. Your Command won't be around tomorrow, and the day after they'll find them in a ditch. Don't you understand? They're taking out all of the locals, all of them. I survived only because I serve the Russians. And you have to serve them too, if you want to survive. They're the bosses now. Forget about anyone else. I looked you up because I remembered you and want to help a good guy. If you do a good job for the new powers that be, they won't bother you. Think about it. Things have changed. 'Bes' is gone. If you want to act like a bureaucrat you'll end up like all the rest."

The effect was immediate. "Actually there is no placement diagram," he said. "I helped plant the explosives and can show you where they are."

"Excellent. Let's go."

"Right now?"

"No time like the present."

*****

The ruined hulk of the abandoned factory resembled the set of an American post-apocalyptic movie. A clear September sky was visible through the shattered windows. Overhead, teetering slabs of destroyed walls leaned against steel girders, threatening at any moment to bury the entire building. Girders and rebar showed through gaps in crumbling sections of the floor.

Mihailo followed Vasya, climbing over piles of stone and rubble and stumbling on the uneven floor through half-ruined machine shops.

Periodically, Vasya would point out the location of a mine in a debris-covered corner. "Over here, and in the basement, too."

Mihailo silently photographed it all with his smartphone and noted the positions on a crude building diagram he had drawn.

"Is that everything?" he asked Vasya after what seemed an interminable period.

"I suppose so."

"You suppose so, or is that everything?"

"That's everything."

They were preparing to leave when footfalls sounded on the other side of the wall and echoed throughout the enormous space. Mihailo froze, and Vasya fixed him with a questioning eye. A camouflaged figure appeared around a corner with a machine-pistol Mihailo recognized as a *Bizon* 9X18mm Makarov, the same weapon he had trained on in Kharkov. The gun was pointed directly at them.

"Who are you?" barked the soldier. "What are you doing here?"

Vasya spoke first. "The Deputy Commander here wanted me to show him where the mines were planted."

"Deputy Commander?" the guard squinted at them, the epitome of suspicion. "I spoke with the Deputy Commander not ten minutes ago, and he ordered me to see who was sneaking around the factory. The patrol reported a civilian vehicle on the property."

"What do you mean?" Vasya stared at Mihailo, a shadow of comprehension clouding his face. He reached for his holster.

Mihailo reacted without thinking. He struck Vasya on the jaw with one hand and grabbed his pistol with the other before diving behind a fallen section of ceiling.

A shot rang out behind him, and then a burst of automatic fire. He sprinted for a door and turned the corner.

He'd last fired a weapon was during training

hurriedly organized by the Donbas Battalion in Kharkov. He'd never fired on a living person in his life. Would he be able to pull the trigger now?

He ducked into another corridor and then another. Cries of alarm and the sound of many feet told him there was more than one pursuer.

Mihailo took a darkened flight of stairs to the basement, tripping over piles of debris, bumping into walls. His life was measured by the length of his stride, his laboring lungs, and the beat of his heart against his ribs. Bare pipes and metal mesh reinforcement crawled along the walls. He found another stairway that took him up to an abandoned foundry with mountains of rubble and iron sheets on the floor. Wind howled through breaches in the walls and roof.

A soldier appeared with his machine-pistol at the ready. Mihailo dove to the floor behind a brick wall covered in chipped whitewash and squirmed behind a large, metal plate. A burst of automatic fire tore the air above him as he pressed his body into the rock dust on the floor. Blood ran down his face from contact with the bricks.

He was a normal man, not a soldier. He was a child, a kindergarten adventurer pretending to be an intelligence operative. He could never in his life have imagined what it was like to be shot at.

An instinctive, animal-like desire to live, overcame him. He could see the figure of the soldier through a narrow space between the metal sheet and brick wall. Not a man, but a figure, rushing toward him, death in camouflage, an occupier prepared to kill him just as he'd killed many others. Biting his lip, Mihailo pressed against the cold wall and tried to move the metal sheet. Its sharp surface cut his fingers, but it moved. The Russian soldier turned toward the sound, but too late. Mihailo was already on his feet with pistol aimed, and he pulled the trigger.

A high, sharp cry followed the shot, echoed off the ruined walls and died. His feet leaden, Mihailo approached the body. He was shaking and encompassed by alternating waves of hot and cold. The room around him dimmed, and he prayed for strength. The enemy in camouflage lay at his feet, a thoroughly dead "little green man." Mihailo picked up the machine-pistol and ran to a breach in the wall.

Finally and unredeemably, the war had caught up with him in all its relentless, bloody essence - with a single shot, his first kill, his first real battle.

He made it to the street and passed through some bushes and a hole in the factory fence.

The fake ID was still in his pocket. It would take some time for his pursuers to pass his name to the road blocks, and Mihailo hoped he could get as far as the recently liberated village of Kramatorsk and from there travel safely to Kharkov.

Chapter 19

Yekatarinburg, Russia

The capital of the Urals greeted Olga with a golden autumn, sunny, full of color, and a clear, bottomless blue sky, gentle and charming. She was met at the train station by a woman of around thirty, a tall, attractive blonde, tastefully dressed in a well-cut cream dress. She displayed a Hollywood smile, the epitome of perfection right off the pages of a fashion magazine. The smile seemed genuine, warm – or Olga simply wanted it to be so.

"Greetings. I'm Nastya," said the vision. "How was the trip?"

"It was wonderful."

"What would you prefer? Shall we go to the apartment immediately, or if you're not too tired, I can show you the center of town."

"I'm not a bit tired," exclaimed Olga. At that moment she could walk through the entire, unfamiliar city if it were necessary. This adventure was so incredibly surreal to her.

"Good. Let's go." Nastya beamed and headed to her parked car.

Olga liked the city center. Of course, Yekatarinburg lacked the scale and majesty of Moscow with its broad thoroughfares, ancient, winding streets and splendid cathedrals. But it was clearly a successful metropolis. The carefully restored old buildings in the center made for attractive architectural variety. Sunlight reflected from the glass expanse of shopping centers and the *Visotskiy Tower* skyscraper.

The *Vayner* pedestrian street reminded her of Moscow's *Arbat*, and the cobblestoned main square, named in honor of the 1905 Revolution was graced by a familiar statue of Lenin with his arm outstretched.

The river walk was just beyond the square, where the Iset River was channeled into a straight canal, bordered by pleasant walkways and parks. There was a small dam over which passed the inevitably named Lenin Prospect.

Nastya was a good tour guide. "A long time ago, there was a factory here, and that was the beginning of our city. This is the oldest part." She pointed to a 19th Century structure with elegant, miniature columns, gothic arches and delicate stucco decoration on windows and cornices, the home of a famous native. Beyond this was the Governor's residence.

Upon closer examination, the river was incredibly polluted, but when the sky reflected from its surface it appeared a crystalline blue. There were more 19th Century estates along the opposite bank, and just beyond were newer buildings, including the local White House with the Russian flag waving above.

They walked along the embankment toward a tall, white cathedral with golden cupolas.

"That's the Temple of the Blood. It was built on the spot where Nikolas II and his family were executed," explained Nastya. "And a little farther is the Resurrection Church."

Without warning, Nastya interrupted her narrative to say, "By the way, I'm not giving you this tour just for fun. Over the next two weeks you must become intimately familiar with the city – all the main streets, public transport, traffic, attractions. Success will depend on it."

Olga was surprised by Nastya's suddenly

serious, businesslike tone in contrast to her former chumminess. It was time to remember why she was here.

"Do you drive?" asked Nastya.

"I took lessons last year, but I've not had much experience."

"You will," Nasya assured her. "Well, shall we go home?" She was smiling again.

"Home" was a small, one-room apartment in a bedroom neighborhood where Olga would live for a month and a half. The outskirts of Yekaterinburg were identical to those in Moscow, the same gray slab, ten-story buildings, the same cozy, slightly overgrown courtyards with their squeaking swings, just like they were throughout Russia.

The apartment was furnished in old Soviet style. There was a stout, heavy table, an old-fashioned chest of drawers and shelves along one wall.

Waiting for them there a man of middle age with a severe air and a big, gray moustache that reminded her either of a walrus or Stalin. The very sight of him made Olga nervous. This man bore no resemblance to outgoing, charming Gleb Solntsev.

"Welcome to Yekaterinburg, Olga Vladimirovna." The mustachioed man spoke with the manner of someone accustomed to obedience as he invited her to be seated. Gleb never used her name and patronymic. "My name is Boris Ivanovich. I congratulate you on your first assignment abroad, and to the States, at that. Do you understand how hard you'll need to prepare for it?"

Olga nodded.

"You'll live here. It looks pretty cozy to me. Nastya will pick you up every morning around eight, so you'll have to be ready. You'll study a lot, well into the night, until you've mastered all the required skills, perfected them. So take it seriously. Are we agreed?"

"Agreed," she replied breathlessly as excitement mixed with panic grew within her, manifested by a lump rising in her throat. *I won't be able to do this! It's all completely new to me.*

"There's a lot to learn," continued Boris Ivanovich, "Surveillance, surveillance detection, working alone and as a team member, the use of special photographic devices, secret writing and encoding, *maskirovka.* Your life will depend on these skills, by the way."

Olga's head was spinning from a strange mixture of fear and exaltation. She curled her fingers in the cloth of the sofa, afraid of showing her feelings.

Things were not nearly so remarkable in practice as they seemed when she heard them for the first time. For two weeks she wandered the byways of Yekaterinburg, sometimes on foot, sometimes driving, but always under Nastya's watchful eyes. Finally, she began to recognize patterns, intersections, landmarks and how they related one to another. Yekaterinburg revealed her face to Olga, an unforgettable diagram of buildings and streets.

Next, she was instructed to follow randomly selected targets around the city and compose thick dossiers on their movements, contacts, and activities. She found this tedious and exhausting, and she wore out her shoes. She soon discovered that heels were not the best footwear for long days on the street. The "targets" were not in the least interesting, and following them everywhere was unbearable. The loneliness was oppressive, and there was no one to help her. Her time was no longer her own, and the absence of freedom was worse than anything else.

She was glued to the "targets" like a marionette on strings as she dutifully followed kept an eye on their backs in crowded shopping centers or carefully maintained her distance on deserted streets at night.

She was often tempted to slack off, and once she did become distracted. It happened in the park next to Resurrection Cathedral. A yellow carpet of fallen leaves and dried grass rustled under her feet as she pushed her way through the thin branches of maple and rowan trees. A duck pond lay in the middle of the park, and a weak breeze carried broad maple leaves to its uneven surface. The water reacted with small ripples and then quieted again to reflect the blurred outline of the trees.

When she lifted her eyes from the pond, she could find no trace of her target. Incredulous, she abandoned caution and cast about in all directions for a sign of him. There were people all around, but the one she wanted was nowhere to be seen. She imagined how she could explain her failure to Boris Ivanovich, the disappointment and sorrow with which Nastya would regard her, and she was ashamed. She would die if she were not successful.

It was at this instant that she realized how vitally important all of this was to her. There was nothing on earth other than this single training assignment.

I've got to find him. I've got to find him. She whispered to herself, still searching in every direction. On the other side of the pond she spotted an islet with a neat, white gazebo that was popular with tourists. A narrow wooden bridge connected it with the shore. Trying act naturally, Olga moved quickly thinking that the gazebo offered an unobstructed view of the area around the pond. She could use the zoom lens of her cellphone. Several people were already on the islet taking photos, and it would be easy to fit in with them.

It wasn't long before she spotted him sitting on a bench a short distance from the water engaged in a lively conversation with someone. Grinning triumphantly, Olga snapped some photos. She wasn't under instruction to do so, but photography from such a distance was perfectly secure.

She didn't let the target out of sight for the rest of the day.

When she prepared her report, she included print-outs of the photos.

"What's this?" Boris Nikolayevich puffed out his moustache.

"It's a photo of the person the target met at 17:15 hours in Kharitonovskiy Park. They were together until 17:32 hours, and then the target ..."

He interrupted her. "I understand. It's dangerous to take pictures from near-by when during an operation."

"I know. That's why I took the photos from the islet. There were three other people there at the time with cameras, so there was nothing suspicious in my behavior. Besides, the target could not have spotted me from that distance."

"From the islet ..." Boris Ivanovich repeated thoughtfully. "That was bold and opportunistic, of course, but ... I gave no permission for you to get that far away from the target. You might have lost him."

"But I didn't lose him." She surprised herself with this retort.

"Humph." He could not conceal a certain satisfaction. "OK. You got lucky, and I won't argue, but I want no such independent action in the future. That's an order. I'm glad that you think for yourself and can be creative. That's important in our business, but even more important is discipline. Our rules can seem boring and meaningless, but they've saved a lot of peoples' lives. Do you understand?"

"Yes, sir." She replied, only somewhat chastened. "I understand."

Nastya observed all of this, and when Boris Ivanovich was gone, she laughed out loud. "Don't take it to heart. It's best not to argue with Ivanich. He a vindictive sort, and your success depends on his final assessment. But I could tell he was satisfied. Your results were excellent, and this time you showed initiative and did more than was required."

"Like the good student who gets all 'A's' and double for good conduct?"

"And people like that are successful, believe me," Nastya was enthusiastic as she retrieved a bottle of wine from a drawer in the chest. "Let's drink to your future success. You'll conquer Washington."

The next day, Nastya began to instruct her in the use of technology. There were concealed cameras, long-range microphones and video systems, an unending variety of disguised gadgets and communications equipment.

"Is this stuff real?" Olga was entranced.

She no longer cared if she appeared naïve or laughable. Nastya was a friend, or at least Olga treated her like one, and it seemed the feeling was mutual.

She was introduced to the arcane terminology of espionage, coded phrases and ciphers, secret writing and dead drops. After a month she possessed practical, if rudimentary skills in all these areas.

Boris Ivanovich paid them another visit at the apartment. His manner was solemn. "So, Olga

Vladimirovna, now we enter the final phase of your training. You will be working with a team. There will be no personal contact ahead of time between team members. You will each be given a code name and instructions to appear at a pre-determined rally point. From there, you'll use standard tradecraft to surveil a target. You will act as team leader and direct the operation.

"When the surveillance ends, team members will retire in different directions. Standard radios will be used for team communication. At the end of each exercise you will write up a full report that describes everything the team observed. You must be especially alert for any indications that the target is engaged in espionage. You might observe the target making a brush pass or unloading a dead drop. Do you understand?"

Olga nodded. She was certain that in this instance the target would be professionals from the FSB, as would the other "team members."

Boris Ivanovich continued, "This training has only a single goal. At the end of the month your task will be to predict with absolute certainty where and when the target will appear the following day, and what he will be doing. You will give your report to the other surveillance team members, but only you will have the responsibility for the prediction. You will be entirely responsible for the success or failure of the operation," he concluded with special emphasis on the words "entirely responsible."

This was an obvious challenge, and Olga applied herself to it enthusiastically. She'd gotten away with near failure in Kharitonovskiy Park, but that was minor league compared to this. She was to become a faceless figure, a genuine warrior on an invisible front.

She spotted Boris Ivanovich on the street several times during the exercise, and she developed a strong desire to please this strict and tedious man. She had to succeed; there could be no other outcome.

By the time she handed her report to Boris Ivanovich, she had memorized the target's pattern of behavior and movement, knew his favorite restaurants, when and where he walked his dog, his arrivals and departures from work. Despite her best efforts, she had spotted no sign of suspicious activity, and this worried her.

She waited breathlessly in the safehouse as Boris Ivanovich and Nastya studied her report. Their faces betrayed nothing. Finally, the former displayed a rare, wide smile.

"Olga Vladimirovna, tomorrow you'll return to Moscow, and we'll meet at an office in the Lubyanka." He handed her a slip of paper on which an office number was written and then left without another word.

She could barely contain herself and ran to embrace Nastya. "Nastya, I did it! Will you be going with me?"

"Where? Moscow or America?" she smiled. "I'm in Moscow a lot, but I live and work here. But America? We don't leave, Olga. Many colleagues and I cannot leave the country because we know a lot of secrets. So I'll wait for you to visit me here sometime."

"I'll be back," promised Olga, "It'll all go fine with me, and sooner or later I'll come back. Just keep believing in me."

Nastya displayed her Hollywood smile.

Chapter 20

Belgorod, Russia – Kharkov, Ukraine

Compared to the rest of Russia, Vlad found Belgorod to be a rather pleasant city – well laid out, clean, with new buildings and swept streets, green parks and a variety of unusual statues of things like an old lady knitting or a happy family. It was as if the city were enveloped in a sort of pre-war bubble, and the noise of war that spread over the rest of Russia had not yet seeped into its quiet streets.

The train station was not especially noteworthy, but it was relatively new and absent the smell and filth characteristic of older stations, especially those along Russian rails.

Vlad's trip took eleven hours thanks to the innumerable stops and engine changes along the way. It was late into the evening by the time he arrived. He took a taxi to the address provided by Golovina. His contact lived in a new 12-story building. Unlike the older, Soviet style structures, it was spacious with clean entrances and a new children's' playground under the windows.

A tall, gangly fellow with an unruly mop of long hair and a cheerful expression opened the apartment door.

"I'm Dima," he said, "or you can call me Mitya, if you prefer. Want a beer? Don't worry, I have plenty. And I have a free sofa. You'll spend the night here while we figure out how to get you across to Kharkov tomorrow."

"And what does that depend on?" asked Vlad as he entered the large, one-room apartment in typical bachelor disarray.

"Depends on what you're up to," serenely replied Mitya.

"What does that mean?" Vlad was not prepared to share with this stranger the details of the case against Solntsev, not even if he was Golovina's best friend in the world. He couldn't condemn yet another innocent person to certain death.

"It means articles or blogs," he said breezily, "extremism, or illegal meetings, or regime change. Regime change is the most difficult. With extremism, they usually push people into exile. Meetings are more difficult here, but they don't follow them too closely. But when it comes to treason they apparently have to fill out a lot of papers listing the evidence." Mitya said all this with an air of authority as he opened two bottles of beer.

"But ..." Vlad finally understood. "No, they've not opened an investigation on me." Then he added, "I hope. No, with me it's something else, a journalistic investigation. They want to kill me. They've already tried."

He accepted the cold bottle of beer and dropped onto the sofa, suddenly aware of his fatigue. But he would conceal from this imperturbable young man the sort of danger that came of contact with him.

"Well, that's complicated," muttered Mitya. "It's the first time, to tell the truth, that I've come up against one like this. Here's how things work. The train to Kharkov takes just over an hour. Get on here; get off in Kharkov. There are no stops along the way. That's why you go through Russian Customs at the station before boarding. If they let you board the train, it's all good, and you're on the way to the free world. Then you have to pass Ukrainian Customs in

Kharkov before you get off the train. If they let you through, get off the train, walk out of the station, and go wherever you like. These days, with the war, the Ukrainians require that any Russian man of military age have an invitation from a Ukrainian citizen. They won't let you through without it. But if someone meets you there and vouches for you, the problem is solved. This is the first and easiest variant."

"What's the second?"

"If there is a warrant out for your arrest and you can't legally board a train, then you go by car. There's a chance of getting across the Russian border illegally, but not the Ukrainian border. The possibilities are practically nil. They're very vigilant about fighters and subversives. In this case, you have to ask for political asylum right at the border. Except that with this variant they normally hold the car at the Ukrainian checkpoint for five to seven hours, so you are still stuck in Russia. During this time they may well search you and then kill you. Well, you said they already tried once ..." Mitya seemed a little abashed.

"Let's try the train." That was an easy decision. He was tired of playing games with killers, so tired he was almost indifferent. If all this ended sooner than he thought, so be it. He was dealing with professional, well-trained killers. If they already knew he was here, they'd be waiting for him at the station and all along the border. On the other hand, he had still been in Moscow only that morning, and Solntsev's people were unlikely to find out so soon that he would be at the Belgorod train station. He didn't thing there was an arrest warrant out on him, and that meant there was a chance that his name wasn't on any watchlist. Time was on his side for the moment, and the thought that he should spend more long hours in

Russia was insupportable.

"OK," sighed Mitya, the train it is. If there's nothing more, we need to get a move on. So, you'll leave tomorrow morning?"

Vlad shook his head. "No. I'll go right now. Check the Internet, will you? There should be a train schedule."

"It'll be very late by the time you get there, and you'll have no time to rest up ..." Despite his reticence, Mitya concluded, "Maybe you're right. In your place, I wouldn't waste any time."

Within an hour, they made their way through the night to the station. The city with its night lights and illuminated fountains seemed incompatible with someone passing through its well-tended streets to escape certain death.

Vlad bought a ticket at the counter, not having wished to alert anyone with an Internet purchase. Ticket purchases were computerized, but he wanted to keep risk to a minimum. The station Customs official gave his passport a thorough examination, squinted at him, but finally let him pass.

Through the window he could see the people still standing on the platform, among them Mitya smiling up at him. There, outside the window was Russia, the homeland he had never thought to abandon. He was certain he would never see it again.

Beyond the thick glass of the train window in the chill September night, he was leaving behind twenty-five years of his life – his entire life: the school years, university, friends, work, his first adolescent love about whom he least wished to think at this moment. There also was the hell of the recent past, his father's corpse stretched on the cold, wet ground, the destroyed ash of his apartment and his deceased mother. He could not bring himself even to bid farewell to the familiar places as he gazed at the lights of another, unfamiliar but still Russian city ... With a slight lurch, the train started to move, and the platform slipped away. Ahead was a different world. *A free world.*

*****

Bogdan Kosti did not disappoint – he met Vlad in Kharkov wearing a camouflage uniform and a prepared invitation. He handed the document to the Customs official, and Vlad passed without delay through the checkpoint.

The khaki uniform awoke an irrational awareness in Vlad, as though he were destined somehow to undo the despicable and senseless war in Ukraine. He could not dispel the thought that this young man who was forced to fight instead of leading a peaceful life, was now helping him – a citizen of the aggressor country.

Reading Vlad's thoughts, Bogdan spoke first. "Don't worry. I understand. Before the war, I was in the international human rights movement. I know a lot of guys from Russia, and they're still my friends. I met Golovina in Moscow a few years ago. What a grand old lady! In Soviet times our Ukrainian dissidents worked with her – and that's why she went to the Gulag. She's pretty famous here. And if she asks us to help someone, no one will refuse. We're well aware of how things are with you in Mordor. You see how this war began."

"I'm incredibly sorry ..." Vlad got a few words out before Bogdan interrupted him.

"Don't apologize. No one in my family has died

yet, thank God, but you – both parents. Marya Fedorovna let me know all about it, so it's not for me to complain to you about anything. You're lucky to get out of there. We know what it's like, believe me, and if we can help, we'll help.

"I hope you don't mind, but my living conditions right now aren't great. I have a two room apartment, but one room is now occupied by a family from Gorlovka. There's a mother and baby, and her husband just arrived today. They left their home there and can't return. You understand what 'can't return' means? We haven't found them a place yet, so I took them in. So we'll be sharing one room. OK?"

"You ask me that? Listen, how can I help you? You know, so that I'm not a burden. Are you accepting people in the Battalion?"

"We really don't need you right now in the Battalion," Bogdan replied. "You rest up and get yourself together. You just got away from a bunch of murderers, and you want to get in a gunfight now? Where do you think you could fight without any training? We'll find something for you, don't worry. Marya Fedorovna said you're a journalist. Do you know how few journalists there are in the cities along the front? All the press is in Kiev and afraid to come out here. Those who do come are amateurs. We might need to get some important information out. Today I asked armed forces headquarters, the VSU, and there's something they want published as soon as it's approved, and it'll have to be written quickly. So you see, you came just in time."

Bogdan smiled for the first time since they'd met.

Chapter 21

"Yevropeyskiy Kharkov" website:

Russian Fighters Mine a City and Its Inhabitants

By: Vladislav Illarionov, Kharkov

The artist Mihailo Korzh recently escaped from occupied Gorlovka and was an eye witness to everything written here. Finding himself in an occupied city, here was no choice but to contact the so-called "MGB DNR" in order to obtain permission to leave. But the normal bureaucratic procedures led to an unexpected outcome: Mihailo witnessed the occupiers' plans to destroy his home town. We met with the refugee in Kharkov, where he told us about how the city was occupied by Russians, Chechens and Serbs, about hunger and repression and even how these occupiers resolved to blow up the city and all its inhabitants.

"Field Commander Bezler, nicknamed 'Bes,' is a fanatic," asserts Mihailo. "He thinks a bunch of 'Bloody Banderists' rule in Kiev. He actually believes what Russian propaganda says."

However, according to the artist, problems in the currently occupied city began even before the appearance of the "Russian Beast." At the end of February 2014 almost four thousand Russian citizens entered the city, practically simultaneously with the events in the Crimea.

"I don't know if there were Spetsnaz among them, but I do know that there were criminals and Russian fascists – I saw their swastika tattoos. The occupied workers' quarters and guest houses on the outskirts of town and were transported to every pro-

Ukrainian gathering in the Donbas where they started fights. For example, they provoked a massacre in Donetsk. They were armed only with knives and rebar, but this was enough," recalled Mihailo.

Then Girkin/Strelkov[6] appeared, and Bezler came with him. In order to control the recently arrived and local criminals, "Bes" made an agreement with the local establishment and even made an ally of the mayor. His next task was to bring the Chechen and Serb bandits under control.

"The Serbs were in charge of counter-intelligence against so-called 'agents of Right Sector[7]' and random criminals. Most of the Serbs didn't even speak Russian and for the most part were happy to arrest people on suspicion and turn them over for torture or execution. The prisoners were interrogated by officials of the Russian FSB. The Chechens handled routine patrols whenever it was necessary to frighten the locals, and they were very efficient at this," says Mihailo. "The Serbs who knew a little Russian said openly that they were there to continue the war they'd fought in Croatia.

Things became chaotic in Gorlovka. Bezler and his men confiscated all the microbuses and four-wheel drive vehicles. Anyone who resisted got a bullet in the head, according to Mihailo. Many of the occupiers actually believed they were fighting NATO and the Americans.

The repression began shortly after Bezler

---

[6] Igor Vsevolodovich Girkin aka "Strelkov," a Russian GRU colonel who played a prominent role in the invasion and occupation of Ukraine and the eventual formation of the so-called "Donbas Peoples Republic." He was sanctioned by the EU for his actions.

[7] Right Sector was a far-right, Ukrainian nationalist organization with fascist tendencies.

organized his homegrown "siloviki." They were quick to deal with any sign of dissent. The beginning of the repression was the death of Rybak, who was a member of the City Commission, but he is far from the only victim of the occupiers. Later came the firing squads for those who refused to turn over their property, demands for bribes from important businessmen, and the arrests of activists.

"As often as not, people simply disappeared, and then either their bodies were found or they were never heard from again. The official line was that these people had fled to Ukraine, but we knew this was not so. At least 600 people disappeared, even if they offered no resistance following the occupation," Mihailo recalls.

It has become even more chaotic in Gorlovka over the past week. Like Girkin, Bezler left the Donbas and returned to Crimea, and at the beginning of September Russian troops entered the city and mercilessly exterminated the former "leadership."

"There were battles between different elements that controlled sections of the city, including use of heavy weapons. According to Russian media, at least half of the destruction was due to these outlaw skirmishes," says the Ukrainian refugee.

In the meantime, the economic situation in the newly declared "republic" worsened with each passing day. No one received a salary for a long time because all the businesses were closed. There was a catastrophic lack of food.

Mihailo confirms that during the recent advance of Ukrainian forces the city might have been re-taken. But this was prevented through filthy blackmail. One side began blowing up the railroads, bridges, and reservoirs while the other threatened not only to destroy the city's infrastructure, but to devastate it completely along with the population.

"At this time Bezler officially notified the Ukrainian side that Gorlovka had been completely mined with explosives. I learned of this by accident, personally from an MGB employee. Later, other local officials confirmed this. Right now in Gorlovka, the water lines are mined, and toxic substances are emplaced that would be released into the water supply when the charges go off. The mined the sewers, the gas lines, and the power plant, and also two large industrial sites – the "Stirol" chemical combine where there is a great deal of dangerous substances and the factory that manufactured explosives for municipal works and for military purposes. There is a mountain of defective and unused explosives that would be detonated by an explosion. If that were to happen, nothing of Gorlovka would be left. It would be like another Chernobyl. Even the factory workers say so," explains Mihailo.

Locals have noted that a great many important sites also have been mined in Donetsk and Lugansk. In recently liberated Slvyansk and Kramatorsk all the schools and means of subsistence were mined. According to Ukrainian sappers, everything was wired to be detonated by a single phone call. Thus, occupied Donbas is literally held hostage by terrorists who threaten to erase it from the face of the earth.

Chapter 22

Vance Johnson took a second to admire the steaming cup of ink-black coffee in the white Navy mug in his hand. It was his personal Sumatra blend, supplied by a coffee shop in Alexandria, Virgina, and the aroma was worth the slight delay before tasting. In fact, it would be his third cup of the morning, having ground the beans and consumed the first two cups at home in the townhouse he and his wife occupied behind the high brick wall along *Konyukovska Ulitsa*. The townhouses were all on the Embassy compound. The Russian "White House" stood kitty-corner to the Embassy on the other side of the street.

Johnson was somewhat of a novelty in the new Central Intelligence Agency. At 47, in the CIA since the early 90's, straight out of the military and with a degree in Russian history and literature. The fact that he was still with the Agency was in itself an anomaly at a time when the average "career" there lasted only seven years. Long gone were the days of the 30-year man.

No, these days Langley was much more concerned with ensuring employee "diversity" than sticking to the business of developing professionals for the collection and analysis of intelligence. But then that was just him. Many of today's crop just went along with the flow because they could resign after a few years and flaunt their credentials as an "intelligence operative." In the old days, even before Johnson joined up, seven years was barely enough time to be permitted to walk across the street unattended in the world of espionage.

Some bright thinkers who occupied desks at Langley also thought it was a good idea that officers should not specialize in any one area or culture. Now a tour in Kuwait might be followed by a posting to Japan. There were still days when Johnson, a fluent Russian speaker, was surprised to have been named Chief of Station, Moscow. Obviously, someone in Human Resources had made a mistake.

As he raised the steaming cup expectantly to his lips, the office door swung open, and Derick Williams rushed in waving a piece of paper.

"Did you see this?"

With considerable regret, Johnson set the cup on his desk. The coffee would never see 197 degrees again. He glanced at his watch. "Christ, Derrick, it's only 7:30, and you're interrupting an important morning ritual."

"You've got to see this." Williams thrust the print-out across the desk still waving it like it was burning his fingers.

Johnson took the paper. It was a print-out of a story from the day before on a Kharkov newspaper's website.

"Look at the by-line," said Williams.

"Vladislav Illarionov," breathed Johnson. "So he made it out, after all."

"He sure did, and he's already in print in Ukraine. He could publish the Ryazan story any day now."

Johnson made a sour face. "I sure as hell hope not. That would be a big mistake."

Williams was as astonished as if Johnson had risen from behind the desk and mooned him. "I don't understand. That information is very important. And the kid has hard evidence. He left the country so he could get it published."

"And because some FSB skinheads wanted to kill him."

"That too," agreed Williams, "but I still don't understand your attitude."

Johnson raised his arm and waved a finger around in the air. "I think we should go to the S.C.I.F. again."

Once they were safely ensconced in the plastic "bubble," Johnson sighed because he was going to have to explain Russian cynicism to someone who should already know all about it. He belatedly remembered the cup of coffee still on his desk.

"Derrick, you know as well as anyone that the Kremlin's strategy is to block the ability of the general public to think critically. Their propaganda exploits and promotes emotion, not thinking. This is especially true of official 'reporting' from and about Ukraine. They call it 'укроСМИ' (ukroSMI),[8] 'Ukrainian mass media,' and they don't mean it as a compliment. The image of the enemy in Russian propaganda is not distinguished by its originality, and has taken form with varying degrees of intensity over the past few years. Of course, it's the USA, and those the propagandists call 'American puppets,' beginning with the Ukrainian authorities and ending with the whole of Western and Eastern Europe."

He hoped his words were sinking in. "So, if young Illarionov is successful in publishing his

---

[8] УкроСМИ: "Ukrainian mass media." In Russian, "СМИ" stands for "Средства массовой информации," i.e. "mass media."

accusations in the Ukrainian press, what do you think the reaction here would be? Do you think it would have an impact?"

Williams' face sank as the import of the CIA Chief's words sank in. "They would denounce it as a fabrication, and no one in Russia would disagree."

"Right. And the reaction would probably be little different in the West. What kind of credibility would an article from a small Ukrainian newspaper on the front lines of a war possess?"

A crestfallen Williams nodded. "None."

"Zip. Zero. *Nada*," said Johnson. "But getting the information out through a respected, major Western publication would find some resonance. The Russians would react no differently, but it might keep American and EU eyes on the ball."

"So what can we do?"

Johnson chewed his lower lip. He experienced an intense need for a cup of coffee. He did not doubt the importance of the information Illarionov possessed. The problem was what, if anything, to do about it. Williams was placing his hopes in the hands of the CIA, but he was probably betting on the wrong horse. No, Vance wouldn't pass this hot potato to Langley, where it would in all likelihood be dropped. There were still too many people in Washington who actually believed they could coax the Kremlin into the international fold if only they treated the Russians as if they were normal people.

"I think this is one for your guys, Derrick."

Williams was surprised. He didn't especially care for the CIA, but he thought they could get things done. "I don't understand."

Johnson leaned forward with elbows on the table. "Illarionov is no longer in Russia. For all intents and purposes, he's already in the West. There are no restrictions on travel out of Ukraine. All he lacks is a visa. Maybe your guys could arrange a study grant or something ..."

Williams was immediately enthusiastic. "That might just be possible. But we'd have to find Illarionov first."

"That shouldn't be too difficult," said Johnson. "I'm sure your press attaché in Kiev would have no trouble contacting the editor of the Kharkov newspaper. That's a pretty good starting point."

Vance's coffee was stone cold by the time he returned to his office.

Chapter 23

Olga met Gleb Solntsev at the *Sretenka* office. With September fading into October, the weather had turned chilly, and she wore her best coat with fur trim over a simple, but elegant dark green dress with a modest hemline. Her calves were encased in fashionable black leather boots.

Solntsev greeted her with an avuncular hug and then held her at arm's length to look her over as though he were the judge at a livestock contest. "Perfect," he pronounced his verdict. "You'll make a fine impression.

He escorted her along the familiar route on *Bol'shaya Lubyanka.* Olga was surprised when he guided her into *Furkosovskiy Pereulok.* FSB headquarters is located in the massive Lubyanka building, a huge pile of yellow bricks that housed an insurance company in pre-Soviet times. Behind the familiar massive façade that faces *Lubyanka Ploshchad* lays an entire complex of interconnected buildings.

The officers of the FSB, formerly the Second Chief Directorate of the KGB, do not envy their former colleagues of the SVR their modern Yasenevo high-rises. Tradition is valued in the Lubyanka.

It was Olga's dream to enter the doors that faced the square. Noting her curiosity, Gleb explained, "The main doors off the square are used only for ceremonial occasions. This is where the operatives enter."

He pointed to an imposing set of solid metal gates with a small traffic signal to one side.

Inside the gates was a featureless courtyard

with a vehicular entrance to a subterranean garage and several other closed doorways without any indication of where they led. Immediately to the right after entering was a set of double doors, and this was where Solntsev led her, explaining that this was Building 1.2, where the executive offices were located.

Olga was thrilled to the bone. She was following literally in the footsteps of real Chekists. Probably *"Iron"* Feliks Dzerzhinsky himself had trod these stones. She did her best to conceal her enthusiasm, but it did not escape Gleb Solntsev's practiced eye. *"She'll do,"* he thought. He detected no doubts or suspicion in the girl. His instincts had once again proven accurate.

He led her down a corridor to an elevator that took them to the third floor, and then down another long corridor covered by a beige runner. They stopped outside a room that bore the number given to Olga in Yekaterinburg.

Boris Ivanovich, his Stalin/walrus face wreathed in a smile, waited for them in a straight-backed chair at the head of a well-polished conference table that could easily accommodate twenty. Today he was wearing an olive green FSB uniform with the three stars of a full colonel on the epaulets.

He waved them to be seated next to him at the head of the table. Just as they were sitting down, the door opened to admit a tall, spare, older man with a full head of iron gray hair and fierce, nearly black eyes under a thick tangle of eyebrows.

Boris Ivanovich and Solntsev quickly stood, and Olga followed suit. This was clearly a man of importance. The older man pulled out a chair half-way down the table and flicked his wrist for them to be seated. He didn't say a word, but those black eyes never strayed from her. She was afraid to return the gaze.

Boris Ivanovich cleared his throat. "Olga, this is an important day for you, and one you will not forget. First, my name is not Boris Ivanovich. I am Colonel Aleksandr Kozlov, and officially I do not exist."

Unsure where this was leading, Olga straightened her spine and kept her eyes on the Colonel, who continued ponderously, "I do not exist on any roster of FSB personnel. I am paid from a special fund that is untraceable. From this moment, your name and records have been expunged from FSB files, as well."

It occurred to Olga that she had been unaware that she even had an FSB file.

"You are known publicly as a member of '*Svoi*,' and nothing can be done to change that, but we can take certain precautions. You will inform your family and friends that you have resigned from '*Svoi*,' for perfectly honorable reasons, of course. There will be no reason for you to hang your head. On the contrary, you have been offered a lucrative position with a think tank in Washington that specializes in Russian affairs. It is called 'The Russian-American Study Group.' You will be paid through them, and you will receive an extra stipend for clothing. Naturally, an apartment will be rented for you."

Kozlov paused to see how she was receiving his words. Satisfied, he continued, "The avowed purpose of the 'Russian-American Study Group' is to promote good relations and understanding between the Russian Federation and the United States. Its true mission is to promote Russian ideas and counteract American propaganda. You will be expected to engage influential Americans, young people, and media in dialogue and convince them to support our cause. This will not always be easy, but Americans are easily corruptible, not very intelligent, and we already have many of them working for us in Washington and throughout the country. We are especially interested in working with Russian émigrés to strengthen their ties to the Motherland. Do you understand?"

Olga gulped and nodded her head. She was not a little daunted by the tasks they were setting for her.

The Colonel smiled benignly, reading her thoughts. "You won't be alone in this work, Olga Vladimirovna. Besides your colleagues at your cover office, you will have regular contact with one of our people at the Embassy in Washington. He will be your case officer, your guide, and is there to support you in any way required. While your work with the 'Russian-American Study Group' is very important, there is another side to your mission that will be handled exclusively between you and your case officer. This is the reason for the training we gave you in Yekaterinburg. Do you think you can handle all that?"

Olga nodded and managed to say, "Yes sir."

The men in the room regarded her somberly for what seemed an eternity until Kozlov nodded and pushed a button at his side. The door opened, and a man in a white jacket wheeled in a cart loaded with delicacies and a bottle of *shampanskoye*.

The tall, older man, who had not uttered a word, rose from the table, nodded at the Colonel and Solntsev, and left the room after a final, judgmental glance at Olga.

When the three of them were alone, Kozlov popped the cork on the bottle with practiced finesse and filled three champagne flutes. He raised his glass and said, "With the dissolution of the Soviet Union and the advent of 'democracy,'" his voice dripped with sarcasm as he pronounced this word, "traitors were suddenly and inexplicably made into heroes, state secrets were revealed to our enemies. And all the while the Americans continued to recruit agents of influence, to dig tunnels under our embassy in Washington, and to expel dozens of our people. I cannot list all the injuries inflicted upon us. But now, thank God and our new leadership, Russian special services are regaining their feet and becoming what they should be – strong, professional, and supported by the *narod*. The *chekist* is once more valued and admired, and you are now one of us, Olga."

Chapter 24

He was an older man, a KGB veteran now assigned to the SVR's Directorate KR, counter-intelligence. Given his intimate familiarity with the control exerted over the capital's streets by surveillance teams and cameras, as well as technology to detect clandestine communications, it was surprising that, among the several in-place assets handled by the CIA, he would insist on personal meetings. This was risky, but he was an extremely valuable source.

The only person Vance Johnson trusted to handle these meetings was himself. The CIA Station Chief was "declared" to the SVR and expected to manage liaison relations. If the SVR knew his identity and role, so did the FSB and its omnipresent surveillance teams. The question was: would his status lull the Russians into believing that a declared officer was unlikely to attempt clandestine activities in Moscow; or, would his status make him a prime surveillance target?

The SVR penetration was uniquely placed to provide invaluable intelligence. In the post-Aldrich Ames era, he was in a position to provide early warning should another CIA officer be recruited, and he enjoyed some access to FSB activities. So, when the source signaled for an unscheduled meeting, Vance Johnson was set in motion.

The techniques of a Moscow surveillance detection route were part of his DNA. He drove through the Embassy gates that afternoon and turned left on *Bol'shoy Devyatinskiy Pereulok*, the left again at the end of the street onto *Novinskiy* Boulevard past the old US Embassy building. It would be a long day.

His first stop was the up-scale "Berlin House" shopping center where after a half-hour perusing the shelves, he bought two books on Russian history. His car was visible through the front windows, and he spotted nothing out of the ordinary, what he would have termed "hostile indicators."

Next he made a second stop farther west across the Moskva River, using the *Borodinskiy* Bridge to funnel possible surveillance behind him. He spent an hour browsing the shops at the huge *Yevropeyskiy* Shopping Center, and still saw nothing that raised an alarm.

He continued in this manner gradually moving to less routine cover stops and resorting to increasingly provocative maneuvers, and still drew out no signs that he was being followed.

At last, he parked his car and jumped aboard a bus, after switching into a leather jacket and clapping a flat cap on his head. In the old days a CIA officer might have ducked into the subway, but now all the stations were packed with closed circuit television cameras, and that mooted the possibility of spotting physical surveillance.

Johnson followed this routine until dusk, each phase bringing him ever closer to the meeting site. Finally, after an exhausting four hours in perpetual motion, Johnson stepped off a bus on *Kutuzovskiy Prospekt* and walked slowly toward the parking lot of a large, circular building that housed a Battle of Borodino Museum.

This was always the most heart-pounding moment when the adrenalin electrified his veins. Had he been successful, or did a team of highly skilled FSB officers have him in their sights? Or had the agent been compromised and he was walking into an ambush?

He spotted the agent's Volvo sedan parked in front of the museum, and there was a white box visible on the rear-window shelf – the safety signal.

Johnson approached the passenger-side door and slid into the car. Colonel Sergey Lopunin beamed at him and tapped his wristwatch. "Right on time, Vance, as usual. You are a good *razvedchik*."

"Thanks, Sergey. I hope this is worth wearing out a pair of perfectly good shoes. How much time do we have?"

"Oh, as much as we need, but this won't take long. I came across a bit of information I think will interest you."

Lopunin switched on the engine, backed out of the parking space and swung into the traffic on *Kutuzovskiy*. He drove carefully and glanced frequently in the rear view mirror.

"Are you worried you're being followed, Sergey?"

"One can never be too careful," said the Russian, concentrating on his driving. "Does the name Vladislav Illarionov mean anything to you?"

Johnson's face remained impassive. "Should it?"

Lopunin gave him a sideways glance. "You wouldn't tell me if it did, would you? That's fine. But you are interested in assassinations planned by the Russian special services?"

"Of course, Sergey. They're becoming all too common here in Mordor and elsewhere."

"I see you've adopted the jargon of the dissidents."

"If the shoe fits ... But you didn't call this

meeting to discuss language. What's up?"

Johnson wanted to finish this business as quickly as possible and return to the anonymity of the streets.

"Our brothers at the FSB are on the warpath for this Illarionov. He's in Ukraine now, apparently not far from the front lines, and they're sending a team to eliminate him. It seems he has some sort of information that would cause the Kremlin a big problem if it came to light."

Johnson concealed his alarm. "Has the team already been dispatched?"

"I don't know, but if not, it will be soon. The FSB has its panties in a wad."

"How will the team get into Ukraine, through the lines?"

"No. They'll enter from the safe side from somewhere in the West, posing as normal visitors. Their local agents will supply the weapons. They'll leave the same way when the job is done."

"Are you sure of your source?"

Lopunin was slightly insulted. "Of course. I don't trade in crap. I heard this directly from one of the Lubyanka planners, an old drinking buddy from KGB days."

"What's his name and position?"

Lopunin was reluctant to supply this information, but after some urging, he did.

After a half-hour of aimless driving, he pulled to the curb and Johnson got out of the car. Before closing the door he leaned back in to say, "Thanks, Sergey. Your efforts are very much appreciated."

"Just see that the appreciation is placed in my bank account as soon as possible. I'll have to get out of here one of these days."

Johnson watched until the car disappeared into traffic. No one was following Lopunin.

It took another 45 minutes to return to where he'd left his car. After another 40 minutes, he drove through the Embassy gates some six hours after his departure that morning. He saw the Russian security guard dutifully note the time of his return.

He didn't go to his office because there was a lot to think about and also because he knew his wife would be on tenterhooks.

The following morning, he was in his office after only one cup of coffee at home. He had not slept well despite his exhaustion.

He was obligated to report the results of last night's meeting to Langley. He would send a single, strictly compartmentalized cable reassuring Headquarters that no security problems had arisen and transmitting the intelligence provided by Lopunin.

The intelligence would be of only passing interest to Langley, maybe a footnote to a report, but it meant a great deal to Johnson. The reason was that the subject of the information was Vladislav Illarionov

Johnson's problem was that he had not shared anything with Langley about Illarionov. His reasoning had seemed sound, but now he was obligated to inform them of Lopunin's warning. Johnson could either give Langley the whole story and wash his hands of it, or figure out something else.

He opted for something else, maybe something that in the end would bring the cautious bureaucrats on board without knowing exactly how it had come about. At least he could give Illarionov a fighting chance to survive.

Chapter 25

So this is America.

Through the plane's window Olga watched as the homeland of the Main Enemy rose up to meet her. They descended along a gentle glidepath, having first circled far west of Washington before turning back above the Shenandoah Valley for the final approach to Dulles International Airport. Through scattered patches of cloud, she saw large wooded areas with Autumn-painted leaves, farmland, highways and smaller roads – the arteries and veins of an arrogant and powerful country that wanted to rule the world.

The eleven-hour flight from Moscow was exhausting, but now a chill of apprehension ran through her as the wheels of the big jet screeched onto the runway.

The cleanliness of Dulles International Airport struck her, and the "people movers," the huge bus-like vehicles on fat, oversize tires that carried the passengers from the plane to the main terminal were unlike anything she had seen before. They debarked into the cavernous immigration and Customs hall where she stood in the queue with other foreigners of all stripes.

She offered the passport control officer a radiant smile and handed over her passport – a claret-red, Russian passport. He took it as though her country of origin made no difference, noted the reason for her visit, stamped it and handed it back with a wave toward the baggage area on the other side of a Plexiglas wall. Olga smiled triumphantly. She had arrived behind enemy lines.

In the reception area outside Customs, she spotted a well-groomed young man in a dark suit holding up a cardboard placard with her name. Perhaps unconsciously, Olga was accustomed to the rough and tumble boys in "*Svoi*," quite unlike this avatar of the "golden youth."

"How was the flight?" he asked. "I'm Stash Dobrovolskiy, the Deputy Director of the Russian-American Study Group. And I understand you're to be my assistant."

She was being greeted by the number two person of the Group, which made her feel even more responsible for carrying out her mission.

"The flight was OK, but I'm tired," she said. In reality, she was bursting with countless quite illogical, even childish questions, the most important of which was, *what is America like?* But she didn't want them to think she was a silly, impressionable girl.

"It wears us out every time," he agreed. "We have an apartment for you in Arlington that is convenient to a subway station. You should get some rest, but try not to sleep. If you stay awake you'll get accustomed to the time difference lots faster. Tomorrow morning, you have to be in the office." He shot her a sympathetic glance.

Outside the terminal the fresh air revived her. Unlike Moscow which already was sinking into the Autumn blues, mid-October here was more like Russian September – the same bright Fall foliage, a still warm sun, and an overarching blue sky. The road from the airport was little different from Russia, only a bit smoother, cleaner, and wider. Olga leaned back against the car seat and sighed heavily. Nothing was impossible for her now.

"What's that?" she asked, pointing to a high

wall that stretched along the Dulles Access Road. "Do all the roads have walls? Are they afraid of being robbed?"

Stash laughed. "This isn't the most picturesque area. It's nicer farther ahead. But don't let it fool you, Olga Vladimirovna. Always keep in mind that all of this was created on the corpses of millions of ruined lives and dead children. Libya, Syria, Yugoslavia, Iraq, Ukraine. American wealth is created at the expense of the poverty of other countries. They don't even deserve the land that was taken from the Indians ..."

She didn't need any schooling in the cant she already knew by heart, and did not reply.

Mistaking her silence for disappointment, Stash gave her a mischievous grin. "Would you like to see something interesting? Let's make a little detour along the George Washington Memorial Parkway past the Headquarters of the CIA."

"The CIA?" She experienced a variety of sensations. Excitement, fear, joy, shock – all at once, that erased the fatigue. "Let's go!"

Traffic clogged the Beltway, and Olga wondered if there was an accident ahead.

"No," said Stash, "this is the way it always is. There's a perpetual rush hour all around Washington."

The Parkway heading toward Washington was less crowded and unexpectedly scenic. It was like being in a forest similar in all its aspects to the forest just outside Moscow. Large trees leaned over the road, shimmering in the slanted late afternoon sunlight in shades of gold, pale green, and burgundy in a joyful confusion of solar sparks. She peered through the trees and caught a glimpse of a large river far below. She suddenly caught sight of thick white tree trunks with broad, black stripes.

"*Beryozi!*" she exclaimed. "Russian birches under the nose of the CIA."

They laughed, and it seemed to her that the forest laughed with them in all its sun-intoxicated transparency.

A few moments later she spotted a sign: *George Bush Center for Intelligence* – the CIA.

"Look up to the right." Stash pointed to an exit from the main road. "Just a short distance up there are the main gates. Unfortunately, they won't let us in," he smirked.

Olga silently peered in the direction he indicated, the direction of the Main Enemy, but little could be seen.

They exited at Key Bridge and Stash pointed back over his shoulder. "That's Georgetown across the river. It's full of bars, restaurants, and rich people. Maybe I'll take you there sometime."

She didn't know how to interpret this. Was he talking about business or pleasure?

He finally stopped in front of an attractive high-rise on a narrow side street. As promised, the subway station was only a block away.

"Your apartment is on the third floor facing the street," said Stash. "I think you'll like it."

He retrieved her bags from the trunk and escorted her to the apartment door where he handed her the keys. "I'll pick you up tomorrow morning at seven o'clock. The fridge is stocked, so you can fix something to eat and get a little rest. But try not to sleep right away," he reminded her.

The place was furnished, if not sumptuously, certainly more luxuriously than the place in Yekaterinburg. There was even a flat screen television.

She busied herself for a while putting away her

clothes and then stepped out onto the balcony. The sky was beginning to darken. The evening air was cool on her skin, and she breathed deeply, taking in the essence of the enemy hidden beneath the appealing surface.

Chapter 26

Derrick Williams poked his head into Johnson's office. "You summoned me, oh Prince of Darkness?"

The Chief of Station acknowledged the sobriquet with a wry smile. "Ah, Derrick, if you only knew the half of it I'd have to kill you."

It was an old joke, but it always elicited a laugh, sometimes a nervous laugh.

Johnson stood and walked around his desk. "Guess where we're going."

Williams groaned and trudged after the COS to the S.C.I.F.

"Derrick," began Johnson, "I'm going to share something with you that I shouldn't. In fact, I'm breaking a cardinal rule. And if you're not careful with the information, I really will shoot you."

Williams' eyebrows shot to his hairline. Like most of the uninitiated, he harbored a secret envy of the spooks. "Oh, yeah?"

A long, tired sigh escaped Johnson before he spoke. "I have it on reliable authority that the FSB is sending an assassination team after Vladislav Illarionov in Ukraine, and I want you to do something about it."

Williams features froze in shock. He might secretly envy the spooks, but he certainly had no yearning to be involved in their business. "Me?" he squeaked.

"Now, don't go all girlyman on me. I don't expect you to charge in with guns blazing. It should actually be quite simple. How soon can you travel to Kiev?"

"Kiev?"

"Stop giving me monosyllabic answers. I just want you to go to the Embassy in Kiev and talk to your counterpart there. The rest will be up to him if you're convincing enough."

That didn't sound too daunting, but Williams was leery. "Why don't you go to Kiev and talk to your counterpart?"

Johnson ignored him. "This is simple, not in the least risky, and I'm not suggesting you do anything out of the ordinary. We talked about this before – your guy needs to find Illarionov pronto and help him get out of Ukraine. I thought you were on board with this."

Williams was immediately abashed as he recalled their previous conversation. Johnson's idea might just work. "You're sure they're going to try to kill him?"

"Scouts' honor." Johnson held up three fingers.

"Maybe we could set up a study grant in the States for him."

"That's the spirit. Now get some travel orders and get your ass on a plane. I don't know how much time we have."

Back in his office, Johnson brewed a fresh pot of coffee as he considered his options. Half-way through the first cup, he made his decision. He lifted the handset of his secure telephone and dialed the number for his counterpart in Kiev.

Jack Kelly's voice, processed through some very sophisticated encryption technology, was clear but slightly distorted and accompanied by whistling and hisses. "Hi, Vance, how're things in the heart of evil?"

"Still evil and becoming more so with each passing day. Listen, Jack, I'm going to share something with you that Headquarters has not disseminated yet, so this call is off the record. Is that OK with you?"

"Hell, yes. We're here, and Langley is thousands of miles away, and they usually don't know what they're talking about anyway."

That's my boy, Jack. The response was what he expected. Jack Kelly was young and had a healthy disrespect for authority. This was not a trait normally admired in intelligence officers, but Johnson could use it to his advantage.

"Jack, I just learned that the FSB is dispatching an assassination team to Ukraine. Their target is a Russian dissident writer who is now in Kharkov. His name is Vladislav Illarionov. By coincidence our Press Attaché, Derrick Williams is on his way to Kiev to help arrange a study grant in the US for Illarionov. You should have nothing to do with those arrangements unless our help is absolutely required. But I thought you might have a chat with your local counter-intel boys and give them an informal heads-up that a Russian snuff squad might be operating on their turf."

"I don't know, Vance. The SBU is riddled with Russian penetrations."

"But I'll bet there are a couple of guys you can trust."

"I think so."

"Good. Tell them the goons will come from the West, not through the battle lines. *Capisci*? Or they might have a team already in place for contingencies. God knows, they're well-practiced at infiltrating Ukraine."

"I get it. No need to tell Headquarters about this, right?"

"I always figured you for a smart fellow, Jack.

And, by the way, keep an eye out there for Derrick Williams, our press attaché."

*****

Derrick Williams was no James Bond, but he wasn't a slouch either. He was pretty sure that Johnson and he were on the same side, but then again you just never knew what games the spooks might be playing. He'd heard stories.

So the first thing he did after making reservations to fly to Kiev was visit Golovina. He'd not risked visiting her often following the confrontation with the "*Svoi*" thugs, but now he was compelled to do so by the sense of urgency thrust upon him by the Chief of Station.

The plight of dissidents in Putin's Russia went largely without notice in the wide world, where so many terrible things were happening. While the West was distracted by terrorists, the Chinese, and insane North Koreans and Iranians, the Kremlin was left free to wield a large club without too much kickback. Ukraine had damaged Russia's international standing and sparked repercussions, but Williams doubted if anyone on main street America even was aware, let alone cared, that a bloody war still raged there.

Today's dissidents went unrecognized except for a few people who cared, and Williams was one of those people. He admired and sympathized with brave souls like Golovina, a woman whose persecution spanned two historic eras but who still maintained the struggle. If there was anything he could do to promote and support their cause, Williams was determined to do it.

Across the rough plank surface of the table that served her as a desk Golovina cocked her head to one side as she listened.

"Marya Fedorovna, I can't tell you everything, but I've got to warn you that young Illarionov is in very real danger, even in Ukraine."

"They're going after him, aren't they?" Sadness and weariness washed over her face, and she suddenly became the old lady she was, a Russian *babushka* worried about her family. The young people she attracted and guided were indeed her only remaining family, and Vladislav Illarionov was one of her favorites.

"I can't say more," said Williams, "but I'm going to Kiev this afternoon, and I'm going to try to find a way to get him to the States."

She stretched a bony arm across the table and clasped his hand. "God bless you, Derrick. You may be his last hope."

"I was hoping you might be able to get word to him somehow. There may not be a lot of time." Williams did not know the extent of Golovina's network and never asked. You never knew who might be listening. But he hoped she had resources to call upon.

She nodded. "Don't worry. I'll get word to him, and he'll be waiting to hear from you. How can he contact you in Ukraine?"

Williams wished Johnson would suggest some safe, secret mode of contact. The best he could come up with on his own was to tell Illarionov to contact him at the American Embassy. He wrote the phone number on a scrap of paper and gave it to Golovina. "I'm afraid that's the best I can do right now. This is happening so fast."

Golovina was a veteran of a thousand conspiratorial meetings, but she was more than grateful for anything Williams might do. In all the world there was no one people like her could count on but the Americans, and although they could occasionally find some NGO money to keep them going, she missed the old days when Western leaders regularly and loudly denounced the Kremlin's repression.

"Thank you again, Derrick, and good luck. Now I must get to work if we are to be successful."

Williams left her there in her "office," a thoughtful expression on her face as she puzzled out her next move. He emerged from the basement door into the afternoon sunlight and scanned the area carefully in all directions to see if he could spot anyone watching. He didn't, but he knew he wouldn't be able to see them even if they were there.

Chapter 27

The Russian Embassy sits high up on Wisconsin Avenue in Washington's exclusive Georgetown, more precisely on Mount Alto, the third highest point in the District of Columbia. The Embassy's web page boasts "a view of the Capitol, the White House, the Pentagon and the State Department," a veiled boast about the ideal line of sight for communications intercepts. They were keeping an eye on the Americans.

The architecture of the buildings on the compound is modern and functional, and the chancery is finished in white stone, as is the sumptuous "ceremonial building" with its lavish interiors of Russian white marble. They were constructed exclusively of materials of Russian origin, proving yet again the superior common sense of the Russian Foreign Ministry over the feckless bureaucrats of the U.S. Department of State. Early on, the FBI attempted to tunnel under the grounds in order to tap into communications lines, but the operation was discovered, resulting in snickers throughout the halls and drawing rooms of Washington.

The chancery with its slit windows glistened like alabaster in the early afternoon sunlight. It reminded Olga of a fortress, a white, shining fortress high on a hill overlooking enemy terrain. She stepped out of the taxi and presented her passport to the uniformed guard in the enclosed checkpoint at the entrance.

After scrutinizing the document and checking it against a list of approved visitors, the guard instructed her to take a seat while he arranged for an escort. She found a place in a row of straight-backed chairs along one wall and glanced nervously at her watch. She didn't want to be late to the first meeting with her FSB case officer and arrived with twenty minutes to spare. As the minutes ticked away, she became more and more nervous.

On the top floor of the chancery, a middle-aged woman knocked on his office door and announced to Valeriy Eduardovich Karpov "The Polyanskaya girl is waiting at the gate."

"I'd almost forgotten about her," was his sour response. "Go fetch her up here."

Karpov slumped behind his desk and reached for a pack of Marlboros.

Why had the Center saddled him with this inexperienced young girl? What could she possibly know about his work? On his desk lay the mottled green cardboard folder containing her dossier, and he flipped through it again. *She's just a little propaganda bitch that works the Kremlin parties. All she's good for is shrieking slogans and waving placards. What the hell am I, a nanny? Do they think I have nothing better to do than mess around with an empty-headed kid from Moscow?* He could only conclude that some powerful friend in Moscow was rewarding her with a "vacation" in the U.S. Or perhaps she was the mistress of some *silovik* who just wanted to get rid of her.

But the orders were clear. *Use her as efficiently as possible, and keep an eye on her.* How was he to interpret that?

There was a light knock at the door. "Come," he said, closing the file folder.

The girl entered the office and stood uncertainly before his desk while he gave her a frankly appraising once over.

She was of medium height with jet black hair and large green eyes, what the Russians would call a real *krasavitsa,* a beauty. Karpov settled on his mistress theory as the most likely explanation for her assignment.

Olga would not have called the man behind the desk handsome. He was dark-haired, around forty with high cheek bones on a sallow face currently arranged into a sardonic expression. He possessed none of Solntsev's masculine charm or the refined courtesy of Stash. In fact, she found something repulsive about him. He was more like a former soldier than a successful diplomat. She was disappointed.

"My name is Valeriy Fedorovich." He shot her an irritated glance. "You're three minutes late," he said, as though no better was expected from her.

He stood and walked around the desk, gesturing for her to follow him out the door. "Come on, we're going to talk somewhere else."

Without uttering a word she followed in his wake. He led her down a flight of stairs to the floor below and to the end of a corridor. He used a key to unlock a featureless door, and they entered a small, windowless room. It contained a small table surrounded by four chairs. He took a place across from her.

"Well, Olga Vladimirovna, tell me what you did in Moscow."

She was confused by the question, although it was not unexpected. This man's unconcealed displeasure erased the words she'd planned to say.

Looking down at her hands, she said, "Officially, I worked as a press secretary, meeting with media and the public. I prepared presentations and made speeches, supervised student meetings and social and charity events."

He cut her off. "And unofficially?"

She swallowed uncomfortably. "Unofficially we followed opposition activities, especially those traitors who were in touch with Americans. We organized counter-demonstrations, interrupted their gatherings, we explained patriotic values and the danger of revolution to young people."

"So you persecuted dissidents." She couldn't tell from his voice whether he approved or disapproved.

"Not at all." Olga didn't bother to conceal her indignation. "We worked to prevent a revolution, so that people can live normally. I took no personal pleasure in 'persecuting' anyone. I just did not want blood and chaos in my country."

She wondered if Valery Eduardovich might be somehow testing her. But it was impossible to penetrate his opacity, and it was driving her crazy.

"Is that all?"

"We recruited volunteers to send to the Donbas."

"Why?" His tone was sharp.

This was a provocative question. She wanted to talk about the terrible Ukrainians, the fascists, about protecting the Russian-speaking population, how New Russia was a historic possession of Russia, but instead she answered, "Because Ukraine is of strategic importance to Russia." She was doing her best to appear professional and cynical.

He gave her another hard stare, and said, "More than anything else, Russia itself is strategically significant to Russia."

She couldn't take much more of this. "The boss

gave me the Donbas assignment, and I don't argue with orders."

For just an instant she thought she detected a hint of approval in Karpov's eyes.

"What kind of training did they give you before coming here?" he asked.

"Solo and team surveillance, counter-surveillance ..."

"And do you understand what you'll be doing here?"

"Only in general."

Karpov leaned back in his chair and lit a Marlboro despite the closeness of the room. "Olenka, our situation is complicated. Our country made a strategic mistake. Possibly, in the course of events, there was no other choice. The invisible Cold War had gone on too long, and at some point it was bound to turn hot. The Yankees grabbed Ukraine by organizing an armed coup, and Russia was forced to act. Those at the top, of course, had a clearer view as to whether there was another way ..." He was silent for a few beats before continuing, "But now it's clear that the States wanted to draw us into a destructive war, and they succeeded. And now they'll do everything possible to extract maximum gain and destroy us in the end."

As his words soaked in, she experienced fear for the first time and to such an extent that it erased her indignation.

Karpov continued as though he were talking to himself. "And they have every resource and possibility. Many organizations serve this American goal, and not only the CIA. There's the State Department, various government commissions, many funds that provide grants to Russian traitors, several research institutes – every one of them working for American intelligence. Our traitors and liberals who've come to the States work with these organizations. And you must sort it all out: their programs, actions, specializations, goals and methods. You should have learned all of this before coming here. Your cover work will place you in contact with all of this, but first you must realize what they are actually doing and what they're after. This can be a dangerous game."

"I'll sort it out," she said with some heat. "Believe me. I'll do it."

"OK." She detected condescension in his voice and eyes. "I'll explain it simply. They may be divided into 'doves,' or 'hawks' - neocons. It's even easier to deal with the latter: they are clearly enemies, and they don't hide the fact that they want to destroy our country. They dream of our collapse. They don't hide their goals from anyone. But the 'doves' are more complicated. They pretend to be the 'party of peace,' but it's far from the truth. They're just more refined and delicate: they pretend to be weak and create the illusion that they're easy to trick. But they actually want to entrap you. At first glance, it seems that these two tendencies work against one another, but it's really nothing more than a banal lust for power. Both hate Russia."

"What kind of traps do these 'doves' have?" she asked, quite taken aback by Karpov's exposition.

"That's what we have to find out, Olenka. That's the task set before us all. Sometimes they can create the illusion that there is no trap, but there is. It cannot be otherwise. If we don't find them, it just means we aren't looking hard enough. The very survival of our country depends on our success here. This is a war of destruction, and it's us or them. You know what will happen if the liberals and national traitors come to power in Russia. They'll demand to get rid of people and to put anyone associated with the present government on trial, and that means you and me. If we lose, we'll lose not only Russia, but our freedom and maybe our lives. There is nowhere we can go; the time for compromise is past. Our real enemies are the Americans - not the ragged bunch of sell-outs you were after in Russia. Our real goal is to save Russia and not to go on some quest in the Donbas. Do you understand?"

"Understood." Olga gulped and then blurted, "Valeriy Eduardovich, I understand that you don't think I'm a professional, that I know nothing and can't do anything. But I was able to fool a lot of people in Russia. They believed me; I could convince them of anything. If I have to, I can lie and pretend to get along with anyone. I love Russia, and I'll do whatever is necessary. You'll see."

"We'll see. Now, let's go over some of your first tasks here."

Her first marching orders against the enemy.

"It may seem obvious, but you must learn your way around, streets, public transportation, etc. This will be very important when you are given surveillance assignments, and there will be such assignments as soon as I am convinced you are ready. In your cover work you must be alert not only against enemy provocations, but also for people who may be sympathetic to Russia, people who may one day be co-opted or recruited as agents. You will, of course, prepare your reports in writing. We will meet here at the Embassy once a week to gauge your progress."

So it was to be the same in Washington as in Yekaterinburg - endless walking, riding buses, the subway, studying maps. The second part of Karpov's instructions was more interesting.

*****

After dismissing the girl, Valeriy Eduardovich made his way to the top floor of the Embassy to the office of Dmitry Nikolayevich Olesnikov, the SVR *Rezident* in Washington. It was not his purpose to brief Olesnikov on Olga's visit. It was time for their regular afternoon chat.

The relationship between the two was tenuous. Officially the SVR was responsible for foreign intelligence and counter-intelligence, and the Washington *rezidentura* was large and capable. But the President of the Russian Federation was the former head of the FSB, and the FSB was more genuinely "Chekist" than the "modernized" former First Chief Directorate that was the SVR. The foreign intelligence service suffered from numerous failures, including having its illegals operations wrapped up in the United States. That was why the President entrusted certain sensitive tasks to the FSB.

Formally, Karpov was to coordinate all of his operations with Olesnikov because, technically, he was on SVR "turf." The *rezident* nevertheless suspected that Karpov did not share everything with him. And the *rezident* was correct. He resented Karpov, but managed to remain philosophical about it.

It was nearing embassy closing time, and Olesnikov was pouring his customary afternoon vodka when Karpov walked into his office without knocking.

Olesnikov downed the vodka in a single swallow and said, "What the fuck do you want?"

"Aren't you going to invite me to drink?"

"Why not?" Olesnikov pulled another shot glass from his desk drawer and filled it after re-filling his own.

Karpov sat without an invitation and picked up his glass. "*Ura!*" he said, and downed it.

"Do you have anything important to share?"

Karpov knew it was not a serious question. "No," he replied, "just business as usual."

"You had a visitor this afternoon, a very pretty little visitor." He leered at Valeriy Eduardovich over his glass.

Of course, the *rezident* would have a list of all visitors and who their contacts at the embassy. "Just a new staffer at the Russian-American Study Group. I gave her the standard security briefing."

"So she's not here to bump anyone off?"

Karpov laughed to cover his embarrassment. "Of course, not, Dmitry Nikolayevich. That joke's getting a little stale."

*****

It was not yet three P.M. when Olga stepped back out the Embassy gate onto Wisconsin Avenue. With nothing more on her schedule now was as good a time as ever to begin her reconnaissance of the District of Columbia. She set off toward 'M' Street with a determined stride, but after several blocks decided it would be too far to walk.

She raised her arm at a passing yellow taxicab, and to her delight it pulled over immediately. The driver was large and black, and this led to second thoughts as she hovered indecisively between getting in and remaining on the street. Finally, she slid into the car, safely separated from the driver by a Plexiglas partition. On a whim, she instructed him to take her to the Capitol building. What better place to start than the heart of the enemy camp?

The cab stopped on Capitol South in front of the Library of Congress, and she carefully counted out the fare before placing it in the slot in the partition. She was taken aback by the fierce glare of disgust from the driver and then recalled the American custom of tipping. Apparently, working people were so poorly paid they depended on the charity of others to make ends meet. This cabbie was a member of an oppressed group. She reached back into her purse and placed an additional dollar bill in the slot. The driver shook his head philosophically and pulled away from the curb with a screech of tires.

Across the wide street the Capitol Building at first seemed quite unremarkable - a building with some columns surmounted by a dense network of scaffolding. But as she walked around it, she appreciated it more as the afternoon sun splashed off its columns and broad steps in contrast to the bright, autumnal colors of the trees. Stash's warning came to mind: "Even if you really like something, even if it's beautiful, always remember that it's all built on the blood and bones of millions of destroyed lives."

This place is the center of evil, she said to herself.

Chapter 28

Vlad stared blankly into the darkened countryside rushing past the window. Four hours earlier he had boarded the train at Kharkov's twin towered station, and in two more hours he would arrive in Kiev. The departure from Kharkov was precipitous, triggered by the urgent message transmitted along Golovina's ratline to Mitya in Belgorod and across the border to Bogdan Kosti in Kharkov.

Bogdan's friendly manner was instantly replaced by marshal determination as he rushed Vlad out of the apartment to the train station.

On the platform, Bogdan pressed a wad of bills and a page torn from a notepad into Vlad's hand. "This is all I have right now," he said, "but it's enough to pay for a hotel in Kiev for a couple of nights. I'm giving you the number of a reliable contact there, but I advise you to contact the Americans as soon as possible." Golovina's warning message included the embassy number provided by Williams.

Escape into Ukraine was not the last step in Vlad's flight, but he hadn't expected FSB wolves to be on his trail so quickly. Maybe he shouldn't have published that article in *Yevropeyskiy Kharkov*. It was a foolish gesture of gratitude to Bogdan, but it revealed his location to enemies who might already be in Ukraine. Maybe they were waiting in the Kiev train station scanning the faces of arriving passengers.

By the time he arrived it was after ten P.M., and an icicle of anxiety pierced his chest as the train pulled to a stop. He remained in his seat for a long time as he surveyed the platform through the window in a vain attempt to spot any FSB operatives lurking in the shadows. Finally, he realized he would never be able to spot them. He lacked the necessary training and knowledge. His only choice was to step out of the train and hope to luck that an assassin's bullet would not cut him down.

No one took a shot at him, and he rushed out of the cathedral-like terminal into the late September night casting frequent glances over his shoulder. He headed straight up *Petlyuri* Street, a decidedly unimpressive thoroughfare. It was much too late to call the American Embassy, and he wanted to get off the street and out of sight as quickly as possible. After a long block, he turned right onto *Zhylyanska* Street and walked into the first hotel he saw, more than relieved to discover the rate was the equivalent of twelve dollars per night. Vlad was worried that his Russian passport would be a problem in Kiev, but the desk clerk assigned him a room with no comment.

There was no question of sleeping. He was much too wound up for that. There's something about being under threat of imminent death that bans drowsiness. His room faced the street, and he kept the curtains closed, a thin barrier against the danger he imagined lurked outside.

He had no idea when the American Embassy opened, or even if anyone there would know who he was. Nine AM seemed a reasonable hour, and he dialed the number Williams had given to Golovina. It was answered by a female voice, "U.S. Embassy, Press and Culture. This is Janet."

In his best English, he said, "Is Mr. Williams there, Mr. Derrick Williams?"

"Who may I say is calling?"

Such a simple request, and yet Vlad was afraid to pronounce his own name on the phone. "Erm, just tell him a friend of Marya Fedorovna, please."

There was a pause before Janet replied. "Hold, please," and one of Kenny G's tunes poured into his ear.

"Hello. This is Derrick Williams. Is this Vlad?"

He immediately recognized the voice. "Yes."

"Where are you?"

"I'm in Kiev."

"Are you safe?"

"I don't know."

"Tell me where you are, and I'll come pick you up in an Embassy car. Be ready to leave immediately. I should be there within a half-hour."

*****

Derrick had arrived in Kiev the day before and went directly to the embassy where he met with his Kiev counterpart in the Press and Culture Section, Brad Peters.

"I don't see a way to get him paroled into the States any time soon. There's really no hard evidence that he would qualify for political asylum."

Derrick started to protest, but realized that Peters was right. There was nothing besides Johnson's unofficial and unauthorized warning. "I know, but I don't doubt that he's in danger. We have to find a way to get him out of here, preferably to the States. We might help him get a tourist visa, and he could ask for asylum after he gets there. Or how about a study grant of some sort? Do you have anything pending?"

Peters was doubtful. "The guy is Russian, not Ukrainian."

"Well, he did write a big article in a Ukrainian newspaper, and there's no way I can help him in Moscow because he can't go back there." He cast in his memory for possibilities. "What about that AEI grant? They're willing to sponsor a six-month internship in Washington. I think they'd jump at the chance to get a real Russian dissident journalist."

"Yeah, well ..." Peters' attitude softened. "Let's work on that. But you've got to find him first."

That problem solved itself.

They were going through the paperwork next morning when Vlad called in to the Embassy. He was on his way to check out a car from the motor pool when he ran into a tall man with a friendly, Irish face and shockingly red hair.

"Are you Derrick Williams from Moscow?"

"Erm, yes."

The redhead thrust out a large, freckled hand. "I'm Jack Kelly. I have the same job here that Vance Johnson has in Moscow."

CIA guys, thought Derrick, have such an elliptical manner of speaking. *I have the same job here that Vance Johnson has in Moscow.* Why couldn't he just say he was the Chief of Station?

"He said I should lend you a hand ... if you want, of course," Kelly finished.

"I'm on my way to pick up Illarionov right now. He's in a hotel not far from the train station."

"Good. Why don't you let me take you in my car?"

Any port in a storm. Derrick agreed without hesitation. It wouldn't hurt to have a friend along when picking up a guy on the FSB's assassination list.

He gave Kelly the name of Vlad's hotel.

"Great," said the CIA man. "Let me just make a quick phone call first."

Kelly was back in ten minutes and led him to a parking lot at one end of the Embassy compound where he directed him to a late model BMW 5 series. Not an Aston-Martin, but nifty, nonetheless.

Less than 30 minutes later, they pulled up in front of Vlad's hotel on *Zhylyanska* which turned out to be an unremarkable one-way street. The hotel was large and equally unremarkable. Kelly pulled up in front and turned on his blinkers. As he stepped out of the car, Derrick caught a glimpse of a shoulder holster under the CIA man's jacket.

"You're carrying a gun?"

Kelly grinned. "I'll probably never use it, but I wouldn't want to need it and not have it on me."

Derrick also noticed that Kelly was scrutinizing their surroundings as he closed the car door. He was doing it casually, but it was a complete 360-degree scan.

They called Vlad from the front desk, and he appeared within a few moments dressed in jeans, a leather jacket, and with a backpack over one shoulder. The young man was obviously relieved to see a familiar face and shook Derrick's hand heartily as he cast a curious glance at the big redhead at his side.

"Vlad, this is Jack Kelly. He, erm, works at the Embassy here and gave me a lift."

"Ochen' rad poznakomitsya," (Glad to meet you). Kelly's Russian was good.

They headed for the exit, and Kelly waved them to stay behind him. He stepped outside and again scanned the vicinity. When he turned back toward them, that big grin was on his face again. "We're good to go."

Outside, a large, black Mercedes sedan sat with its engine idling right behind the BMW. It contained four men with their faces turned toward them.

Derrick skidded to a halt and grabbed Vlad by the elbow. "What's going on?"

"That's our escort," said Kelly. "I called some friends in the SBU for back-up before we left the embassy."

"SBU?" Derrick was unfamiliar with the term.

"The Ukrainian Security Service. We'll be perfectly safe. Now, hurry up and get in the car." He continued toward the BMW with a nonchalant wave at the men in the Mercedes.

"I wish he'd said something," grumbled Derrick. He and Vlad slid into the back seat.

*****

The peculiar warble alerted Vance Johnson of an incoming call on the secure line. Jack Kelly's distorted voice greeted him when he answered. "I just wanted to let you know that your fugitive dissident is safely inside the embassy here."

"So, you met Williams?"

Kelly chuckled. "Yeah. Rather a nervous type, isn't he?"

"Maybe he has a good reason to be nervous. Putin's Nazis haven't made his life pleasant here."

"Is that a fact? They've caused some problems for the Ukrainians, too."

"So I've heard. Are they going to get Illarionov to the States?"

"I think so. Williams was talking about some sort of internship in Washington."

"That'll work, if he can get out of Ukraine alive."

"About that: I called in some markers from the SBU, and guess what. This afternoon the editor of that Kharkov newspaper started getting calls asking about Illarionov. The SBU boys were sitting with the editor at the time. To make a long story short, the editor invited the caller to his office to collect the information, and a couple of very interesting Serbians turned up. They're being interrogated as we speak. The SBU is very grateful."

"That's good news, but it won't slow them down long. Can you guarantee Illarionov gets out of the country safely?"

"He'll be behind a cordon of SBU tough guys. Nobody will get to him in Ukraine before he gets away."

"Let me know when he's on the way."

Johnson replaced the receiver and closed his eyes. He needed to think, and he needed to get back to Washington for a few days.

Chapter 29

There was one building in Washington where Olga could be assured of finding likeminded friends. The offices of the Russian-American Study Group were near the intersection of 17th and 'M' streets in the heart of the business district within easy walking distance of The White House. The exterior reminded her of the Russian Embassy, and she looked upon it as a sort of outpost on the front line.

The Group's small suite of offices was on the third floor with a view of the National Geographic Building on the opposite side of 17th Street through a narrow window.

"So how do you like Washington, Olga Vladimirovna?" The head of the Group, Valentin Gyorgievich Zartetskiy greeted her. Olga returned his smile. In contrast to Karpov, Zaretskiy was gentle and charming. He could not, of course, compare to the charismatic Solntsev who was capable of igniting the spark of heroism in even the most mediocre of people. Nevertheless, Zaretskiy's friendly and caring manner was reassuring.

"Bright and pretentious, but Moscow's better," she replied.

"True," said Zaretskiy, still smiling, "There would be nothing to do here if it weren't for the work. And we have a lot of it. Take a seat."

He led her into a small conference room where they found Stash already at the table.

Zaretskiy said, "Olga has only just arrived, and already we have a very important job for her. First, you may be surprised to learn that we have friends in

America, even important people. And one of our most important jobs is to help them."

Unlike Karpov's emphatically dismissive attitude, her "official" boss treated her with respect, although with a certain informality. She could be quite successful here.

"Do you know the name Alan Sandburg?" asked Zaretskiy.

This was a name familiar to viewers of Russian television. She recalled an image of a rather dry, no longer young man talking about the dangers of aggressive American policies that could lead to conflict with Russia. He accused his own country of unleashing a new Cold War and interfering in Ukraine.

Stash bent so close to her that she could feel his breath on her ear. "He's an analyst."

Embarrassed by Stash's closeness, she leaned away and said, "Yes, I've seen him on RT."

"Mr. Sandberg is one of the most senior so-called Russian specialists in the States," Zaretskiy continued. "He understands that the security of the United States depends on maintaining good relations with Moscow, and that American interference in our sphere of influence led directly to the present crisis. He works at an influential 'think tank' and is considered their primary Russian specialist. I'm sure you understand how important his help is in supporting our interests. People at the highest levels pay attention to what he says."

Olga was intrigued. Here was an American in the very heart of the enemy camp who served Russian interests. She was certain there must be more here than met the eye. Otherwise, why would Zaretskiy and Stash be talking about the man?

Her thoughts were confirmed by Zaretskiy's

next words, pronounced with a certain solemnity. "What is not evident is that he could do none of that without our help. In fact, we provide a great deal of material and guidance to him." He paused for emphasis before saying, "And we pay him well for his efforts."

"He's one of ours, and frankly it's amazing he's gotten away with it for so long," added Stash.

Zaretskiy said, "Yes. For years his 'think tank' has trusted his analyses and acted on his prognoses. His policy papers are sent to Congress, the State Department, even the Pentagon. Alan Sandburg frequently visited Russia, even in Soviet times. No one questions his competence. But he does have his detractors, and they are becoming more vocal. It is more important than ever to continue to support him in every possible way."

Stash leaned close again. "And that will be your main job for the Group, Olga."

Anxiety fluttered in her chest, like a bird trying to escape a cage. She was to be entrusted with such an important task? "How will I do this?" she asked. "And what do you mean by 'one of ours?'"

Stash smiled indulgently. "I mean that he's our creature, but he probably actually thinks he's his own man. He's quite egotistical, and that makes him easy to manipulate."

Zaretskiy broke in. "Olga, you are a young girl, and this old man will be susceptible to your obvious charms. He'll continue to do as we say, and he'll like it. In Washington our Group is just one 'think tank' among many, and it will be perfectly natural for you to be in regular contact with Sandburg. No one will suspect a thing. You'll be perfectly safe."

This was a lot to take in at once. "So he

actually does not believe what he says? He just does it for the money?"

Stash laughed out loud. "Oh, he probably believes it. But all Americans love money and will do almost anything to get it."

"How does it work?"

Zaretskiy said, "Moscow sends talking points and guidance at least once a week. All you have to do is deliver them to Sandburg."

Her initial anxiety now melted into something like disappointment. After all this build up, she was to be nothing more than a messenger.

Reading her thoughts, Zaretskiy sought to reassure her. "Olga, this is a very important operation, and the fact that we are entrusting it to you should make you proud."

"And that's not all you'll be doing." Stash laid an arm around her shoulders. She was uncomfortable at the familiarity but didn't shrug him off. She was still feeling her way.

Zaretskiy smiled slyly then turned serious. "Having a person like you on our staff is really a good thing. You have a lot of practice meeting new people, and we'll put that to good use. There is a lot of Russian garbage here who dream of profiting from the troubles of their own country. It's just a bunch of filthy hipsters and shrieking gay activists. What they want is asylum, and so they complain about the 'bloody Kremlin.'

"The Yankees don't pay them much attention. Occasionally some local politician will meet with them and snap a few photos to show the voters that America is protecting human rights, and then they forget about them. Since 1991 there has not been much interest in Russia here in Washington. But our liberals often organize ugly meetings and protests at our consulates. We never took them seriously, but we still have to keep an eye on them."

Olga was filled with resentment, and there was fire in her voice. "Filthy cosmopolitan scum. What can we do?"

"We must gather as much information as possible. And this means you must go among them, get to know them. Your task is to find out all you can about their activities and plans, who are the leaders. We must discover their weaknesses, for example, find out about their families still in Russia."

"You think they'll really talk to me?"

It was Stash's turn to speak. "This isn't simple, Olga. I'll give you some names of reliable, pro-Russian activists in the Russian community. These are regular people, but they are still patriots. The community is not large, and they all know one another. They go to the same Russian theaters, put their kids in the same Russian kindergartens and Russian-language schools. If they're believers, they go to the same churches. There are even Russian dentists. Be discreet. Get to know them. We'll help you."

"Quite correct," said Zaretskiy. "With Olga's charm, we should be quite successful. Above all, remember not to become angry. Try to act naturally and unobtrusively. As soon as we can arrange it, Stash will introduce you to Alan Sandburg. We'll prepare all of this in a few days for you.

Olga left the meeting with the weight of the world on her shoulders. Zaretskiy placed a lot of faith in her "charm."

Chapter 30

"No foreign enemy can do as much damage as a traitor," said Valeriy Eduardovich Karpov.

His eyes bored into Olga as though he were trying to read her innermost thoughts. The girl remained somewhat of a mystery to him. Could there be anyone, he wondered, as truly dedicated as she insisted she was? And yet, despite his misgivings, she was highly recommended by Lubyanka.

Karpov's physical resources in Washington were limited and left him with little choice but to entrust the new arrival with a task of considerable importance. The main players had been in place for several weeks already, but everything depended on timing.

Olga remained silent under Karpov's measuring gaze. She sensed that her FSB handler was about to impart something important to her. The Russian word for handler is *"kurator,"* which literally means "caretaker," and she found the term distasteful. She required no "handling;" all she needed was an assignment, and she would surely succeed.

Karpov's eyes never left her. It was a technique developed over many years interrogating enemies of the state while serving in the KGB's Second Chief Directorate. But he detected nothing in the girl that might betray a doubt.

"There is a so-called 'dissident' in Washington. His name is Mark Lvovich Shtayn. He's winning a reputation and has the ear of influential people. Apart from the normal liberal whining about 'political prisoners, he recently published a report that damages our work: the names of euro-deputies loyal to us, pro-

Russian political groups throughout Europe, the influence of Russian business on certain foreign politicians. And that's not all. Shtayn is beginning to frighten people with the notion that Russia is determined to destroy American relations with Europe and destroy NATO. And they believe him because in the 90's he was an influential banker with direct access to the Kremlin leadership. He knows state secrets."

"And this man is a Russian?" asked Olga.

"A corrupt, venal Jew, like I said, a banker, a money man." muttered Karpov. "And worst of all, he somehow has access to our military secrets in the Donbas, including the identification of various units and their weaponry. You can only imagine where this shit gets his information."

"What do we know about this Shtayn?" asked Olga ignoring the vulgarity.

"He fled Russia right after Putin was elected president and received political asylum in Ukraine where he made outlandish accusations against the president. When Yanukovich came to power, he moved to the States. He's been here four years on a green card, so he's still officially a Russian citizen. We didn't pay too much attention to him until now, but he's become loud and dangerous."

"That's a shame," said Olga. *Why was Karpov telling her this?*

"Olga Vladimirovna," Karpov smiled thinly, "I have an assignment for you, a real assignment. Not that cover work you do for Zaretskiy."

Olga was thrilled.

"First, Olga Vladimirovna, we must gather as much information as possible on the traitor. This will be up to you. Your task is to discover all you can about his activities in the States, about his work, his friends, his habits, his contacts, but most importantly – his weaknesses, anything that may be used to compromise him."

"You think he'll talk to me?" Olga was dubious.

"No, Olga, under no circumstances should you have personal contact with him. This man is your target, the subject of your investigation. Remember the lessons you learned in Yekaterinburg. Your immediate task is to gather basic information, but you must be discreet."

"I'm already developing contacts in the Russian community. It's part of my work for Zaretskiy."

"That's an excellent place to start." The girl was smart. He gave her that. "You will report to me, and only to me, what you turn up. The next phase will be to surveil the man, map out his patterns. This will be important. It may well reveal his sources."

Stash provided a contact, an eager and reliable informant named Andrey Petrov. He was a naturalized American citizen who lived comfortably in a two-story house in the Washington suburbs. But this was a matter of convenience only, and he believed the US was teetering on the brink of destruction. For this reason he made it his business to preserve relations with his former country. He was an established realtor and made quite a good living from the Russian community.

It was easy to arrange a meeting with Petrov, who received her at his Fairfax office. He was a man of average height with thinning black hair and a bad comb-over. His eyes roamed over her body, but his manner bordered on the obsequious.

She decided to adopt an indirect approach and told him she was gathering opinions in the Russian diaspora about events in Russia, even if they were negative.

"We want to be as objective as possible in order to show our American colleagues the entire spectrum of opinion," she said.

He gave her a dubious look, as though the idea of objectivity might never have occurred to him. "Olga Vladimirovna, you're an expert and know more than I, but ... we have some real assholes in the community who hate their own country even more than the American 'hawks.' Some of them spread blatant lies. When they are confronted by someone who speaks the truth it's even worse. They love to expose Russia's secrets. They make money by inciting hatred of the Homeland. It's not worth your time to write about such opinions." He was warning her that such opinions were dangerous, maybe even to her.

"You mean these people are actually taken seriously?" She injected feigned surprise into her voice. Her talent for dissembling was growing like the first shoots of a young tree as it puts down roots and blossoms.

Chapter 31

Совершенно Секретно
Eyes Only Colonel Kozlov

Subject   : *Black Widow*
From   : *FSB Rezident, Washington*

The initial operational phase of *Black Widow* is complete. Phase 2 is underway.

Subject's activities already are well-known, but additional information was successfully elicited by our new operative.

Subject continues to publish liberal slanders against the Motherland concerning so-called "political prisoners" and "Mafia connections," but even worse are his revelations about our external work. He names Euro-deputies loyal to us, delineates the pro-Russian sentiments in various European countries, and the influence of Russian business over certain foreign politicians. He also has collated what our European friends have said against the United States, with emphasis on anti-NATO sentiments. The similarity of these statements leads to the conclusion that all are based on guidance from Moscow and are aimed at disrupting the North Atlantic Alliance.

It is also clear that Subject possesses sources of highly sensitive information concerning the Russian military and its strategic planning, especially in the Donbas.

Subject is winning influence among American policymakers and elements of the right wing press. It is fair to speculate that if he is allowed to continue his subversive activities, his trajectory in Washington will continue only to rise. It is clear that he still has sources inside the Motherland, as well as in Ukraine where he resided for a number of years. Some of these sources may be official, and it is even possible that he is a witting agent of the CIA or FBI.

The Rezidentura has launched Phase 2 of this operation, the surveillance of subject. This task is simplified by the work of our asset in locating Subject's home and office. We should be in a position within a matter of weeks to accurately predict Subject's movements. The Center will be advised as soon as sufficient data has been gathered.

The full report of our operative is attached.

END   *END*   *END*

Chapter 32

Olga used the Russian-American Study Group's resources to review open-source information about Shtayn. There was a website, and she was surprised that his office address was openly available to the public and actually quite close to her apartment.

Shtayn must be on the U.S. Government payroll. How else to explain a couple of invitations to the White House? He had testified before Congress and frequented the State Department. He was a fixture in Washington's densely populated analytical community.

Shtayn didn't fit Zaretskiy's characterization of activists in America as "filthy hiptsers and shrieking gay activists" that no one took seriously. No. Shtayn was something else entirely. He was a clear and present danger to the Motherland.

No matter what Russia might do, no matter in whose business she meddled, and no matter whether she was right or wrong, no one should act so cold-bloodedly against their own country. To collect information in order to pass it to the enemy was intolerable.

On Shtayn's website she found photos of him with some Euro-deputies. This coincided with Petrov's information that Shtayn spent a three-month study grant there when still a law student.

Petrov was useful in other ways, too.

"How do you know about this travel?"

"My son's nanny is his neighbor," he whispered as though he was divulging a great secret. "You know how it is here. Immigrants receive citizenship, apply for family reunification and bring their parents over. The fathers and mothers don't know a word of English and try to get illegal work, as often as not as nannies for Russian-speaking families. This woman is one of these. She a nice old lady who likes to talk. I brokered her children's purchase of a small house for her in Fairfax, and it turns out that this traitor lives next door. When he went to Europe she looked after his dog. I know when he was there right down to the very day. As I understand it, he went to Strasbourg and got to know some Europeans. That's when he started following our activities there. He obviously recruited informants and they spy on Russian diplomats. I can only guess at the rest."

He shook his head sadly.

For an instant, his words evoked school-day memories of reading about informants and firing squads during Soviet times. Petrov was just like those old schoolbook caricatures of informants. The realization did not deter Olga but rather gave her a new sense of self-worth.

Here was Petrov – a worthless little man doing his best to convince her of his value - to serve her. He was obsequious and fished for compliments. She was far above him and his sort – she was an official, a true Chekist, and people like Petrov saw in her the personification of the government they served.

She smiled condescendingly in unconscious imitation Karpov.

"You are a true professional," she said. "It's simply remarkable that you've been able to dig all of this up. You've been very helpful. Could you please let me have the address of this old lady? One of my friends is looking for a nanny."

Petrov gave her a cunning look out of the

corners of his eyes. She wasn't fooling him. He knew exactly what she was doing. He wrote the address on a piece of his company stationery and handed it to her. "Here it is. Her name is Nina Valentinovna Guskova. No need to talk politics with her. She's one of us – watches Russian TV, but she doesn't understand the subtleties. That's why she can get along with this corrupt Jew. She's a simple soul and doesn't understand what he's doing. If it were me, I'd punch him."

Petrov slapped himself on the chest as though he expected someone to pin a medal on him.

Olga flashed a brilliant smile. "I'm just looking for a nanny."

She accepted Petrov's silent admiration and left.

Olga debated whether to pay a visit to the nanny. Karpov might not approve of her getting so close to the target, but she wanted to see where the man lived.

Guskova lived in a modest house surrounded by shrubbery that undoubtedly would explode in a riot of color in the spring. But gray skies dominated now, and a gentle rain was falling when she knocked on the door.

She introduced herself and was invited inside by a white-haired but robust appearing woman in her mid-70's – Nina Guskova. The cozy house was filled with the aroma of baking cookies. On one wall of the living room was a small shelf with dried flowers, icons and family photos decorated the walls.

Olga experienced a brief regret that she was here under false pretenses. But she kept in mind the image of herself as a steel-nerved professional. She was in a war, and she would fight it with every smile and word, every nod of her head, in her smallest gesture, in the firmness of her gaze, in the tension she did not betray. An invisible war.

Olga recited the story she had concocted as a pretext for the visit. "My friend has a two-year-old daughter. She's very precocious and runs everywhere and talks. The only problem is that she doesn't live near here. You don't drive, and it would be hard for you to get there. It's possible that my friend could bring the child here on her way to work in the morning and pick her up after. You have such a nice garden where the little girl could play. But I do have a question. Are your neighbors OK?"

"Oh, the neighbors are very quiet." The old woman waved vaguely at a window. "On that side there is a very nice elderly American couple. Their children visit occasionally, and they're very nice. And a nice Russian boy," she gestured to the other side, "lives over there. Well, not a boy, but he's young and quite charming, a handsome Jew," she smiled. "He says clever things that I don't always understand. He lives alone with his dog. I don't know much about dogs, but this is a good-sized one. But he's nice. He always runs to give me a kiss."

"So this man is smart and handsome, but he's not married?" She wanted to encourage some gossip.

"Oh, he's always busy, like all the Americans." Guskova shook her head. "He used to study all the time, to be a lawyer, I think. He also worked as a paralegal for one of those lawyers that help with political asylum. I asked him, 'Marik, what is all this about asylum – escaping from one's own country?' And he says, 'Oh, Nina Valentinovna, it's best that you not know.' And what does he know that I don't? I lived my entire life in Russia and saw much that he did not ..."

This was easy. It didn't take much to get the garrulous old lady started. "And what did he do when he finished his studies?"

"He went to Europe for about three months and asked me to look after his dog. He was with me so long it was hard to give him back. Such a good dog. But then Marik founded some sort of organization and spends most of his time there. He helps all sorts of people, refugees, I think. I tell him, 'Marik, you should have a family instead of helping others all the time.' And he says, 'These people help me, too. Thanks to them I always know what's going on, and know that I'm not working in vain.'"

As she listened to this naïve old lady praise a traitor, Olga experienced an unwelcome nausea. She breathed in the aroma of fresh cookies and through the window saw the sun break through the clouds outside. Something in her soul could not be reconciled to what was happening, and she could not shake it.

This work is complicated, and I only now realize it completely. Aloud, Olga asked, "So he hasn't traveled to Europe again. He's still here?"

Guskova waved a hand in the air. "He's always traveling. He went to Ukraine just a couple of months ago. I said to him, 'What do you do over there, Marik? There's a war and fascists,' but he said, 'No, Nina Valentinovna, there aren't any fascists like they say on television.'"

Guskov's eyes went wide. "And how is it possible that the television could lie? They have smart people, and they know everything. But Marik just laughed and said, 'I talk with generals, with professional soldiers, and they know more than the television.' But can one believe generals if they aren't our generals?"

The television does not lie, but Shtayn lies every time he opens his mouth. Olga wanted to say this but did not, and the old lady continued like a water tap that could not be shut off.

"I saw a girl with him a little while ago, maybe his secretary. They work together, and she's started to come home with him. She's young, but then so is he. She's pretty. I like her looks. I saw her through the window." It was a habit of *babushkas* to watch what their neighbors were doing.

"Does he have family in Russia?"

"In Russia, yes. He complains about not seeing them for so long, but what can I do. It's his fault. My daughters weren't refugees, and they came home every year to visit me while I lived there." She turned a disapproving eye in the direction of Shtayn's house.

And that was everything she could wring out of the old lady for her report to Karpov: information on his repeated trips to Europe, his contacts with foreign generals, about his family and his supposed girlfriend. It didn't seem like much to her.

Chapter 33

The Shenandoah Valley, Virginia

This is what the old man knew.

Age strips us of our vanities and illusions until, like an oak in winter denuded of its autumnal glory, we stand naked against the bleak winter with all our faults exposed. But unlike the oak, there is no promise of quickening sap in the coming spring, no prospect of summer's renewed vigor. Man's cleverness has mauled the circle of life into a straight line, a mortal continuum with a definite beginning and an inevitable end. What happens in between is largely a matter of chance.

A hollowness had expanded inside him, like the empty, icy expanse of space, and it led him to decide that he no longer liked nor needed people, either as individuals or, more generally, as a species. There were those he had called friend, and two women he'd truly loved. But they were lost like stones dropped into deep, dark water to sink from sight forever.

People were best avoided. Perhaps this disdain always had been a part of him but temporarily overcome by youthful enthusiasms. The old man knew too much to retain those deceptions.

There were ideals worth fighting and dying for. He had met evil and vanquished it time and again, only for it to reappear in some other guise, sometimes springing from the same soil he thought he had salted. The lives of some who defended what had once been called an evil empire were snuffed out by his hand, but these had been only temporary, ephemeral victories.

By taking sides, he also accepted a burden of responsibility that in the end was too heavy to bear. Evil would always be with us.

And so in the end, he abandoned mankind to its foolish devices and stopped caring if it repeated the same ancient mistakes. His participation was at an end.

He much preferred the company of dogs, a species he viewed as vastly superior to man in spirit, decency, loyalty, and truth. Dogs do not require a surfeit of conversation, and deception is unknown to them.

The smoke from a large Cuban cigar, a Partagas Lusitania, in fact, wafted toward the fire in the native stone hearth. A chocolate Labrador Retriever named Sadie rested her head in his lap. The furnishings in the log cabin were spare and solidly masculine. There was a lot of leather and heavy, oak pieces. The walls were adorned with a few oil paintings, identified as seascapes of the Irish coast if one were to examine the small, brass plaques affixed to the frames. A glass-fronted liquor cabinet with a copper top contained a collection of Islay single-malt scotches.

There were no photographs because reminders of the inhabitants of his former life evoked unfailingly painful memories.

Book shelves lined one wall. There were so many of the great books still to be read. There was a gun safe concealed in another wall containing a variety of weapons. Beside the door, a coat rack was mounted on the wall. It was currently inhabited by a hooded parka and several hats. A sturdy blackthorn walking stick leaned against the wall below beside a pair of fur-lined boots. If one were to enter the cabin, one would encounter the pleasant aroma of tobacco mixed with furniture polish and pine-scented cleaner, but there were never visitors.

The cabin was situated on fifty acres of unimproved, forested mountain land on Supin Lick Ridge, a part of the Appalachian range, overlooking Virginia's Shenandoah Valley. The old man paid a ridiculously inflated price to a delighted real estate speculator. The place had been abandoned decades earlier and sold at a tax auction before passing through many hands. He found the neglected cabin nearly in ruins and spared no expense in its restoration, which included a powerful generator to guard against frequent power outages, a state of the art perimeter alarm system, and a kitchen that sparkled with the most expensive and modern, stainless steel equipment. He also installed a sturdy gate at the entrance to the only access road. He added a garage on one side to house for the Land Rover.

There was no television and no computer, only an ancient but powerful, multi-band radio of German manufacture. A phone line was connected, but he kept the phone unplugged. There was no one from whom he wished to hear.

He was comfortable here, alone but for the dog, and isolated from the world by acres of forested mountainside. The cabin represented a return to beginnings, to self-sufficiency.

Once a month, the old man would drive with the dog to the nearest city to re-stock his supplies. He discovered Costco, which except for the scotch satisfied most of his needs.

An early frost already had begun to turn the leaves by mid-October leading Shenandoah Valley residents to predict a long, hard winter. The leaves turned earlier than usual, bringing in carloads of tourist gawkers who bought locally produced apple cider and colorfully decorated hand-carved whirligigs in the shape of roosters or other animals. In another month hunters would begin to move through the forests in search of deer, turkey, and bear. The prizes from these hunts would feed many families throughout the year.

It was time to top up the 500-gallon underground propane tank, assure a good supply of dry firewood, and stock the larder.

In the check-out line at Costco the old man noticed a man in a military surplus jacket with a woman in a hijab, not in itself so unusual, even in Harrisonburg, Virginia. The man was young and handsome. He and the woman ferried two loaded trollies piled high with bulk food items toward the check-out counter.

Shoppers avoided the line like scattering birds to head for other lines that promised a faster pass through. The old man, his own shopping cart heaped with a month's supply of meats, frozen goods, and sundries, fell in behind the two.

It was a spur of the moment decision, his interest slightly piqued. It was not so much the fact that the couple aroused his curiosity, but rather the outline of a large caliber pistol traced through the fabric of the man's jacket when he bent to the trolley to lift items onto the counter.

Virginia is a concealed carry State, but the combination of a Muslim couple and a large caliber weapon in a store full of shoppers flipped an interior switch which activated reflexes too much a part of his make-up for too many years to ignore. Entirely of its own accord his hand snaked inside his jacket to unsnap the safety strap that secured a Heckler & Koch

.45 Tactical in a shoulder rig.

Nothing untoward happened. The couple paid for their purchases with cash and trundled toward the exit. Except that when the man spoke to the woman the language he used was Russian. This shifted the old man's speculation geographically northward, toward the Caucasus.

The old man paid and pushed his own cart to the parking lot where he loaded his purchases into the Land Rover.

The couple was still loading their purchases into the bed of a beat up F-150 with sun-bleached red paint and a sagging rear bumper. The woman did the heavy lifting while the man stood aside lighting a cigarette. When she was finished, the woman headed back to the main building tugging both empty trolleys behind. After crushing his cigarette beneath his shoe, the man climbed behind the steering wheel and started the engine, which emitted a well-tuned purr that belied the trucks appearance. He waited for the woman to return and clamber into the cab before backing out of the parking space.

The old man filled the Land Rover's tank with cheap Costco gas and headed for an ABC store to pick up a couple of bottles of single malt.

*****

Some days later he spotted the F-150 again on the narrow gravel road that led up to Supin Lick ridge. It was stopped in front of a gate that guarded a narrow dirt road leading to a former turkey farm. On certain hot summer days when the wind was right, the stench of the old breeding barns drifted up the mountain over his fifty acres that lay just to the west.

As the Land Rover passed, the man opening the gate stared hard, his eyes following the old man's progress until he was out of sight. In the Land Rover's rear view mirror, the F-150 passed through the gate.

His didn't like his new neighbors' profile. The location was remote. Given the extent of the old man's property it was possible that the new occupants of the turkey farm didn't know he was even there. But he knew about them now in the way a man knows about a splinter in his flesh that is otherwise invisible; the irritation would fester.

Chapter 34

Surveillance of Mark Shtayn was simplified by the fact that the man travelled between his home in Fairfax and his office in Arlington via an unchanging route. He left the house every morning at the same time, caught the same Metro train at the same time, rode it to Clarendon Station and walked the short distance from the station to his office with almost no variation. In the evening, he reversed the route. Those times he would elsewhere were often publicized, and so he could be found speaking at a university one night or attending a symposium at a Washington think tank on another. To make things even easier, his public appearances were punctiliously published on his website.

It didn't take Olga long to figure this out, and she told Karpov she would not require assistance. Shtayn never once so much as looked over his shoulder. He felt completely invulnerable in America.

Curiosity drew her to one of Shtayn's appearances at Georgetown University. She didn't seek Karpov's permission because he almost certainly would have denied it. But she wanted to see for herself why this man was such a successful anti-Russian agitator.

She arrived at the auditorium five minutes before the presentation and found a cozy spot in in the back row. The audience was an eclectic mix of students in jeans and hoodies, not so different from what she recalled of her own time at university in Moscow, well-dressed older men and women, and everything in between.

By the time the speaker was introduced, the place was about half-full. Shtayn's lecture on the Russian-Ukrainian conflict was open to the public. Olga could see him clearly across the expanse of auditorium seats. As he took his place behind the dais the air seemed charged with electricity that tingled on her skin and caused her heart to beat faster. This was the enemy, her target, and her goal was to see him disgraced. She feared that her animosity was so great it would be noticed by Shtayn as though assaulted by a physical force.

Shtayn began, "The Russian incursion into Eastern Ukraine was carried out under the control of the Western Group of Forces – one of four strategic formations created in 2008 when the Russian Armed Forces were reorganized. At that time Moscow created the Western Group of Forces to counter NATO. The Eastern Group is to conduct operations against China. And the Southern Group against the Caucasus and Central Asia. The Central Group serves as a strategic reserve."

Olga sucked in her breath. *This is our military. How can he talk like this in enemy territory, and how does he know these things?*

"The Western Group has two headquarters levels and was used in military operations in Ukraine, both in traditional and non-traditional ways. The non-traditional, for example, include airborne divisions and regiments, as well as special operations brigades. It was actually these forces that were used at the beginning of the war to destabilize Eastern Ukraine and gather intelligence on strategic targets in the region. These were the forces known as 'little green men,' and they were involved in the invasion and annexation of the Crimea. As for regular forces, as the incursion got underway they consisted of tank and motorized divisions that supported mechanized and armored brigades. These forces were reinforced by elements from the Central command."

Images of men in camouflage with darkened faces and without identifying unit patches appeared on a large screen behind Shtayn, as well as tanks and other military equipment that Olga did not recognize. But she knew they were "ours." The strength of Russian arms was being shown at a Washington university – could this be permitted?

There was a question period after the lecture, and several people raised their hands. One of them leapt up not waiting to be recognized and in a voice shaking with emotion began to speak.

Olga barely contained a laugh. She recognized Petrov who was doing his best to keep his voice calm.

"What you are saying is totally unconvincing. First of all, there is no proof that these are actually Russian soldiers. You yourself say that they have no unit designations. And as for military groups ... Military formations exist throughout Europe, there are secret CIA prisons in other countries, and for some reason no indignation about that. Besides that, Russian troops had every right to be in the Crimea. The Russian Black Sea Fleet is there."

This was getting good. Petrov was *her* man, and she was proud of his effort to spoil the traitor's night.

"You talk about Russian saboteurs, but obviously not even the best prepared saboteurs could ignite a rebellion without the support and participation of the local population. Without massive support you can't establish logistics or guarantee communications, or gather intelligence. And it goes without saying that you can't ignite a civil war in a happy country where there is consensus and where the government has legitimacy – that's just conspiracy theory. Try dropping some saboteurs into Finland. Such things are obvious to clear-thinking people, but not for you and your American sponsors." Petrov finally lost his temper.

The room went quiet. Shtayn spotted Petrov with a slight grimace of disgust, as though he recognized him. But his response was restrained and dignified.

He squinted at Petrov. "You want to ask if I am aware that there were problems in Ukraine and that some citizens were pro-Russian? Of course, I'm aware. In fact, you just admitted to the entire audience that if there are contradictions in a country, then saboteurs could be effective. In other words, the existence of problems in a country, in your opinion, is sufficient basis to unleash a civil war and armed invasion. That's your position?"

Petrov snorted loudly.

"And so," Shtayn continued coldly, "I remind you of the fact that I passed my childhood and youth in just such a country. A country full of social contradictions that make the Maidan events look like child's play. This country is called Russia. Do you recall the separatist tendencies in the Urals? More precisely, Sverdlovsk Oblast only demanded more local control and independence, and no one even thought about armed uprising or calling in foreign troops. The project was known as the Ural Republic, but even the weak Yeltsin government would not permit it, and nipped it in the bud. And do you know, I'm grateful that there were no egotistical cynics in America that wanted to send armed soldiers to our streets to 'support the Ural Republic." I know very well that Yekaterinburg would have been destroyed within a few days. At the time, the majority of Russians suffered from hunger and dreamed of living in another country, no matter where. But the States did not make matters worse, but only tried to help. And what did we get in return?"

"Help?" Petrov was screaming now and rolling his eyes. "They tried to destroy our country for ten years and nearly succeeded. They stole from her every day, broke her to pieces. If it hadn't been for Putin ..."

"Destroyed?" Shtayn's voice was filled with irony. "Mr. Petrov, believe me, if they wanted to destroy you, they would have done it long ago."

There was a sprinkling of laughter in the auditorium, and Olga clenched her fists.

"Immediately after the fall of the Soviet Union the remains of the KGB became tightly involved with the criminal class. You know very well that after Yeltsin it was former 'Chekists' who monopolized resources and power in Russia. I find it strange that against the background of an orgy of crime, banditry, so-called 'new Russians,' mafia gunfights and all the other unsavory realities of the 'wild 90's,' you still blame it all on democratic reforms and the West. In the 90's crime was due to people from the Soviet KGB, not young reformers. The West was not happy with this symbiosis and even suffered from it. I've collected a lot of information about how these 'respectable' *vory v zakone*[9] laundered their ill-gotten gains in foreign banks, all the while establishing espionage networks. The activities of their agents are directed primarily

---

[9] "Thieves in the law" a traditional Russian term for certain criminals

against the West to discredit and corrupt its basic institutions. If you, Mr. Petrov, should have friends in the KGB, I suggest you ask them about it."

The laughter that greeted this remark petrified Olga with shock. *That's wrong. He can't be right. It was a miracle that Russia survived the 90's. The West failed then, but they would try it again.*

She wanted to flee the auditorium. It became physically difficult to listen to Shtayn. But she dared not bring attention to herself. *She should never have come. This was disaster.*

A young female voice rang out from the audience. "Isn't it hard for you to do this? Russia is your country. Isn't it hard to work against her?"

To Olga's astonishment, Shtayn did not try to justify himself or hide behind a smokescreen of pretty words to the effect that he was doing this for Russia and not against her – no false patriotism. He simply said, "Miss, have you visited any local parks?"

What kind of answer is this?

He continued, "Sometimes it's very good go visit parks, simply to walk around, unwind a little, breath fresh air. Children play there, just like they play in the courtyards of Russia. Can you tell which children are 'ours' and which are 'theirs?' Just go and take a good look and them and their parents for maybe a half-hour. Stroll around the streets and see the houses, everything around you. Then ask yourself – is this worth defending?"

The girl replied with some heat, "But there are parks in Russia, too, and a peaceful life."

"There are, undoubtedly there are," said Shtayn, "But Russia is an aggressor. Either through brute force or deception Russia strives to bring destruction to other countries. I've seen the results with my own eyes. I've seen how they try to destroy everything others have created. I've followed them for many years and seen nothing apart from a permanent desire to destroy. They bring only strife to the world, only eternal blackmail with their oil and gas. What kind of future is Russia preparing for her children? To be sent as cannon fodder in the Donbas, to kill foreigners? To end up in prison for a careless cartoon posted in a social network? Or to quietly drink themselves into a stupor, fearing to say what they think? Is it worth defending such a place?"

"But that place is your homeland." The question reflected Olga's thoughts.

"Yes, it is my homeland. I don't have American citizenship, and I don't know if I ever will. But the fact of my birth does not cloud my ability to distinguish the guilty from the innocent, freedom from slavery, happiness from force. For me, the innocent will always be dearer than the guilty. I don't wish ill for Russia, but I will always defend those who are innocent against aggressors and thieves. And for me, a country which can provide its own citizens and others happiness rather than despair is worthy of defense. Do you see how simple it is? It's nothing personal, nothing more than an objective view of the world. Truth and conscience should not depend on where one was born."

His logic was perverse, openly and rudely unpatriotic. He spit on his country and didn't hide it, but he possessed some special power that demanded respect and did not jibe with her image of a traitor. *Could treason be worthy of respect?* The man was an enemy of her country. He did not even pretend to be a patriot. What more was there to think about?

She left the auditorium, hiding herself in the

crowd, as she cast a venomous glance back at her target. She and her colleagues must spoil his plans, compromise him somehow.

All of what Shtayn said, the clever manner in which he manipulated people would go into her report to Karpov. Her mission was almost complete.

Chapter 35

"Life on earth is suffering on the path to Heaven."

Mid-November is early for a snowfall in Washington, but white flakes were falling from an iron dark sky over Arlington. Forecasts said there would not be a heavy accumulation, but road crews were out in force with their clumsy trucks, distributing salt and sand.

Mark Shtayn carefully increased his pace as he approached the entrance to the metro station and the anticipated warmth inside. A ten-minute ride would take him to the Dunn-Lorring Metro Station where he expected his car to be covered with the white stuff.

He did not notice the woman behind him.

For someone in his position, he was habitually unaware of his surroundings and the people around him. This was attributable to the fact that he was usually deep in thought and today the snow forced him to pay close attention to his footing in the slush on the pavement.

The young woman was unremarkable, unless one were to look closely into her eyes and notice a glassy vacancy which might be associated with drug use, an almost trancelike state. Even that was unremarkable these days. She wore a snow-dusted heavy winter coat that almost entirely covered her, and a knit hat pulled far down. Her hair was dark where it strayed from under the hat.

She had no idea where she was, not even the name of the city. The drive had been long as she rode docilely between the two men in the old truck. She followed the man onto an escalator that sank under the curved, metal and glass roof sheltering the entrance to the Metro station. Behind her, cars with their wipers working crawled along the wet street. Such cars, and so many of them, the likes of which she had never seen in her mountainous homeland.

The two men had deposited her on the street a few moments ago, but she could still see them where they waited on a side street ahead. Their eyes were upon her urging her on.

She was weary, and the clear liquid the older man had given her to drink made her feel as if her feet did not touch the ground, as if she were caught up in a current that effortlessly carried her along like flotsam on a great, heaving sea. Her will was not her own but was subordinated to a greater volition, something glorious. Try though she might, she could recall only imperfectly what her life had been before and so far away. Now she was someone with a purpose, someone almost holy.

What was it she was supposed to do? Oh, yes, find the center of the crowd on the train platform.

The escalator carried her down, down until she was on the platform surrounded by people bundled against the cold, all of them too intent on their own cares to notice a lone girl in a long, dark coat. She struggled to concentrate on her task as the train slid into the station.

In the pocket of her coat she wrapped her fingers around the triggering device that would detonate the explosives strapped to her body. She need but to push the button and the misery of her life would be transformed instantly into the joys of Paradise.

Just before she pressed the detonator she

intended to say, "*Allahu Akhbar*," but Instead, she only whispered, "Oy!" as though she were shocked by what she was doing.

When the investigators later found what was left of her body, they remarked on how her face was untouched, long dark hair spread beneath, blue eyes still open as if in surprise at the havoc her action had left, her lips half open as if about to speak. "*Oy.*"

*****

In the F-150 half a block away on North Highland Street Arbi Basaev blinked as the whump of the explosion was felt more than heard before black smoke and flame vomited from the Metro station entrance, cascaded against the Plexiglas shelter and spread out over the street in a malevolent cloud.

"I was afraid she wouldn't do it," he said as he put the truck into gear.

The bearded older man beside him smiled thinly as Arbi drove carefully south toward 10th Street. The area would soon be congested with fire trucks, police, media, and lookiloos.

The older man with his narrow, ascetic face, white beard and dark eyes could have been Iranian or even Arab. In fact he was a Chechen named Bolat Zakayev, and he possessed a doctorate in chemical engineering from the Bauman State Technical University in Moscow. He patted Arbi affectionately on the shoulder as he maneuvered the van into the slow-moving traffic heading toward Route 50. "She did well, Arbi, your little 'bride.' We didn't have to use the remote detonator." *They could trust their suicide bombers only so far.*

The girl's name was Esila. She was a young,

widow from Dagestan, where her in-laws, having no use for a childless daughter-in-law, sold her to Arbi. They took her to a safehouse in Baku where Zakayev put her on a steady diet of psychotropic drugs that left her pliable with no will of her own. The operation was meticulously planned: a ship from Baku to Havana, transfer to a smaller fishing vessel that carried them to Nicaragua. And then northward, guided by a well-paid *coyote* into the United States where the old, but reliable truck waited as promised at a truck stop in Arizona.

"The remote signal might not have reached her so far underground." worried Arbi.

The older man stared straight ahead as the snow increased and obscured the windshield. "You should have more confidence, Arbi."

It would be best to avoid main roads until they were completely out of the metropolitan area. The truck was equipped with a GPS unit, and Arbi had spent many days becoming familiar with the tangle of roads that surrounded Washington.

By the time they fought the traffic onto Route 50, which would take them west out of the metro area into Virginia, the snow had begun to taper off, but true to their reputation Washington area drivers were in a state of panic, abetted by reports of a possible terrorist attack that spilled from every radio.

As always, it was the unanticipated that changed plans. The snow was falling more heavily now and turning the roads into slushy toboggan runs. To make matters worse, darkness was falling fast. Cars were losing traction, sliding off the roadside or crashing into one another as panicked drivers failed to maintain safe distances.

"We cannot afford to be involved in an

accident," said the older man. His brow furrowed in thought. "We must find a place where we can stay the night until this passes and the roads are clear. We'll never make it all the way back to base tonight in this."

"It could be dangerous," said Arbi with a sidelong glance at his companion.

Zakayev replied. "The greater risk is to be involved in an accident and questioned by the police. We have no choice." He waved his hand in the direction of the road ahead. "Look at the way these idiots are driving. It's as though they've never seen snow before in their lives."

Ahead they spotted the neon sign of a motel blinking redly through the falling snow. "Pull in there," said Zakayev. "We can take a room for the night. I'll remain in the van."

Arbi, with his youthful good looks and winning smile, won an admiring glance from the young woman manning the desk. It was a modest establishment near the Seven Corners shopping center, but the room was clean and comfortable with two beds.

Women were never a problem. Arbi was darkly handsome and magnetic, so much so that women fell in love with him on sight. All he need do was gaze into their eyes, squeeze their hand, whisper something, and they were his.

Behind the warm façade he was cold as ice and calculating. He knew exactly what he was doing, and the women were little more for him than transitory entertainment before they were initiated into the ways of martyrdom. There were always plenty of women.

Once in the room with Zakayev, Arbi punched a number into his cell phone. The call was answered immediately.

Arbi told Valeriy Karpov that the snow

prevented them from clearing the metro area as planned and that they would have to wait out the storm.

Karpov was displeased. "Make sure you're out of town in the morning.

Chapter 36

Snow.   Welcome back to Northern Virginia.

The sharp chill hit Krystal Murphy as soon as she ducked out into the Jetway at Reagan National Airport.   The warmth of the Florida sun abandoned her like the fleeting memories of a daydream.   The heavy clothing of the crowd milling inside the brightly lit, vaulted expanse of the airport bespoke of the cold waiting for her outside.

She shivered at the unwelcome thermal difference between Washington and Miami and hoped the Miami memories would keep her warm.   The most lingering of those were of Dade County Police detective Ray Velazquez.

Several months earlier, when the heat had not yet abandoned Washington, Velazquez had been nearly killed by a .45 caliber slug from a serial killer's gun.[10]   This was followed by weeks in the hospital as his lungs and bones healed, and then a long convalescence in Krystal's small Arlington apartment. Chief Everett Fogerty of the Arlington County Police Department where Krystal was a Detective Lieutenant gave her "as much time as it takes," and had been only too happy to stand before the cameras to describe the investigation that led to the bloody denouement of the murderers Krystal had brought to justice.   She was content to remain out of the media spotlight.

She had flown south with Velazquez when he was sufficiently recovered to return to Miami.

In the queue for a taxi outside the terminal a

---

[10] KRYSTAL, Michael R. Davidson, 2014

frigid, snow-laden wind quickly dispelled memories of the Miami nights and replaced them with a single-minded desire to return to her apartment, turn up the heat, down a slug of scotch, and flop on the couch in front of the television. An evening of mindless entertainment, she told herself, would prepare her for the return to the office the following day. Or maybe it wouldn't. She had no idea what to expect.

A long tedious cab ride later, she surveyed her small apartment from the vantage point of the galley kitchen as she poured herself a generous dollop of ten-year-old Laphroaig single malt.

During his convalescence Ray had slept in her bed, which would more than have delighted the Cuban lothario had the circumstances been different, and she took the couch. Fortunately, the building was wheelchair friendly, so she had been able to take him for short outings as he regained strength. Even after they returned to Miami, the doctors said it would be at least two more weeks before he could begin a modified work schedule, and possibly a couple of months before he would be fully recovered.

The idea of being cooped up in the small apartment with a recovering Velazquez had not at first filled her with joyous anticipation. Ray was a great guy. There was undoubted romantic heat between them that she wanted to explore further, but she feared that 24/7 propinquity combined with her Irish temper might sour them.

To her surprise, it had not.

She had just downed the Laphroaig when the phone rang.

Chief Fogerty's voice was immediately recognizable. "Krystal, thank heaven your plane was not delayed. I'm sorry to bother you now, but something's come up, and all leave is cancelled. "

"I'll be glad to help, Chief. What's up?"

"I guess you've not heard the news yet. Turn on your TV, and you'll catch on soon enough. I'll send a black and white for you."

The Chief cut the connection before she could ask why he thought she needed someone to pick her up.

She grabbed the TV remote from the kitchen counter and turned to a local channel. The screen was immediately filled with images of first responder vehicles of every description, blue lights and red lights flashing, and people in uniform moving about with grim expressions. A female reporter in a heavy parka looked seriously into the camera as she spoke of an as yet unexplained explosion at the Clarendon Metro Station. Greasy black smoke drifted in the air behind the reporter.

Bad. Really bad.

She switched off the TV and went to the bedroom where she pulled a heavy turtleneck sweater out of a drawer and grabbed a pair of high-topped boots from the floor of the closet. She had a police issue parka in the hall closet and figured she would need that too. It could be a long night.

Ten minutes later she was downstairs when the black and white arrived. The snow had not stopped and was becoming thick on the streets. The distance from her apartment to the scene was only a few blocks, but walking it under these conditions would have been tedious. She hated Washington winters, and she hated Washington summers, too. The Capital was a city of extremes of both weather and politics. How had she ended up here? Because the best job offer came from Arlington, that's why. At least spring and autumn were nice. Miami didn't really have that.

Chief Fogerty was in earnest conversation with a small knot of men when she arrived. She sloshed through the slush toward them, her boots making splashing noises in the salt-laden snow. When Fogerty saw her, he waved impatiently for her to join them.

Fogerty introduced the solemn-faced man beside him as FBI Special Agent Nick Ferguson from the Counter Terrorism Task Force, the CTTF. Ferguson may have been in his mid-forties, but it was hard to tell with the watch cap pulled low over his ears and the heavy parka with FBI emblazoned on the back in big, yellow letters. He could have been almost anything under all that, but his face was Bureau-issue square jawed and his brows were black Irish dark. He wasn't happy. But, of course, who would be under the circumstances? The other two guys were from Homeland Security.

"This is detective Krystal Murphy," Fogerty said to the men. "She's the best I have, and she'll be your primary liaison contact on this." He waved vaguely behind him toward the Metro station entrance.

The scene was like something right out of a Hieronymus Bosch painting with fire hoses tangled like spilled intestines everywhere over a now ice-coated surface. First responders moved about carefully as salt was spread wherever possible. EMT's emerged in soot stained gear from the darkened Metro entrance carrying heavy plastic bags that they lay in an irregular line in a roped off area. There were a lot of these bundles, too many.

Ambulances were backed into the area from all directions still being loaded with survivors, and others were queued up to take more. Glancing back over the seen she decided most of them would be heading for the morgue.

Fogerty's words finally penetrated the shock of horror the scene generated. He'd said "primary liaison contact," which meant he was dumping all of this on her. She could not imagine how she and the entire cadre of the Arlington County Police could even begin to cope with the scope of this tragedy, but then the gears in her head creaked into motion and she realized it would be Homeland Security and the FBI that would be in charge with all of their abundant resources. But the event had occurred in Arlington, and that meant the ACP also had an oar to dip into the bloody water.

Another reason for the assignment, she realized, was that Fogerty must be aware of her standing relationship with FBI Executive Assistant Director Enoch Whitehall, the Bureau's *eminence gris*. This could be good or bad.

She caught Ferguson eyeing her warily from under his watch cap and wondered if he, too, was aware of her relationship with one of the highest ranking officers in the Bureau. That could be a problem if he was one of those feebies who was jealous of position and resented anyone who could leapfrog his chain of command. Of course, he was one of those. Weren't they all?

Ferguson finally spoke. His voice was scratchy, probably from the smoke. "I think they're about finished recovering victims. You want to go down and take a look-see with me?"

Murphy certainly did NOT want to go down and "take a look-see," but she would do it anyway because that was what cops were obliged to do – witness the worst humanity had to offer.

"Yeah," she said.

She turned to Chief Fogerty. "Are you coming?"

Fogerty's face went pale with a greenish tinge, and his eyes widened slightly as he imagined what awaited them below ground in the station. "Uh, no. We've still got a few things to discuss here," he said nodding at the Homeland Security guys.

She turned to Ferguson with a resigned shrug. "Lead the way."

They skated across the icy sidewalk and over the firehoses to the entrance where they were assaulted by emanations that might well have arisen from hell. The dark odor of greasy smoke, burnt plastic and electrical fires laced with the petroleum imbued perfume of spent explosives. But worst was the sickly smell of the carnage that waited below.

An EMT handed them surgical masks at the top of the steps. "Most of the smoke has been cleared out and the flames extinguished," he said. "And we've set up emergency lighting. There's nothing down there I ever want to see again, though." There were tears rolling down the EMT's cheeks, whether from the sharpness of the overloaded air or from weeping, she could not tell. She wouldn't blame him for the latter.

The steps had been liberally salted and were wet but free from ice. She and Ferguson descended, salt crystals crunching under their feet, and arrived at the blackened train platform. There were still some bodies covered with bright blue blankets and circles drawn in neon yellow chalk on the floor around body parts. Ferguson stopped and she heard him catch his breath.

"Is this your first bombing?" she asked, her voice muffled by the surgical mask.

"So you've concluded already that it's a bombing?"

The presence of the CTTF suggested that terrorism was the likely cause of the explosion. She sniffed the air. "Yeah. No doubt about it. Is this your first?"

"Yes. How about you?" His voice was strangled.

"I spent a good while in Iraq with the military and saw my share over there. Those were all in open areas, though. This is worse. You never forget the smell."

The vaulted ceiling and walls of the station had served to focus the blast back onto the train and platform thus multiplying the destruction and carnage. The train must have just pulled in when the bomb was detonated. The side of one car had been ripped completely away, creating even more shrapnel than had been in the bomb itself to tear at flesh. The blackened tile walls were pockmarked where the shrapnel had impacted. The effect on human bodies would have been horrific.

A man in a white hazmat suit, or a suit covered in suet that must have at one time been white, caught site of Ferguson and waved them over. He was standing near the center of the blast area holding a bag with something inside.

"Larry," he shouted at Ferguson, "over here. We found something."

They walked over to him, carefully avoiding the chalk circles. He pointed at the bag. "We think this is our bomber, or what's left of her."

When suicide vests are detonated the force of the blast disintegrates the body, but can detach the bomber's head and leave it relatively intact. Murphy guessed that was the case here.

Ferguson was no slouch and had come to the same conclusion. "Man or woman?" he asked.

Murphy guessed that the guy in the suit was a member of the FBI's forensics team. Ferguson introduced him as Sam Helger.

"Woman," answered Helger. "Wanna see?"

Ferguson sighed with resignation and disgust, "Shit, yes. Why not? How much worse could it get?"

He turned to Murphy. "You OK with this?"

It was not, unfortunately, the first time Murphy had seen a head in a bag. "I'm OK."

Helger placed the bag on the floor and carefully unzipped it. When he pulled it back the bomber's face was upturned. It was almost completely undamaged. The brown eyes were open wide and the lips were parted in terminal surprise. Long, dark hair spilled from behind.

"Jeez," said Ferguson. "She was young, probably no more than twenty or twenty-five. What the hell drives these people?"

"Death," intoned Helger. "The bastards are in love with death."

"You think this was an Islamist terrorist attack?" she asked. This was not the first time Murphy had heard fanatical Islam described as a death cult.

"Most likely. The M.O. fits, but we'll know more once we get all the pieces to Quantico."

The Bureau techs would examine every scrap of evidence, including bodies in a process similar to what the Flight Transportation Safety Board did in the wake of an airline disaster. Nothing would be too trivial for examination.

"How long will it be before we have something concrete to go on?" asked Murphy.

Helger reclosed the bag. "This will take several weeks. You can't hurry these things up."

"The public will be clamoring for a statement,"

said Ferguson, "Already is. There are mobile crews from every news network out there."

"That's not my problem," said Helger.

"It will be as soon as the White House comes down on you," said Ferguson.

"Oh, well," said Helger, "in that case we'll just label it workplace violence."

Ferguson snorted behind his mask. "If anyone labels this as Middle East terrorism before the results are in, there'll be political hell to pay."

Murphy remained uncharacteristically silent. Everything in this town was linked somehow to politics, and she had had her fill of politics. Way more than her fill. She was often accused of having too black and white a view, but wrong was wrong and the truth was the truth. But truth could be a gauzy thing in Washington.

She finally spoke up. "Maybe someone will claim responsibility. That'll be hard to cover up."

Chapter 37

Olga welcomed the end of the operation against Shtayn. The mental effort of dealing with the difficult man wearied her more than the physical effort. His words left her disoriented and confused, which only made her angry.

It was nearing six P.M. and snowing when she emerged from the Metro station a block away from where she lived. It was nothing like a Moscow snowfall, of course, but she would be glad to get back to her cozy little apartment nonetheless. She decided not to cook tonight and ducked into the small pizzeria on the corner of Wilson and Herndon. The New York style pie there was good, and on a chilly evening, pizza sounded like a good idea.

As she stood at the counter, she sensed as much as heard a deep rumble that rattled the plate glass window and the china on the counter. She turned her head in time to see the ugly black effluvia of an explosion disgorged from the Metro station entrance across the street and stared in incomprehension along with others who had sought temporary refuge from the snow and a slice in the small establishment.

What the hell was going on?

The Metro station entrance was a gaping mouth emitting flame-tinged smoke that Olga thought surely must resemble the Gates of Hell. There were people in there, trapped underground where only moments before she had stepped off her train. This was the very station used by Shtayn every morning and evening, and with a start she realized that the traitor might well have been in the station.

She'd done her job well, she knew, as she went over events in her mind. She'd picked up Shtayn as he left the office building a few blocks west. Careful observation over the course of the past several weeks had confirmed the man's pattern. Olga had ridden the Metrorail several times to the suburban station and watched as the target walked to his car and drove away.

Through the restaurant's fogged window she could see as people slowly, fearfully began to move toward the blackened Metro entrance. A few, very few tried to go inside but were driven back by roiling, greasy smoke and fumes. Faintly at first, then louder, the wail of sirens came through the glass.

She realized that long minutes had passed. Police, fire, and emergency vehicles arrived at the scene, and the streets were being blocked off. Witnesses would be sought out, and questions would be asked. It would not do for her to remain.

She slipped out the door and headed away from the scene toward her apartment. She must talk to Karpov as soon as possible tomorrow.

Chapter 38

The snow was tapering off by the time Olga made it to her apartment. It was a short walk from the pizza restaurant, but she was shivering not only from the cold. The subway explosion was the worst thing she had ever seen.

She took a long, hot shower and curled up on the couch to watch the television news reports as one tense-faced reporter and talking head after another made the logical assumption and intoned solemnly on the latest visitation of jihadist terrorism to America.

The next day, she made excuses at the 17th Street office and took a taxi to the Russian Embassy.

Karpov greeted her with a broad grin, an expression so uncharacteristic of the normally dour FSB man that she was taken aback. Perhaps the half-empty bottle of vodka and the shot glass on his desk explained it.

He led her to the safe room, the bottle and two glasses dangling from one hand. "Have a drink with me, Olenka. You look like you might need one."

"I was almost killed yesterday," she said, and told him about the subway explosion. "It was terrible. I was right across the street and saw the entire thing."

His brow furrowed, and he gave her a quizzical look. "You were in the area?"

How could he not know where she lived?

"I live only a block away from the Metro station. I use it every day. I almost called you on my cell phone. I left the station only moments before the attack."

"It's a good thing you didn't call." He placed a

finger alongside his nose. "Radio silence. The Americans will undoubtedly check every cell phone call made in the vicinity before and after that explosion."

If she expected sympathy, she wasn't finding it here.

Karpov pointed at the bottle. "You really do need a drink."

Olga leaned away from the table. The chair was wooden with a faux leather seat and back and not particularly comfortable. "The whole damned subway just blew up."

All the television channels this morning were still filled with images of emergency vehicles and excited reporters at the metro station.

"Well, I'm happy nothing happened to you," he said in the kindest voice he could muster.

Olga nodded.

"It was not intended that you should be anywhere near when the operation came down. You never mentioned you lived so close to the metro Shtayn used. But the really good news is that we can confirm the kill, and that means you did your job well. *Molodets!*" He unscrewed the cap on the vodka and poured liberal slugs into both glasses. He shoved one toward her. "Drink!"

Olga stared uncomprehendingly without picking up the small glass. "'... *confirm the kill?*'" Her voice trailed off.

Karpov peered at her through slitted eyes before answering. "Think about it this way: our target is just one of many casualties, which means his death will not be particularly suspicious, which means no suspicion will fall on us. That's a good thing."

He downed his vodka and poured another. The

clear, viscous liquid spilled over the rim and puddled on the table. "Have a drink, and calm down." He pointed to the glass he had filled for her before tipping his glassful down his throat.

Karpov's words reached Olga through a swirling fog. She was tempted by the vodka, but she resisted as his words sank in.

"You're telling me that the explosion was *our* doing? That it was done in order to assassinate Mark Shtayn?" She was nauseated and struggled not to vomit.

"Don't give me that shit, Olga Vladimirovna. You know all about handling scum like that. This isn't the first time you've fingered someone for elimination. Don't tell me you're beginning to think like an American with his head full of all that shit about tolerance and love?"

Olga was seized by terror of a sort she had never in her life experienced – a mindless, paralyzing, inexorable collision with the inevitable. *This could not have anything to do with her.* In her mind's eye the scene at the Metro played out again, and the demons in the hellish inferno grinned at her complicity. *No, I can't have killed anyone.*

Fear whispered in her ear, *here is a murderer.* An instinct of self-preservation from somewhere deep inside asserted itself, but the quiver in her voice betrayed her emotions. "I'm not sure I like this, Valeriy Eduardovich, "tracking down people so they can be, erm, eliminated."

Karpov rendered a chuckle that was completely devoid of humor and shook his head in mock dismay. "There's a popular Russian song, by Shevchuk, I think, where he's drinking with an FSB general who says, 'One must believe in something. If our leaders are deceiving us there is no reason to live.' For guys like us, *dorogaya*, there is only one rule to live by, and that rule is duty. That's what we have. That's all we have. That's what you have to believe in, just like Shevchuk's general. It's not complicated."

"So we're not supposed to ask any questions?"

"Never ask a question unless you already know the answer."

"But I do have one question."

Karpov raised his eyebrows.

"What did you mean when you said this wasn't the first time I had 'fingered someone for assassination?"

Karpov clicked his tongue against his teeth. "Don't play the ingénue with me, Olga. I've read your file. You were given high marks for your denunciation of Sergey Illarionov."

Bile rose to her throat, bitter and acidic, filling her mouth with its unpleasant taste. She'd denied her own suspicions so strongly that she'd almost forgotten them. Almost. But the seed was still there, buried and waiting.

She pondered Karpov's philosophy and could not fault the logic. Yes, it was simple, maybe too simple. It was a quintessentially Russian point of view. All of her country's actions were seen as part of a zero sum game. There are only two choices for a Russian: be Russian or be a traitor. There is no middle ground, so it's impossible to be neutral.

The memory of that sun-lit day in the Kremlin dining room and Vlad's burning eyes as he revealed his father's plans – all of that swam before her eyes, as well as what she had done afterwards.

Karpov poured himself another shot and frowned into the glass. Maybe Polyanskaya was not cut out for FSB work, after all, no matter her pedigree. She was acting like a frightened child. But maybe it was just youth and the reality of an operational mission on foreign soil – something a bit more than simple denunciations at home.

He recalled his initial doubts about her.

"Duty is what we have as operatives," he said.

"Anything goes?"

This was a question he did not like. He threw the drink back and slapped the glass onto the desk bottom up. A thought struck him. This could be a teaching moment. "Do you know what SMERSH was?"

"Everybody knows that. 'Death to spies.' It was a GRU operation during the Great Patriotic War."

"Exactly. And it was very effective. But just because we won the war doesn't mean we still don't have enemies. And today, we have enemies within and enemies without."

The immediacy of Karpov's words struck Olga as strangely out of time. The Great Patriotic War, as Russians termed World War II, had ended 70 years ago, and the Cold War allegedly ended in 1989. Karpov made it seem like only yesterday that the Red Army had stormed the Reichstag.

Karpov continued without pause. "Depending on the level of danger or betrayal they represent, these enemies must be eliminated for the good of the *Rodina*, the Motherland." Karpov did not have much use for nebulous, easily manipulated concepts such as patriotism, but it might appeal to the girl.

She nodded. "You mean people like Litvinenko."

"That was a sloppy job. The two idiots entrusted with the mission left a radioactive evidence trail all over London and created a lot of problems for everyone. They should have swallowed their own polonium."[11]

Karpov smacked his fist into his palm. "That *sukin syn,* Litvinenko, was doing - had already done - enormous damage to us. He was a shitfaced traitor. Hell, yes, we took him out. We had every right, even a duty to do it. But it was not handled professionally. Now we use more delicate means to track down and eliminate traitors."

The words slipped out before she could think, "And killing a hundred people to get to one is 'delicate?'"

He scowled, his anger rising, "Sacrifices have to be made. The vodka was loosening his tongue, and he decided on a different tact to make his point, an incident farther in the past and therefore safer. "Ask your hero Solntsev sometime about 1999 and the bombings in in Buyansk, Moscow, and Volgodonsk."

Karpov thought about opening another bottle, but discarded the idea. "But that operation was flawed, too. Three of our guys were caught planting explosives in Ryazan." He paused to lean across the desk, so close that Olga felt his vodka-charged breath on her face. "That was unfortunate. But it won't happen again, at least not on my watch."

Olga leaned farther back in the chair to escape the verbal onslaught. Her stomach churned. She did not want to think too much about what Karpov was saying. Over two hundred Russian citizens had died and over six hundred were injured in the 1999

---

[11] Aleksandr Valterovich Litvinenko was a rogue FSB officer who went public with accusations of assassination committed by the FSB. He escaped to London where he was murdered through polonium poisoning.

bombing of apartment buildings. Olga had been only a teenager at the time. Officially, the butchery was attributed to Chechen terrorists, but in Ryazan three FSB operatives were discovered planting explosives in another apartment building. This gave rise to the horrifying suspicion that the atrocities were intended all along to raise the popularity of a longshot candidate who was running for president. Indeed, that candidate, Vladimir Putin, won the election and initiated the second Chechen war. This was what Sergey Illarionov planned to expose. Did anyone really knew the truth, whether Illarionov was just spinning a yarn? But here was Karpov saying it was true. She just wanted the conversation to end.

"What now?" she asked, keeping her voice neutral.

This was better - a proper question. "As a Chekist you will learn that the ability to recognize an opportunity and take advantage of it is your greatest weapon. Now we'll take advantage of this situation and stir the pot with a little *desinformatsia*, misinformation."

"How?"

"We send a message to the media laying responsibility for the bombing on the *vahabiti*,[12] the damned Muslims. That will scare the shit out of the Americans. As a matter of fact, my young friend, that's your next job."

"Me? Why me?"

"You speak perfect American English," he said. "We'll keep the Americans off balance. It's all good."

---

[12] Wahabis – the term used in Chechnya and Dagestan to refer to Islamist terrorists.

Karpov stood a bit unsteadily on vodka loosened limbs, extracted a plastic baggie from his pocket and dropped it in front of her. Inside were a half-dozen envelopes addressed to various major media outlets.

"Find a mailbox somewhere and drop these in. Be sure you don't touch the envelopes unless you're wearing gloves. We wouldn't want any of your DNA or your fingerprints on them. Do this tomorrow morning."

He handed a piece of notepaper to her. "These are the phone numbers of four local television stations and a short statement. Make the calls from one of the burner phones you have, and then toss the phone. Make sure there are no surveillance cameras near-by. Then go back to your work at the Russian-American Study Group and carry on as usual."

She stared at the plastic baggie. Karpov's instructions were simple and straightforward. The only thing she had to worry about was avoiding surveillance cameras when mailing the envelopes and making the phone calls. She could accomplish everything within the space of fifteen minutes. But could she "carry on as usual?"

Karpov stood scrutinizing her, swaying slightly. "Is everything clear?"

"Yes. Of course."

"Good," said Karpov. "Now, go."

She left the Embassy on rubbery legs. Karpov had tricked her into participating in a mass murder. She had been part of an indiscriminate massacre, even if unwittingly. *Was this what it meant to a Chekist?*

When she was gone Karpov returned to his office and threw himself wearily in his chair. He was still for several minutes staring at nothing then shook his head and regarded the nearly empty bottle of vodka. The thought came to him that he was very like the bottle – mostly empty with only the dregs remaining. He missed the old days when the KGB had been a serious organization. When he had been the girl's age there had been important work to be done. Now, he found himself little more than an appendage of a machine that he both feared and served. It was all such a squalid business.

Karpov would never be as unimaginably wealthy as some of his former colleagues, but was a survivor and would continue to survive by unquestioningly following orders. Did his superiors in Lubyanka even realize that the subway bombing was an act of war? If the Americans discovered the truth, would the missiles fly and bring all the madness to an end?

But the bombing had had another goal besides just killing Shtayn. The geniuses in Moscow thought that Islamist terrorist attacks on the West coincided with Russian interests. Soon the Europeans and Americans would decide that they needed Russia on their side in the war against terror more than they needed to worry about places like Ukraine. Put enough pressure on them, so the thinking went, and sanctions would be dropped, and the Russians would be viewed as saviors. And the Americans would never connect Russia to the bombing, would they?

He very carefully refilled his glass and drained it.

The bottle was now completely empty.

Chapter 39

Krystal Murphy and Special Agent Ferguson grabbed a table by the window at a Starbucks on Courthouse Plaza, not far from her office. This followed an uncomfortable impromptu press conference at the crime scene. Without his parka and watch cap, the FBI agent was solidly built with a shock of unruly jet-black hair that matched the dark shadow of a beard on his jaw.

She didn't get on well with the press, but Chief Fogerty introduced her to the gaggle of reporters as his primary investigator and the go-to person for questions. She'd had no choice but to politely say to the microphones that it was too early to speculate on what might have caused the explosion and that the Arlington police were working hand in hand with the FBI and Homeland Security.

After the scene inside the Metro Station, neither she nor Ferguson harbored any doubt about what they faced. This was no gas main explosion, no electrical malfunction; this was a terrorist suicide bombing, and it scared the hell out of her.

Random acts of terrorism by self-motivated extremists were at the top of the law enforcement's threat list. Without forewarning about a specific individual who might be contemplating such violence, it was impossible to predict where and when an incident might take place. Heretofore, terrorism on American soil had been perpetrated almost exclusively by men. But now this unknown, apparently lone woman had blown herself and dozens of others to bits and increased the suspect pool by a hundred percent.

Ferguson stared glumly into his coffee, his thoughts as dark as the brew. "We need a starting point," he said.

"Agree. There won't be much, if anything, to go on until we have the forensics results, unless we get a break. What does your gut tell you?"

"My gut tells me there's going to be hell to pay. We might not be able to confirm to the press what we suspect, or even what we may find, but the speculation is already out there, and before you know it we, the FBI, Homeland, even you cops, will be blamed for 'missing the clues.' Then the politicians on one side will demand scalps, and the ones on the other side will say it was only the action of a single deranged person and has nothing to do with religion. Meanwhile, people are dead and maimed, and we could be in store for more."

"Maybe someone will claim responsibility for the bombing," she said.

"Yeah, and maybe there'll be fifty claims from nutcases all over the place, and we'll have to track down every one. Like you said, Murphy, if we don't get a break, a big juicy break, a lead we can't see right now, we might never solve this case. Or if today's bomber has friends, they could all blow themselves up before we find them."

"Jeez, Ferguson, you're just a bundle of optimism, aren't you?"

He gave her a rueful grin. "Sorry. What we just saw isn't exactly a confidence builder."

"No need for apologies. But you feebies have the lead on this."

He sighed. "Yeah, I know. We'll start by checking the alerts and potential bad guys we have on file. Maybe something will pop from the travel lists.

Leads aren't quite so easy to come by since they clipped the NSA's wings. Assholes!"

"The NSA?"

"No, the politicians and the gullible idiots who believe the hype, the absolute falsehoods they've been fed about metadata."

"Copy that. The way I see it, you guys and the intel types are damned if you do and damned if you don't. That's why I like being a simple cop."

Ferguson regarded her with what might have been envy. He gulped the dregs of his coffee and said, "I'd best get downtown. It's going to be a long night. Can I drop you anywhere?"

She didn't want to go to the office where she would face a barrage of questions to which she as yet had no answers. So she hid out at home in the hope that more information would be available tomorrow. She hadn't been in the apartment long enough even to unpack before Fogerty's phone call. Frankly, she just wanted to close her eyes and wish it would all go away.

Chapter 40

Like Olga, Vlad Illarionov walked into the reception area of Dulles International Airport clutching his backpack, unsure of what awaited him. He was surprised and relieved to spot the familiar, loose-jointed figure of Derrick Williams striding toward him, a broad grin on his face.

"Derrick. I didn't expect to see anyone I knew."

The two embraced in Russian fashion in a reunion more emotional than expected. After the violent deaths of his parents, Vlad had been through a lot since his abrupt departure from Moscow. The tense border crossing into Ukraine, a Russian death squad, and temporary asylum in the American Embassy in Kiev combined to tell him his fate was no longer his own.

Williams and Peters had accompanied him to Boryspil International Airport under the watchful eye of Jack Kelly and a bevy of SBU men who followed them in a black Mercedes. The last time he had seen Williams was the departure area of the Kiev airport.

From Kiev, Vlad flew to Amsterdam where a man from the American Consulate General who introduced himself only as "John" escorted him to a small hotel not far from the Waterfeitsen Canal. He remained there for several days while his visa and documentation for the United States were prepared. And now, he was in America.

"We seem destined to see one another in airports," said Williams. "But this is an arrival, not a departure. I rented a car, and I'll drive you into town. We'll get you settled in your hotel. You can rest up from the flight, and I'll pick you up for dinner later, if that's OK with you."

"That would be great," said Vlad. He switched from Russian to English. "I'd like to speak English now. I guess I should get used to it as soon as possible."

"That's a good idea," grinned Williams.

Vlad had no luggage other than the backpack which contained a few changes of clothing and his father's precious papers and the recording.

Williams checked him into a Best Western called the Old Colony Inn in Alexandria, just off the George Washington Parkway. "It's an old place, but it's comfortable." He handed Vlad a wad of American money "for expenses" before leaving.

At seven that evening Williams picked him up and drove the short distance to Alexandria's Old Town, turning into a busy street that led several blocks down to the Potomac River. Vlad was fascinated by the red brick architecture and the people crowding the sidewalks of the brightly lit streets.

He didn't consider himself to be particularly impressionable. There had not been sufficient time to sort everything out, but the unfamiliar, peaceful scene was balm for his scorched soul. He was not so arrogant as to believe that his heretofore feeble efforts might somehow topple the brutal Russian regime, but at least he could light a warning fire on the shores of America. The idea that he was on the same side as these carefree people gave him the moral right to rejoice in their innocence.

Williams gave him a brief history of "George Washington's town" as they searched for a place to park. Alexandria is an old city by American standards, but a blink of the eye compared to the millennium and more of Russia's existence. After a thousand years, might America too fall victim to despotism?

On-street parking was hopeless, so they left the car in a public garage and walked through the crowds on the sidewalk almost to the end of King Street, finally stopping in front of a restaurant called Landini Brothers. But rather than entering the restaurant, Williams led him to a discrete door a few steps farther, which led up a flight of stairs to a sleek, multi-level space that Williams explained was a private club devoted to the enjoyment of fine cigars.

They climbed narrow stairs to an upper level and through a door into a dining area where Williams led Vlad to a table occupied by a man of about fifty with brown hair graying at the temples. When he stood, Vlad saw that he was of average height, trim, with intelligent blue eyes. He held a lighted cigar in his left hand.

"Vlad, this is Vance Johnson. He works at the Embassy in Moscow like me, and he was instrumental in seeing that you made it to the States safely.

Vlad accepted Johnson's firm handshake, and the three took seats around the table.

"I'm very happy to meet you at long last, Vlad. I hope you don't mind cigars," said Johnson raising he one he was smoking to shoulder level and waving it in a little circle.

"I'm totally unfamiliar with them," replied Vlad. "In Moscow, only the big shots smoke them." He used the Russian term "bol'shiye shishki."

Johnson gave him an easy smile. "Well, Vlad, here in the States you don't have to be a big shot to enjoy yourself."

Vlad was uncertain how to respond and said

only, "Thank you."

A white-jacketed waiter bustled up to take their orders. At a loss, Vlad deferred to Williams and Johnson, and the latter selected items from the menu. "Would you care for something to drink?" asked Johnson.

Vlad shook his head. "Just water, please. I'm a little jet-lagged."

Williams ordered water, as well, but Johnson asked for a martini with olives. When the drinks came, Vlad was fascinated by the conical, stemmed glass placed in front of Johnson. He had seen this only in movies, specifically James Bond films.

After taking an appreciative sip of his drink, Johnson said, "I understand you have some important materials concerning certain past events in Russia. Did you bring them with you?" He plucked a large olive on a toothpick from his drink and popped it into his mouth.

Vlad cast a questioning glance at Williams, who nodded and gave him a reassuring smile.

"Erm, yes, of course. I have them with me here." He held up the flat leather folder he had carried in his backpack. He never allowed the folder out of his sight."

"And you're convinced they're genuine?"

Vlad flushed with anger. "Genuine enough for my father and mother to be murdered."

Williams placed a hand on his arm. "Don't be upset. This is an important question if the material is ever to see the light of day."

Johnson took another sip of his martini while Vlad cooled down, then said, "Vlad, I'm on your side. Derrick here has told me a lot about you, and I may be in a position to offer some discreet assistance in getting your story published. You shouldn't be thinking of putting such material out in some insignificant blog on the Internet. The Kremlin can too easily discredit such things, and next thing you know, you'll become the target of a horde of Russian trolls from St. Petersburg. The material should be published in a reputable medium."

Vlad had been worried about the same thing, but he had no idea how to overcome the obvious obstacles. "I'd hoped that Derrick might have some contacts at VOA ..." he began, but Johnson cut him off.

"That's possible, of course, but don't you think it would be better to find an outlet that has nothing to do with the U.S Government? For some reason, there is a lot of distrust of the government these days, even here in the States. You need a more independent publisher."

Williams grimaced, but nodded his agreement.

"What do you have in mind?" asked Vlad.

"I'd rather not say right now. I just got into town yesterday, and I need a few days to check some things out."

"In the meantime," said Williams, "I'll get you introduced to the folks at AEI and see what they have in mind about your internship.

Chapter 41

Vance Johnson was in Washington on a ruse, claiming that his elderly father was ailing. He'd reported briefly into Langley to touch base with the Russia House, but they had been sympathetic and set him free to see to his personal business.

It wasn't that he distrusted his Headquarters colleagues, it was just that he knew the bureaucratic routine and the strictures they had against working with the press. He would do this solo, hope he didn't flunk his next polygraph, and if things worked out, he would make no waves. In fact, he would remain entirely invisible. Vance liked being invisible. He had made a career of it.

Ethan Holmes was a senior reporter for the *Washington Post*, and his beat was the Intelligence Community. He was one of Washington's most knowledgeable people when it came to the wheels and gears of the "wilderness of mirrors." He knew who was who, who hated whom, and how the rank and file felt about their leaders. In order to be successful, Holmes had learned to respect the people who inhabited that obscure world, and he had won their trust. It was why he was so successful.

Holmes had known Johnson for several years, dating from the time the reporter got wind of a highly placed Russian asset. The culprit was a loose-lipped staffer on the House Intelligence Oversight Committee. When he called Langley for comment, he found Johnson on his doorstep within an hour. The soft-spoken spook had convinced him that if the story were published, the agent would surely perish, and Holmes agreed to spike the piece.

The two had seen one another on and off since then, and so Holmes wasn't surprised to receive an invitation to lunch from Johnson. "I thought you were in Moscow," he said.

Johnson's chuckle reached him across the ether. "I'll be heading back there soon, but in the meantime, I have something I think will interest you."

Holmes' ears perked up at that. In the past, Johnson had been willing to discuss things of which Holmes already was aware, but he had never volunteered anything.

At noon on the dot, Holmes entered the Capitol Grille and spotted Johnson beckoning him from a corner booth. They greeted one another like old friends, but friends who nurtured a rivalry. Reporters like Holmes are fond of saying their job was identical to that of intelligence officers. Johnson's response was that intelligence officers are the guardians of secrets reporters want to reveal. In that sense, reporters were akin to enemy intelligence officers. Between Johnson and Holmes, though, the rivalry was not hostile.

Johnson observed the usual formalities at the outset by telling the reporter that everything he said today would be off the record, and he was confident that Holmes would obey the rules of the game.

"I want to tell you a story about a dissident in Moscow," began Johnson.

Holmes interrupted, "There's not a lot of interest in Russian dissidents like in the old days, Vance."

"I know, and more's the pity because most Americans don't know and don't care to know what's going on over there, and your colleagues aren't doing much to correct the situation."

Holmes sighed and pushed his Caesar salad

around with his fork. "Terrorism is front and center now," he said.

"Yes, and the Agency has regressed into the OSS to fight that battle. But the Russians are still there, and they still have ICBMs. The current regime is as bad as anything we've seen since Stalin. It looks different since 1991, but behind the façade of Gucci stores on the Arbat, the same bad guys are pulling the strings. Life is getting harder since they invaded Ukraine, and that means the regime is cracking down more. And speaking of Ukraine, how much coverage of the war does the *Post* give its readers?"

Holmes shook his head, "Almost none, I'll admit. It's not what's on peoples' minds."

"If it's not on people's minds, it's because the American media does a shitty job of informing them."

Johnson noticed that Holmes was cutting into his sirloin as though he had a grudge against it. He was getting off track, and his purpose was not to alienate the reporter. "Let's start over," he said.

The story of Vlad Illarionov, his father and mother, the escape to Ukraine and the Russian death squad held Holmes spellbound for the next half-hour. To protect his source in Moscow Johnson attributed discovery of the death squad to the diligence of the Ukrainian SBU, but he provided the facts about everything else. The story of Sergey Illarionov especially touched Holmes. Illarionov had been an investigative journalist just like him, after all, and had died for his efforts. By the end of Johnson's recitation, Holmes was hooked, and he agreed to a meeting with Vlad.

"Ethan, I can't emphasize enough the importance of keeping my name and any hint of Agency involvement out of this story. It would give the

Kremlin the ammunition it needs to discredit everything Vlad Illarionov has to tell. And, in fact, the CIA has never been involved officially."

Holmes nodded his understanding, and Johnson continued, "That also means that your name likewise should not be associated with the story. Your connections with the Intelligence Community are simply too well known."

Holmes didn't like this one bit, but he could see the logic, and Johnson pressed his point.

"Ethan, almost 200 Russian journalists have been outright murdered since 1991, including one American, and only one person has been jailed for the crimes. If there is such a thing as honor among journalists, you owe it to your colleagues to see to it that Vlad's story sees the light of day."

Holmes raised his hands in mock surrender. "OK, Vance, I promise that if the material this kid has is everything you say I'll find a way to get it into print."

"That's all I ask. You'll be performing a great service for both countries and for journalism, as well."

He told the reporter how to contact Derrick Williams to set up a meeting with Vlad Illarionov.

There was nothing more Vance Johnson could do, so he made preparations to return to Moscow.

Chapter 42

Williams took Vlad on a short driving tour of Washington before introducing him to AEI. It was nearing the end of October, and the air had acquired a chill. But as if to welcome Vlad, the alabaster monuments and buildings shone a brilliant white under a cloudless sky. Everything looked so new, and like Alexandria, there was a limit on the height of buildings that somehow imparted a sense of human proportion that emphasized that government here was subordinate to the people. Vlad was well aware that even here that concept was not universal, but for the moment he chose to ignore it.

The headquarters of the American Enterprise Institute are on 17th Street, just a few steps from the venerable Mayflower Hotel. It was a bit late in the year, but Vlad had been accepted into the fall internship program's Russian Studies group under the aegis of one of the institute's resident scholars. Unlike most interns, Vlad's expenses would be paid while he was in the U.S.

The meeting with Ethan Holmes was more complicated because it was to be confidential. So they gathered one evening in Vlad's hotel room.

It required several hours to tell the whole story and finally show the American reporter the report written so long ago by Zhuravlev and play Sergey Illarionov's recording of Tretyakov's jailhouse confession. Holmes did not understand Russian, but he had seen and heard enough to be convinced.

The next task was for Holmes to convince his editor of the value and validity of the story.

Fortunately, the news cycle was nearly stagnant with most attention focused on domestic matters. Although the editor was not particularly interested in the fate of Russian dissidents, Holmes sold the idea as a human interest story. He thought there was enough material to serialize over several editions and also would appear on the *Post's* web page.

In the meantime, as agreed with Holmes, Vlad began work on the article. He would write very little about himself but rather focus on his father and the man's dedication to getting the truth into print, even at the risk of his own life. He decided to entitle the article "In the Shadow of Mordor."

Vlad had no choice but to write in Russian, and he was immensely grateful for Williams' offer to stick around long enough to complete a translation. The article, complete with photos of his father that Vlad had stored on his camera was ready for publication at the end of November. But it was postponed.

That was when the Clarendon metro station exploded.

A cab dropped Vlad in front of the AEI building. The entire Metro transit system was at a halt on orders from the Department of Homeland Security. Snow had stopped falling early yesterday morning, but there was still a sharp chill in the air. He stepped carefully over the curb with his eyes down, wary of slipping on a patch of ice.

When he raised his gaze, he stopped cold and stared at the last person on earth he ever thought to see again.

Chapter 43

Salt on the sidewalks and streets produced rivulets of dirty water that washed away the remaining slush. The patchy snow remaining in parts of Arlington and the sharp bite of the frigid air somehow reminded Olga of Moscow in the autumn or spring. The thought cut through her like a knife. The faint reflections of Moscow reminded her mercilessly of the bombings of Russian apartments, of Solntsev's bold countenance and broad smile, Vlad's burning eyes, and Nastya's approving look following her training in Yekaterinburg.

The memories pursued her more doggedly than any professional surveillance team. There was no escape from them. She could slip around a corner, jump onto a bus, enter a shopping mall from one side and exit from another, run as fast as she could, but not one of these maneuvers would permit her to escape.

Some recollections exuded warmth while others struck her like physical blows. It was unbearable that what had so recently been dear to her should now consume her with hatred; that which had attracted now repelled and horrified. Today the city around her no longer felt like enemy territory and became simply alien – as alien as all the rest of the world. Never in her life had she been so alone.

Nothing was as it had been before and would never be again. The black smoke of the explosion poisoned the present as well as the past, Moscow and Washington, reason and emotion. She still had Karpov's envelope in her purse, and she feared it too might burst into flame. When she touched it her skin seemed to burn as though the paper itself were impregnated with poison. Mechanically reminding herself of the task she must perform, Olga covertly scanned the street to see if she was being observed. She started when she realized she was searching for Shtayn. But unlike her triumph in Kharitonovskiy Park, she would never find him again. Shtayn was no more, and the thought was unbearable. But still she searched for him in the dim November evening.

She somehow carried out Karpov's instructions. There had been no video cameras near-by and no one in sight. She performed the task perfectly and hated herself all the more for having done so. The streets were filled with ghosts, as if the victims at the Metro station had risen and mingled with the living.

*****

The following morning she arrived at the office building on 17th Street somewhat earlier than usual, having been unable to sleep the night before. She did her best to concentrate on the day ahead and the all-important meeting with Sandberg. Her habitual confidence had deserted her.

She froze in mid-stride when she recognized the figure approaching her. She fleetingly thought this must be another ghost, but the man was clearly flesh and blood. *It can't be. Vladislav Illarionov was walking straight toward her.*

Her thoughts a tumult of joy and fear, Olga started backward. There was no explaining the sudden onset of joy. Maybe it was because in this world turned upside down, Vlad remained unchanged, not only reproach incarnate, but also the embodiment of childhood's innocence – their common childhood and the naïve dreams of the 1990's.

Too late, Olga realized that Vlad should not discover her presence here. But he already had spotted her, no less amazed than she. She didn't know what to say to him and struggled to conceal her distress.

"Vlad! I never expected to see you here. What are you doing here?"

What happened with her ability to lie? Not long ago there was no role she was incapable of playing. Now she could feign neither nonchalance nor affability under his wrathful gaze.

"I think I should be the one asking what *you* are doing here. Just last summer you were telling me how much you hated America. So now you've forgotten all that?"

Realization crossed his face even as he spoke. It was a look with which she was familiar since childhood – the sudden spark of insight that lit his eyes as he grasped the truth. The years had not changed him. So why had she changed so much? He knew why she was here. He knew everything about her. Strangely, this no longer frightened her. It made no difference, at all.

"I'm working in a research organization ..." she began.

His voice dripped with sarcasm. "Of course."

"I'm happy you're here." At least this was the truth – the only true words she had uttered in this conversation. But he was having none of it.

"Do you know what?" Vlad said, an undertone of menace in his voice. "In Moscow you and your thugs could do anything you wanted. You're the reason my parents are dead. But you and Solntsev got away with it because there you're the lords of the world. It's my fault, too. Only a complete fool would have entrusted such a secret to a creature like you. I acted like a naïve child trying to convince you. But I've given up on that. I won't lecture you; I'll just warn you that it's better to leave this place. This isn't Russia, and you won't get away with murder here. If you try the slightest foolishness in this country, I'll do all I can to make sure they put you away for as long as possible. You love Russia and Putin? Well, go back to them. You won't be able to poison our lives here."

Her first instinct was to beg for forgiveness, to let him know that she had not desired his father's death, had not realized that things would turn out that way. But the words died before passing her lips. He would not believe her. All her pain, the hellish fire that consumed her conscience - all of this could never penetrate the steely wall of his distrust.

Vlad reminded her of herself during that conversation in the Kremlin. But he was defending a new country while she had defended their old one.

She now understood why he could not defend his homeland.

Vlad had devoted much to his country but received only hostility in return. Too late Olga understood that Shtayn's life was quite similar to Vlad's, but now she could never ask the clever Jew how this had come about.

To Vlad she was an enemy, and he was prepared to stand in her way just as she once stood in his. A remnant of pride spurred by despair lent heat to her response. "Don't you dare threaten me. I have every right to be here. I'm not breaking any law. If you're such a defender of human rights, tolerance and all that other crap, act like it. "

She feared she might cry out in pain so unbearable was his contempt.

"You're a spying whore," he gritted, "an accomplice to murder. I can't imagine how much blood you have on your hands."

He turned away and entered the building, the same building where Olga worked. What was he doing there? But this was already unimportant. She turned into a side street and leaned against a wall, bursting into tears and hoping no one noticed. There was nothing left in her life, past or present, not in Russia or America. And she lacked the courage or even the right to beg Vlad's forgiveness.

Chapter 44

"She's late." Valentin Zaretskiy said irritably. He laid some papers on the table and shot a glance out the window at the street below. Only a few patches of yesterday's snow remained. *How could she have forgotten how important today was to be?*

Stash was nervous, too. "There's barely enough time left." He wasn't sure which bothered him the most: the task itself, or the possibility that he might have to go to the important meeting without his prize subordinate. A pretty, attentive young woman could do wonders to motivate an older man like Sandberg.

"Women," growled Zaretskiy. "They specialize in being late, and here I have all this material prepared – the dollar rises and there is a serious crisis brewing in Russia. There's trouble again in Chechnya. We're in trouble even if the sanctions are lifted. I have all of her talking pointed prepared: documents, ideas about how Russia could be an effective ally in the fight against terrorism. It's very convincing stuff, and all she has to do is make a nice presentation. And now she can't even make it here on time."

"She was very enthusiastic about meeting Sandberg," said Stash, "and she's never been late before. Maybe something happened to her, an accident. Or maybe something came up *there.*"

He pronounced the word in an almost conspiratorial manner with a vague glance at the ceiling. This tradition – to refer only in a roundabout way to the *special services*, was ingrained in officials of all levels during Soviet times, and Stash adhered to the old *nomenklatura* habit now.

"They must know over *there* that we have an important meeting today with our best man in the States," was Zaretskiy's dry response. "They normally would tell us if she were, erm, otherwise occupied. We'll wait another half-hour."

Zaretskiy made several calls to Olga's apartment while they waited, but there was no answer.

When Olga still did not appear, Zaretskiy made his decision. "Stash, you'll have to handle the meeting alone."

He stood and grabbed his coat and hat off the rack by the door. "I'm going to the Embassy."

It took longer than he would have liked to traverse the distance from 17th Street to Georgtown and up Wisconsin Avenue, and he arrived at Karpov's office red-faced and sweating despite the cold outside.

"Valeriy Eduardovich. Something may have happened to Olga Polyanskaya. We waited for her at the office all morning, and I've been unable to contact her. She had an extremely important meeting this morning, and it's very unlike her to be late. "

Karpov furrowed his brow and was silent for a few beats as he considered the possibilities from the most innocent to the worst. Had she overslept? Had she been in an accident? Had the FBI arrested her? Or, worst of all, had she become unreliable?

"Thank you, Valentin Gyorgievich," he said. "I'll try to get to the bottom of it and let you know."

*****

The tears left her empty and exhausted. She wouldn't be going to work, and it mattered hardly at all that today was to have been important. She simply could not face anyone in this condition. What difference did it make anyway? Did all these meetings, gatherings, plans, phony smiles, and empty words mean anything? Did they make it easier to commit murder? Vlad's words struck her like hammer blows. *"I can't imagine how much blood you have on your hands."*

How much, then? Vlad's mother and father, hundreds of innocent people at the Metro station – and this was what she had only just discovered. How much more had she not guessed? How could she go on? How can a murderer continue living under such a burden? How was it possible that she was guilty of the deaths of hundreds? She had never in her life held a weapon in her hands.

She tried not to think of the families, the terror when they saw the news on television and didn't know the fate of their loved ones but could think only the worst. Olga could only imagine the horrible premonition that must have swept over the relatives of the victims, how they hoped it wasn't true, how they would have tried to contact their loved ones but heard only the empty ring of a cellphone that would never again be answered.

She barely contained a desire to run headlong as far away as she could get. But there was nowhere to run, and she walked aimlessly until she arrived at a small park. When she took in her surroundings, she realized she was facing the White House, and a wave of panic engulfed her. She turned on her heel and rushed away with no idea where she was going.

After what seemed hours, fatigue caught up with her. She ducked into a small coffee shop and collapsed at a table. The place was small with only a dozen or so tables and a lunch bar guarded by a rank of round, backless stools. The flat-screen TV on the wall behind the bar was tuned to a sports channel, and Olga was grateful to be spared more news coverage of yesterday's tragedy.

A middle-aged black woman wearing an apron approached the table and asked what she would like. At first, Olga didn't hear what the woman was saying. The waitress, seeing her despondency, put a hand on her shoulder and said, "Are you OK, darlin'? Can I bring you something, a glass of water?"

The touch on her shoulder startled her, and she looked up with frightened eyes. The kindness and concern on the waitress's face only fed her guilt. *Would she look at me this way if she knew ...?"*

She fled the coffee-shop, leaving the waitress shaking her head.

*****

Valeriy Karpov was seriously concerned by Zaretskiy's news. At least the civilian was clever enough not to have used the telephone thus alerting the FBI. Any mention of Olga's name in connection with his own would have unfortunate consequences.

He had no idea where the girl could be, and the possibilities alarmed him. Their most recent conversation had left a bad taste in his mouth. The girl's shock and confusion were troubling. She was, after all, not a seasoned professional. It might have been best to leave her in the dark regarding the explosion, but the vodka had loosened his tongue, and now she was missing. Could it be that his initial suspicions about her had been correct despite the glowing reports from the Center? The blood froze in his veins as he considered the implications and possible repercussions. The feel of the axe on his neck was palpable.

He pulled a burner cellphone from the pile in his desk drawer and dialed Olga's cellphone. There was no answer. Repeated tries yielded the same result.

Deciding he could wait no longer, Karpov grabbed his coat and left the embassy. What if the girl had become disillusioned and gone to the FBI? Or had she simply forgotten her cellphone at home? Perhaps she had fallen seriously ill or been in an accident. He could not avoid the hope that it had been the latter, and she was dead. *From the beginning I knew that such a pampered little girl from Moscow should not be involved in serious matters.* The bitterness of his recollection spurred him to move faster. Whatever was going on, it had to be controlled before a disaster occurred.

The only thing he could do was go directly to her apartment, and that would take precious time as he had to be certain he was not followed.

It would be risky to enter the apartment. If the worst came to pass, he could walk into a trap. He decided to wait on the street and found a comfortable spot by the window in a café across opposite the entrance to Olga's building. After what seemed an eternity he saw her approaching unsteadily along the sidewalk. He hurried out of the café to intercept her, scanning carefully in all directions for signs of danger.

"What are you up to?" He grabbed her roughly by the elbow, his alarm lending unnecessary force to his grasp. "Why didn't you go to the office today?"

She jerked her arm away. Her face infused with rage and her voice shaking, she said, "I'll never go to the office again. Not to yours and not to theirs, never! Never. I'm going back to Moscow. I've had enough, and I'm sick of these abominations. I can't take it anymore. I'm finished."

"Hold on." His voice was hard, and he grabbed her arm again. "You can't do that."

"Don't touch me! Take your hands off me or I'll call the police. I never want to see you again, you damned pig, you murderer! It's your entire fault, everything."

Startled by her heat, he stepped back from her. The girl was insane. He adopted a conciliatory tone. "Olga, wait. I see that you're terribly upset, and it really is my fault. You weren't prepared for this. If you really want to go home, I'll arrange it immediately. It will take several hours, but just wait in the apartment, and I'll send someone from the embassy to pick you up. I promise to have you on a plane to Moscow tomorrow."

Olga was not mollified, but what else could she do? She was alone in a foreign land with no friends, no one to help her. At least there would be some comfort in returning home.

She glared at Karpov, the incarnation of her own self-loathing, and merely nodded agreement.

Karpov waited until the door closed behind her and he was satisfied she was going to her apartment. Things had taken a dangerous turn for the worst and required immediate action.

There was no way he could permit Olga to enter the embassy. His mission in Washington and the actions he had taken, especially the Metro bombing, were known to no one else outside the Lubyanka. If he cut her free at an airport teeming with American security personnel, she could do anything.

The Chechens were his only hope.

Chapter 45

Krystal Murphy must have been more tired than she realized because she passed the night in dreamless sleep despite the horrors of the day before. She awoke with a start and it took a moment to remember where she was. This prompted thoughts of Ray Velazquez, which warmed her a bit until her bare feet hit the frigid floor and brought her with an almost audible thump back to wintry Arlington.

After a long, hot shower she discovered nothing but stale cereal in the pantry and pickles and beer in the refrigerator which she had cleaned out before going to Florida. She decided to grab a pastry and coffee at Starbucks on the way to the office and bundled up for the drive.

She cursed as she swept snow from her old Corolla. Fifteen minutes later she was at her desk where she found numerous notes asking her to contact various media outlets. She immediately dumped them into her wastebasket. She saw no sense in calling people to tell them there was nothing she could say.

She hadn't kept up with the news, having collapsed into bed the night before, so she switched on the television and a bulletin flashing on the screen caught her attention: **_METRO BOMBERS IDENTIFIED_**. She turned up the sound in time to hear the talking head say the explosion was definitely a terrorist act. A claim of responsibility had been received from a heretofore unknown organization with the ominous name "Islamist-American Liberation Front."

She recalled Ferguson's comments of the day

before and dialed his number at the FBI.

"We're watching the news over here, too," he said. "In each case, a woman speaking American-accented English called the media outlet to claim responsibility. She promised a more detailed written statement soon."

"What do we say to the press?"

"Nothing, if possible; as little as we can, if we must. We've heard the claim of responsibility, but there is no evidence it's real. Like I said yesterday, there are nutcases everywhere, and that's the official line for now."

Outside her window, snow had begun to fall again.

Chapter 46

Curiosity dragged the old man unwillingly, and not without complaint from joints that were becoming stiff with age, to the edge of his property, but there was little to be seen. If this were a training facility for terrorists they were being damned quiet about it. The old farm house was visible from the tree line, and hours of patient watching revealed only a few occupants. Peering at them through his LRB 7 X 40 New Con laser range finder binoculars, he recognized the Russian-speaking man from Costco. There was another man, too, but he saw no sign of the woman.

Just for the sake of prudence, the old man set more perimeter alarms in the tree line above the farm house. Prudence was an important facet of his personality. Prudence kept people alive. For some it could be an excuse for doing nothing, for foregoing risk. Not so for the old man, but he had learned not to rush into things.

His ideas about the North Caucasus and the practitioners of Wahabi Islam there were not exactly politically correct, but it was entirely possible that this was a family group seeking only to escape the violence of their homeland and live in peace. If they were armed, it was likely an expression of well-founded caution and ingrained tradition. When this thought crossed his mind, the old man reminded himself with a curse that he did not believe in rainbows and unicorns.

*****

The first heavy snow arrived in late November. Hunting season was signaled by the annual appearance of camouflaged coveralls on the Valley men as they appeared in local shops or drove their pick-ups loaded with crated bear-hunting dogs that howled along the mountain roads. Bow season came and went quietly, followed by black powder season and finally by an all-out assault on the forest wildlife. The deer population was culled and many black bears did not make it back to their dens for the winter's hibernation. The people of the Valley were not bloodthirsty thrill killers. They depended on game to put meat on the table as much now as they had a hundred years ago.

The old man did not hunt. He had no desire to kill and he posted his own acres against hunting. The occasional black bear that lumbered past the cabin heading down the mountain to forage were objects of admiration rather than targets.

The snow fell from great, dark clouds invading as usual over the low peaks of the Appalachians from the south west, leaving a blanket of white silence over the forest and the Valley floor. Isolation was nearly complete, which suited the old man.

He celebrated the occasion by selecting an especially fine and rare Cuban *Hoyo de Monterey* double corona from his humidor and appreciatively caressed its tip with a long match. He stood at a window watching Sadie the Lab cavort in the snow outside. Satisfied that the tobacco was burning evenly, he decided a fresh pot of coffee would be a good idea and by the time the pot was brewing, Sadie had decided she wanted back into the warmth of the cabin. She stood quietly as the old man toweled off the snow and wiped her feet then shot into the kitchen and sat, tail thumping the floor, bright eyes fixed on the canister where the doggie treats were stored.

Night had fallen when the dog tensed, alerted by something only she heard. She pricked her ears and cocked her head before emitting a low, prolonged growl. The old man, who had closed his eyes long ago with his head resting against the back of the couch, soaking in the warmth of the fire that crackled in the stone hearth, put a hand on the Lab's head to calm her. An animal, perhaps a deer, had passed close to the house. The dog shook him off and leapt from the sofa to stand by the door where the growl turned into a frantic bark.

Annoyed, the old man rose and went to the door where Sadie continued her disturbance unabated.

Before he could decide whether to pull on some boots and a coat to go out and inspect, there was a weak knock at the door, really more like a scratch, accompanied by a voice. He couldn't make out the words. He flung open the door and a dark-haired young woman, clad much too lightly for the weather, stumbled against him and would have collapsed had he not caught her beneath her arms.

Sadie's barks now turned to solicitous whines, and she followed as her master half carried the visitor to the sofa in front of the fire. She was mumbling something unintelligible through lips turned blue and stiff with the cold. She wore only a nondescript dress with a man's light jacket over it. Her dark hair was wet with snow. On her feet was a pair of sturdy leather shoes several sizes too large for her.

He placed her on the sofa and went to the bedroom to gather a heavy, quilted comforter in which to wrap her and a towel to dry her hair.

His mind was racing. How had she gotten here

without setting off one of his perimeter alarms? The answer had to be that the sensors were covered with snow where she had passed them, and he mentally kicked himself for relaxing the entire day when he should have been out checking his security system.

What worried him was that she could have come from only one place -- the old turkey farm downslope. He wasn't sure what this might portend, but he did not think her arrival was a good sign.

He covered the woman's shivering form with the comforter and did his best to dry her hair while she stared at him with large, dark eyes. She was little more than a girl, not at all unattractive and was of no distinctive ethnicity. Any ambiguity in this regard, however, was immediately cleared up when she managed to pronounce her first intelligible words: "_Pomogi mnie._" Help me, in Russian. That left no doubt where she came from.

Switching to Russian, the old man asked, "Are you lost?"

She raised her eyes to him incredulously. This was a country of miracles where this cadaverous, bearded old man even spoke Russian!

She shrugged the comforter from around her shoulders and grasped the front of his checked flannel shirt. "We must leave now!" A hard light entered her eyes as she said this, but it was followed by a spasm of sobs. "They'll come after me."

This definitely ruined his day. The snow had stopped falling before noon, and the sky was clearing. The girl's tracks through the snow would be easy to follow even in moonlight.

"Slow down," he said, pushing her gently back onto the couch. "Who will come after you? Your friends? Are you lost?" He repeated the question because if she answered yes, things would become much less complicated.

"They are not my friends. They want to kill me."

The damned Wahabis! What the hell were they doing in Virginia?

He may not emerge as the winner in a long stand-off, besieged in his cabin. They had to get away before that happened.

Options available were limited because of the snow. He doubted he could drive out through it, and that meant that even if he called for help, no one could get up the treacherous mountain roads. But maybe the sturdy Land Rover could make it.

*****

The old man glared through the snow-obscured windshield at the unbroken expanse of white ahead. Even the sure-footed Land Rover was slipping as he drove at a snail's pace down the slope towards the gate at the main road. The deeply rutted trail from the cabin was invisible beneath at least two feet of snow, but he knew the way well.

Before they reached the gate, however, the snow resumed with reinvigorated fury, the wind driving the white stuff horizontally.

They weren't going anywhere.

The old man swore under his breath.

Carefully, he backed the Land Rover up the slope to the cabin. Curse words he hadn't uttered in years shouldered their way to the front of his brain.

The girl was alarmed. "We must leave this place."

"There's no way we're getting out of here for a long while. That's the bad news. The good news is that your friends will have a very hard time getting to us. That means no one will be able to take anyone anywhere until this storm is over."

She stared as if he were some alien creature, this lanky old man with long hair and a patchy white beard covering his cheeks and chin, slitted eyes, and gnarled hands. A man who spoke Russian like a native. A man with a past.

"You won't hand me over to them." It was both a statement and a question

Back at the cabin the generator had cranked to life indicating the power lines were down. The noise of the motor would signal their location. He stepped out of the Land Rover to close the garage doors against the gusting wind, and the dog leapt out after him and darted outside. Between the cabin and the garage she sank into snow already so deep that her head was barely inches above the surface. Apparently considering this to be an insult to her character and race, she barked sharply and plowed ahead toward the cabin door, undoubtedly wishing her master would decide whether he was coming or going.

They followed the dog inside. The fire still glowed. A few moments and some additional logs later, it was blazing again, and the girl stared into the flames.

She was startled when the old man shoved a glass of whiskey toward her and settled onto the sofa beside her.

"Drink this. It'll help," he rasped.

A tentative sniff told her the glass contained alcohol, strong alcohol, and she hesitated, eliciting a snort from the old man.

"You need something to warm you up and calm you down. Then you can tell me what the hell is going on. First, you can tell me your name."

She stared at him as though he had asked an incredibly difficult question and had to think hard about the answer.

After several seconds she said, "Olga. My name is Olga Polyanskaya."

Chapter 47

How much time? It was unlikely that trouble would not follow quickly on the girl's heels.

The problem was that he didn't know how much time he had before one or both of the men from the turkey farm would be knocking at his door, led there by the woman's tracks. They would have to come soon if they were to follow the tracks through the fast accumulating snow. If they were Chechens they were familiar with mountain terrain.

He told her to stay where she was and concentrate on keeping warm. "Don't be alarmed if you hear some loud noises."

She was not reassured when he opened his weapons cabinet to select what he would carry outside. He wasn't happy, but he was ready. He was always ready.

A short-barreled, suppressed M-4 fitted with night sights and his M&K .45 with extra magazines would serve, he decided. He pulled on fur-lined boots and a camo cover-all, shooting gloves, and shoved a cap with ear flaps onto his head before heading for the back door of the cabin.

If the men followed the woman's tracks they would not necessarily cover the rear of the cabin, and they had no idea who lived there. There was nothing in their experience that could have prepared them to meet the old man.

He slipped out the door and moved to the cover of the trees before circling to a position where he could observe the approach. Selecting a large oak tree, he settled behind the trunk to wait, his eye to the reticule of the night sight. Not as limber as he once had been, he realized he would be unable to move quickly once the shooting started -- if there was to be shooting.

There were two of them, just as the girl had said. They struggled up the slope through the snow following the tracks with a powerful flashlight. When they spotted the cabin both dropped to their knees and watched. There could be no doubt in their minds that this was the girl's destination.

Their manner suggested that these were experienced fighters, and after studying the cabin for several minutes they did what experienced fighters would do. They split up, one covering the back while the other cautiously made his way toward the front door. Whether the route the first man took would bring him across the old man's tracks was a crap shoot. He was approaching from a different direction than the old man had taken, and it was likely he would establish a position some distance from the house to guarantee a wide field of fire. The old man watched until he was out of sight. He automatically catalogued possible solutions to taking out the second man. Stalking a trained mountain fighter in the dark in the woods was a formidable task. Deception might be the better option.

The first man was now within a few steps of the front door moving stealthily. He held his weapon, the ubiquitous AK-47, at the ready. The Chechens were planning a down and dirty home invasion. Smash the front door, and if anyone tried to escape out the rear, the second guy would take them out. Simple.

The old man cherished his front door.

The Chechen mounted the front steps, his rifle at the ready. From inside Sadie's furious barking was audible. The Chechen raised his leg to kick the door in.

His leg never completed the action. The old man's hands did not tremble. His breathing was calm, his aim was true, his trigger pull smooth, born of a life-time of experience. A .223 round from the M-4 penetrated the Chechen's skull and rattled around inside his brain pan, turning the contents to mush. The man dropped instantly, his AK dropping silently from dead hands into the snow.

The question now was whether the second man would become curious enough about the lack of action that he would come to the front of the house to check on his companion. That would suit the old man, and the sooner the better. His knees were on fire from holding the cramped position behind the trunk of the oak.

The M-4's suppressor reduced the volume of its report to a sharp cough. The sound nonetheless would carry in the stillness of the forest, hopefully to be absorbed somewhat by the fallen snow. The old man decided not to move. He was not sure his knees would permit it in any case. He would wait it out. If the second man entered the house from the rear and found the girl, so be it. The Chechen would be faced with the decision of whether to kill her or try to return her to the turkey farm. Either eventuality was controllable. It was cold-blooded, but it was his only choice.

He cursed the girl for finding her way to his door.

The killing had only just begun. He waited as he scanned his field of fire through the night sight.

In the past adrenalin would be surging through his veins, energizing his body, bringing increased acuity to his vision and thought processes. The old man found it curious that on this occasion he experienced none of these things -- only the cold and the desire to get it over with, one way or another. Had he become so jaded that killing no longer elicited the same responses? He was about as excited as a carpenter preparing to drive another nail. This was dangerous. What was the old adage among spies? When you no longer feel fear or trepidation going into a clandestine operation, it's time to quit. There was no such thing as luck.

He got lucky.

The second man appeared around the side of the cabin, moving stealthily, rifle at the ready. When he saw his companion sprawled on the front stoop, he flattened himself to the ground and began to back pedal into the deeper shadow. The old man's first shot caught him in the shoulder, driving down through his clavicle, and he screamed in pain and rage. With his good arm he pointed his weapon toward the woods and sprayed bullets through the trees on full auto, shattering the night with the AK's distinctive chatter.

It's hard to control a weapon like the AK with one hand. The shots will march skyward with each recoil. The old man was not worried. He knew the man was firing blind. There was plenty of time to aim and fire a second time with the M-4. The bullet found his mark and scrambled a second Chechen brain to jelly.

And still he did not move. There could be another one out there somewhere in the woods, waiting for his chance.

But after twenty minutes his aching body no longer could tolerate the cramped position. When he tried to stand he found that his knees were locked, and he had to grasp the tree trunk with both hands to pull himself painfully to a standing position. Long ago, someone had told him that age would catch up, that it was time to retire and enjoy life. Well, damn it, he had retired, and just see what it had brought him now.

He slogged toward the cabin with short, old man steps, struggling against the snow until his joints warmed and locomotion became easier. The Lab was still barking and apparently doing his best to tear the door down from inside, and the old man spoke a few words to calm him. He rolled the Chechen's body down the steps from the stoop, cursing his diminished strength.

He found the girl huddled in the bathroom, her features distorted by fear and panic. She'd grabbed a kitchen knife which she held before her defensively, and it took her a moment to realize that he was not one of her pursuers. When she at last recognized him, she breathed "*Slava Bogu*" over and over as she grasped the old man around his aching knees.

He led her back to the living room and instructed her not to move. He had to go back outside for a while, but would be back shortly. The dog jumped onto the couch and settled herself against the visitor.

The first task was to hide the bodies. Fortunately, the snow made it easier to drag them behind the garage and heap some snow over them. The weather being what it was, the cadavers would freeze in short order.

Before covering them, he searched the Chechens but found no documents or other items that would identify them.

He thought they were safe for now. The girl assured him that no one other than the two dead men had been at the turkey farm.

After she had calmed down sufficiently, she was able to tell him her story. It had been a long time since he had heard anything that surprised him when it came to human depravity, but he needed a long drink when she finished.

He hoped the telephone lines were not down. He knew exactly who to call.

Chapter 48

The storm attacked Washington overnight and dumped over a foot snow on the capital. Krystal Murphy contemplated the view through her apartment window and cursed as a truck with a snow blade crawled down the street. She cursed because her parking lot had not been touched. She would have to call the office to send a squad car to pick her up.

It was ten A.M. by the time she reached headquarters, and her cellphone rang before she reached her desk. The caller ID told her it was an old friend, Bob Strachey. He had once worked for the CIA but was now a lobbyist in DC.

"Bob," she said, "how did you know I was back in town?"

"We saw you on TV. Amy says hi."

Amy was Strachey's wife. They probably wanted to invite her to dinner so they could hear all about her and Velazquez. She wondered what she would tell them.

"It's great to hear from you, but I'm afraid it'll be a while before we can get together. My plate is suddenly pretty full."

His tone switched from social to serious. "I can only guess, but that's what I'm calling about. I need to see you right away."

"What is it?"

"It's nothing I can talk about over the phone, but you'll want to hear it, believe me."

Strachey, she thought, would never outgrow the spookery of his former life.

"Bob," she said, "I really can't get away right

now."

"Dammit, Krystal, I wouldn't call you if it weren't important." He paused for a beat before adding, "I have information pertinent to what you're working on, and it's pretty urgent."

"Can you come to my office?"

"I don't think that would be a good idea. Listen, just meet me. I'll tell you what I know, and then it'll be up to you to take the next step."

"Sorry, Bob, it'll have to wait."

She was startled when Strachey raised his voice. "Murphy, drop your goddamned bullheadedness and get your Irish ass to the bar at the Mayflower at twelve noon. I'll be waiting for you. And I assure you that if you don't come, you'll regret it."

He closed the connection.

What the fuck? Who had put the wind up his ass? He had never spoken to her that way before. Murphy decided she'd better make the meeting at the Mayflower, although it would take her a solid hour or more to fight her way into DC and find a place to park. She decided to call Ferguson over at the FBI.

"Nothing has come in from Quantico yet, has it?" she asked, already knowing the answer.

"Only that they've identified the explosive as C-3, pretty common stuff, but it's more confirmation that we're dealing with terrorists. The lab is working 24/7. At best, we might learn something more late today."

"I'll be in town this afternoon," she said, "Can I stop by the Hoover Building to catch up?"

He agreed, and she headed for the parking lot and commandeered a heavy police cruiser for the drive downtown.

The few people who had ventured onto the roads were driving like demented Italian taxi drivers, and there was no place to park on streets piled high with plowed snow. Therefore, by the time she made it to the Mayflower after leaving the cruiser in a public garage and trudging four blocks through slush and falling snow, Murphy was in a black mood.

She found her friend sitting in the venerable hotel bar nursing a martini. Just shy of fifty, Strachey retained a rugged athleticism. His fashionably cut brown hair was just beginning to show some gray, and he was dressed impeccably in a dark blue suit, the standard uniform of the well-heeled "K" Street lobbyist.

He raised his glass to her. "Want one? You look like you need it."

She shrugged out of her Arlington Police parka and took a stool next to him. "A little early in the day, isn't it, Bob?"

His lips twisted into a wry smile. "It's after six o'clock somewhere. Can I buy you lunch?"

"That would be small repayment for making me come here, but I'll take you up on it."

They ordered sandwiches from the barman and headed to banquette along the wall in the back.

"I don't have time for small talk, Bob. What's this big deal you couldn't tell me on the phone?" Recalling his earlier outburst, she added, "And it better be good."

Strachey lowered his head in appropriate contrition. "Sorry about that, Krystal, but old habits die hard. I received a call this morning from an old friend.

Krystal allowed her impatience to show. "What's has this got to do with what I'm working on now?"

"I'm coming to that. It's about the Russians. I think I have a lead to the person who made those anonymous calls to the news services. If everything my friend told me is true, there is a definite Russian connection to your case, and probably a lot more."

That got her attention. "That doesn't make any sense."

"It wouldn't be the first time they've killed people outside of Russia. Remember Litvinenko."

"Yes, but this was mass murder, random violence. I don't see a Russian connection."

"Technically, the Litvinenko assassination was a Russian nuclear attack on British soil. That didn't make much sense either. I think they've gone completely off their nut in the Lubyanka. My friend isn't prone to fantasy or exaggeration. You need to talk to him."

Despite her doubts, Krystal was all too aware that every lead, however tenuous, had to be followed.

"When can I see your friend?" she asked.

"It'll take some doing. He's a long way from Washington, and there's the snow to contend with. But now that I have your attention, let me tell you the whole story."

Their sandwiches forgotten, Krystal listened in fascinated silence to the tale of a Russian girl and a gun battle at an isolated cabin in the Shenandoah Valley. When he was finished, she said, "That's simply unbelievable."

"Yeah, I know, but the old guy isn't a nutcase. His name is only whispered in the halls of Langley. You need to find a way to get to him and the girl before anything else happens."

She was still dubious, but Strachey was as serious as a heart attack. She said, "The Bureau has the lead on this case. I'll have to bring them in."

Strachey made a sour face. Old habits die

hard, and his generation of Agency officers had not enjoyed particularly good relations with the feebies. "The feds might not have enough imagination to take this seriously."

"No choice. And I know someone who will listen. But I'm surprised you didn't go straight to the Agency with this."

"Hells bells, Krystal, the way they're running that place now I doubt they'd know what to do any more than the feebies. And if even half of the story is true, this is nothing you want spread over half of Washington, and Langley leaks like a sieve."

"I'll do what I can."

Chapter 49

Krystal called Nick Ferguson from her car. She told him she would be at the Hoover Building in fifteen minutes.

She knew Ferguson would hate the idea, but the potential involvement of the Russians meant that Executive Assistant Director Enoch Whitehall should be brought into the case. She trusted Whitehall.

Ferguson met her in the lobby. "What's up? Do you have something solid?"

"Erm, maybe. But you might not like what I want to do with it."

Ferguson's winter pallor went a bit whiter at the mention of Whitehall's name.

"This is something he will have to decide," she concluded

"Nobody just walks in on Enoch Whitehall," he said. "It'll take hours even to get a request through to him. And you're supposed to be working for me and the JTTF, remember."

"That's not exactly correct. I'm in charge of liaison with the FBI on behalf of the Arlington County Police. That means I get to decide what part of the FBI I talk to."

That's right, she thought, vintage Krystal Murphy, adept at making enemies. She was almost sorry for Ferguson. The Special Agent was staring at her with a mixture of anger and astonishment.

She grabbed her cell phone from her belt and scrolled for a number Whitehall had given her a long time ago. She hoped it was still viable.

Ferguson continued to stare as the wise-ass

Arlington cop spoke her name into the phone, listened for a moment, mentioned Ferguson's name, nodded and ended the call. She flashed what might have been a triumphant smile and said, "We have an appointment on the third floor. Follow me."

A short elevator ride and a walk down a corridor via a route with which Murphy appeared familiar, brought them to a door with a brass plaque bearing the name of Enoch Whitehall, Executive Assistant Director for Counterintelligence.

Ferguson numbly followed Murphy through the door. This was a sacrosanct precinct that he had never before entered. The office belonged to a legend at the Bureau, a man about whom much was whispered, but few had seen. And now this local cop was leading him to meet the man behind the legend.

They entered an anteroom presided over by a dragon in the form of a woman of indeterminate age, and undeniable hostility that hinted at hidden super powers. She eyed them suspiciously from behind an enormous desk. Krystal knew that the woman's name was Jeanne. The hostility subsided when she recognized Krystal. But she lifted an eyebrow at Ferguson.

"It's OK," said Krystal, "he's with me."

He's with me? Wasn't this HIS headquarters building? Suddenly he was like a new kid on the first day of school, and he didn't like it one bit.

The dragon selected a button from a console and said, "They're here, Director Whitehall."

"Show them in."

The dragon pointed to a solid-looking door behind her.

Krystal pushed the door open with Ferguson hovering behind her and entered the Executive

Assistant Director's inner sanctum, the very air of which seemed redolent with intrigue. No one knew how long the spectral figure of Enoch Whitehall had been at the FBI. The only hint was a framed black and white photo of a much earlier version of the man shaking hands with J. Edgar Hoover. It was the sole adornment on the wall behind the work table that served as a desk.

Whitehall had not changed since the last time Krystal had spoken with him in this very office. He wore what might have been the same dark gray suit that hung from a cadaverous frame. If he had an aura, it would be gray to the point of disappearing into his surroundings. But when he turned his attention to you, the hatchet face with its blade of a nose and deep-set gray eyes, was mesmerizing, and undoubtedly frightening to evil-doers and subordinates alike.

Whitehall unfolded his body from behind the table and, like Dracula rising from his coffin, stood to greet them. "Detective Murphy, what brings you to see me?" The voice was surprisingly resonant for a man more wraith than substance. Murphy wondered if one day he might just fade into the ether and haunt the halls of the Hoover Building for eternity.

"Well, sir," Whitehall was the only person she would call sir without hesitation, and now that she stood before him, she wasn't certain how to begin. She silently cursed Strachey and simultaneously prayed he was not leading her on a wild goose chase. She finally found the words. "You know the case I," a quick glance at Ferguson, "I mean, we, are working on?"

"The incident at the Clarendon Metro. Of course, but that's not my turf, Krystal." An interrogatory eyebrow rose.

Ferguson experienced a small vindication, but then Murphy said, "I received information this morning that might change that."

Whitehall invited them to a small conference table in one corner of his office. "Go on," he said.

When she was finished no one said anything for several beats.

"That's very melodramatic," said Whitehall. "I understand why you would want to tell me about it, but you haven't determined whether this alleged Russian woman actually exists."

The admonition punched Krystal in the gut. Whitehall had never shown her anything but kindness and trust and had actively helped her in some tough situations when no one else was on her side. She had let him down.

Ferguson dropped his head to hide an involuntary smirk.

"But," the gray man said, "it does present some interest, however bizarre."

Krystal perked up. Ferguson lost his smirk.

Whitehall frowned slightly as though deciding how much to tell them. "The interest of which I speak centers on one of the victims of the bombing. His name was Mark Lvovich Shtayn, and he was a sharp thorn in the side of the Russians. In the 90's, Shtayn worked at a rather influential level in the Russian banking sector. Moscow was wild in those days, and Shtayn had an insider's view of just how absolutely corrupt the system under Yeltsin became, and how it continued and deepened under Putin. Putin was infamous for his loyalty to his former benefactor, Sobchak. The two had become wealthy together by diverting millions from projects in Leningrad. Yeltsin needed someone like this, and sure enough, as soon as Putin was elected, he gave Yeltsin and his family immunity from prosecution. Shtayn knew it all – collaboration with the mafia, graft, you name it. His death can only benefit the Kremlin. The assumption was that he was just unlucky, like the rest of the victims. Islamist terrorists have little interest in Russian defectors.

"But the Russians have kidnapped and murdered their enemies since the Bolshevik Revolution, and they've not changed their stripes. Even in their own country they've murdered journalists who refused to toe the Kremlin line and delved into forbidden subjects, like Shtayn."

"There is a lot of interest now in international money laundering, and this was something Shtayn told us about in private – yes, he was a source, but refused any payment. He was going public with what he knew about the dirty dealings of the Office of the President and Putin's circle of friends. So it's not surprising that they would target him for assassination."

Ferguson could not contain himself. "But, sir, isn't it unlikely they would try something on American soil? And previous assassinations have been carefully targeted on a single individual. This was mass murder. Such a plan would be insane."

"Yes, it most assuredly would be insane, but we must check it out nonetheless. Don't forget the Boston Marathon bombing. Despite what they claim, the Russians never warned us specifically, and I for one do not doubt that they were fully aware of the Tsarnaev brothers' plans.

"From what I've seen of late, there is no lack of the kind of arrogance and recklessness in Moscow that would stay a wiser, less desperate hand." He stood and cast a stern gaze over them. "Until we know more, you are to say nothing to anyone about this. As of this moment I'm declaring this a need to know matter. There are too many ears and too many wagging tongues in Washington to risk such a story getting to the public. I'm sure you must have realized that if true, such an outrage could bring about a crisis the likes of which we haven't seen since Cuba in 1962 or the Twin Towers in 2001."

Chapter 50

Ferguson commandeered a Humvee from the Bureau's motor pool, and he and Krystal set out on the 100-mile drive to the Shenandoah Valley less than an hour after the meeting with Whitehall. It was not a pleasant journey. Ferguson was sulky behind the wheel and made occasional snorting noises to indicate what he thought about Krystal's "lead." She remained silent, studying the map and instructions Strachey had given her at the Mayflower.

Strachey warned to approach the place carefully. Bob wanted to go with them, but both Ferguson and Whitehall had vetoed the idea. He would call ahead and advise his friend that they were on the way.

U.S. 66 and 81 were mostly clear of snow, and there was little traffic other than trucks as they barreled west and then south into the Shenandoah Valley. Once they got off the Interstate at Woodstock, it was a different story. Much more snow had fallen over the Appalachians. Conditions were worse on the unpaved road that brought them eventually to the cabin. Without the Humvee, the drive would have been impossible.

The entrance to the property was barely visible and barred by a metal gate. Neither Krystal nor Ferguson had boots fit for two-foot deep drifts, but he managed to get the gate open and drive through. Having been a farm girl, Krystal insisted he get out again and close the gate behind them. His face told her he was unenthusiastic about the task, but he obeyed nonetheless. Clearly, the Special Agent was not adjusting well to a subordinate role.

The cabin lay about three-quarters of a mile beyond the gate, around a sharp curve and up a steep grade. Heedful of Strachey's precautions, Ferguson sounded the Humvee's horn long before they reached the cabin.

A tall figure in a parka and a fur hat emerged from around the corner of the cabin with an ugly, military-style weapon aimed directly at them. "Don't make any sudden moves," Krystal said to Ferguson who was taking male umbrage at having a weapon pointed in his direction and reaching for his own.

She opened the door and stepped out into the snow with her hands away from her sides. "Bob Strachey sent us," she said.

The old man's stance did not change. "Who are you?" he asked.

"I'm Lieutenant Murphy of the Arlington County Police, and that's FBI Special Agent Ferguson behind the wheel."

"Tell your friend to get out of the car and keep his hands where I can see them. Then you can show me your credentials." The old man approached the Humvee carefully, taking slow steps in the deep snow.

Gritting his teeth, Ferguson stepped out of the Humvee and said, "Pointing a weapon at an FBI agent is a federal offense."

"Fuck the FBI," was the old man's prompt response. "I never had much use for Hoover's attack dogs. Now, move in front of the car to stand beside the young lady." He couldn't cover both of them from up close if they were on opposite sides of the wide Humvee.

They laid the documents on the hood and stood back. When he finished examining them, his voice turned to a low growl as he said, **"А сейчас, подонки, я вас убью."**

Krystal and Ferguson looked at one another. "What did he say?" asked the latter.

"I don't know, but it didn't sound friendly," she answered.

For the first time, the old man gave them a crooked grin and lowered his weapon. "Good," he said, "you don't speak Russian. I guess you're who you say you are." He eyed Krystal for a moment. "Young Strachey said you were a good-looking redhead. He didn't lie. Come on inside and let me introduce you to my guest."

But at the front door he paused and said, "I'd better show you something else first. Follow me."

He led them between the cabin and the garage to a pile of snow which he gave a good kick. When the snow fell away, they saw the face of a man whose departure from this life had been precipitated by a large hole in his head.

"There're two of 'em in there," said the old man. "It took two shots to take the other one down."

When Strachey told her about the two dead men it had seemed farfetched, yet here they were, dead as doornails. The weapon in the old man's hands was more than just a threat.

He kicked some snow back over the Chechen's face and led them again to the front door. The interior of the cabin was warm and inviting, definitely masculine with a lot of wood and leather and the scent of cigar smoke hovering in the air. A fire crackled in the fireplace and a yellow Lab stood in the middle of the room wagging her tail.

Divested of parka and hat, their host was tall and thin with long white hair and a short, scraggly beard. His eyes were sharp and intelligent. He wore jeans and a heavy turtleneck sweater. "There's a fresh pot of coffee on the stove if you'd like some. Take those coats off and make yourselves comfortable while I get the girl. She's scared out of her wits and very nervous, which is understandable after what she's been through. She's telling the truth to judge from the two assholes in the snow outside, and there are going to be several sleepless nights in Washington while the morons who run this country try to figure out what to do."

Olga was shaky. This was partly a natural reaction to shock and partly because running lightly clothed through the snow had left her with a bad cold and a fever. The uncontrollable shivering had diminished since the horrific events of the night before, but was giving way to despair. The two thugs who had taken her forcibly from her apartment were dead. The strange old man at least believed her story. In her hysteria she had at first feared that the Chechens would somehow rise again and break down the door, but now the fear was replaced by alarm of another sort.

There was nothing left of her life. She had no doubt that her captors acted on Karpov's orders and doubtless would have killed her had it not been for their drunken carelessness. Not a trace remained of the inspirational ideal of "the Motherland"; it had collapsed and died in the Metro explosion along with the other victims, and lay buried under the ruins of all her former convictions. Her friends and companions, members of a closely knit team had become her worst enemies, murderers, and she was in the hands of her former foes.

Exhausted, frightened to death, she had

absolute faith in the strange, dark old man to whom through wracking sobs she had poured out everything: "*Svoi,*" Solntsev, her American mission, Karpov and Shtayn, and even for some reason Vlad Illarionov and his father, and the apartment bombings in Moscow. She needed to confess, to somehow lift the weight of her guilt. The old man provided the outlet she needed.

The more she talked the more the pain and horror faded to be replaced by uncertainty. What would happen to her now? The old man had been patient and even sympathetic, at times asking perceptive questions. Afterwards, he went into another room where he remained for a long time.

When he returned she asked directly what would happen to her now. He took her by the shoulders. His face was kindly, but his voice was firm. "You must tell everything to the FBI."

The FBI? Her terror returned and she shook out of his grasp as though he had suddenly turned into a monster. The idea of the FBI aroused an instinct other than fear, an instinct born of her training in Russia, all the talks with Solntsev, and even with Karpov – the entirety of her experience over the past several years. This combination of letters pushed a button that launched a sense of uncompromising animosity. She couldn't tell such things to an enemy special service. It would be a kind of suicide.

"But they'll imprison me for espionage and taking part in a terrorist act! I can't ... Please ..." She stared at the old man in unfeigned anguish, but he remained adamant. The wheels were already in motion, and the authorities would arrive soon. She finally understood that she could do nothing and sank onto the sofa with no idea what might happen to her next.

Her revelation to the American of what she had done in his country left little hope for clemency. To escape from this godforsaken house was impossible, and she had nowhere to go in any event. Sooner or later Karpov would realize the Chechens had failed and send someone else to kill her. That was to be her fate. She had no friends in this country, and she was convinced that everyone she knew would gladly hand her back to Karpov if she asked for help. She could imagine how sleek Stash or slimy Petrov would run to the embassy to betray her in exactly the same way they had reported on Shtayn and other dissidents.

It was foolish to resist he American authorities. On the other hand, confessing to the FBI would mean life in prison, and the thought of a slow extinction behind bars was only slightly better than death. In spite of everything that had happened, she could not escape the notion that to tell all to yesterday's enemy would be a form of treason, and this she could not imagine. No matter how they had treated her, would it be possible for her to cross that line?

Somewhere deep inside glimmered a forlorn hope that Gleb Solntsev was unaware of Karpov's actions. What if it was a stupid independent decision of the Washington *rezidentura*? Gleb, Nastya, Boris Ivanovich – surely they could have nothing to do with what happened here. Would it be right to betray them, too?

The insane hope that she still had friends in Russia and that she must somehow get back home unexpectedly possessed her. In this empty world where not the slightest hope remained, the memories of something familiar and eternal were her only chance. These people might appreciate what she had done in refusing to be a part of Karpov's dirty work and understand that she had betrayed no one. In spite of everything, Gleb could save her.

Still consumed by these thoughts, she did not hear the arrival of the Humvee. But she was called back to the present by the old man's gruff challenge to the new arrivals. She couldn't make out the details of the verbal skirmish. Horrified, she rushed to the bedroom window but could see nothing.

She fell back onto the bed and curled up like a hunted animal. She was ashamed of her weakness and hysterics, for her excessive openness, her tears and her demeaning and useless pleas. How could she explain to the Americans what had happened without admitting her own guilt? How could she trust people who had so recently been her enemy?

Chapter 51

Vlad Illarionov was angry and impatient. His article on the Moscow apartment bombings was complete, the editorial board had approved its publication, but the Metro outrage knocked everything else out of the news. Several days passed with little or no official progress. There was a claim of responsibility that may well be specious. Homeland Security and the FBI were still studying the evidence, so press speculation ran the full spectrum.

Most of the stories by now concerned the victims and the families left behind. America was a strange place where mourning, sympathy, and pleas for unity came before rage and vows of revenge. Aside from a few publicity-seeking hotheads, no one was demanding the invasion of another country or "turning the desert to glass." The public debate was all about determining the truth before leaping to conclusions.

The Kremlin immediately offered condolences and solidarity in the face of international Islamist terrorism and issued a statement about its own struggle with terrorism. Given what Vlad knew, he could only scoff at such cynical opportunism. Every emanation from the Kremlin was aimed at advancing only the Kremlin's agenda.

The chance meeting with Olga Polyanskaya was a shock. His childhood fondness for her had curdled into sour loathing. He could not imagine what that lickspittle of Gleb Solntsev was doing in Washington. He was certain it was nothing good, and he vowed to look into it after his article was published.

Right now he hurried along the wet sidewalk

toward the *Washington Post* building on 'K' Street for a meeting with Ethan Holmes. The reporter's phone call a half-hour earlier was the first contact with Vlad since his article had been postponed. Maybe the day had come.

Holmes greeted him with a hearty handshake and a slap on the back. "We're going to publish your story in Sunday's paper on the op-ed page with a photo of your father. We'll have to compose a shorter version because of space allotments, but it'll cover all the main points. The full version will appear on our webpage, and we'll include excerpts from the recording of Tretyakov's confession along with translation."

He expected Vlad to be pleased.

"It will be published as an *opinion* piece rather than factual reporting?" Vlad didn't hide his disappointment. In his mind, the piece should be on the front page with a screaming headline – GLEB SOLNTSEV IS A MASS MURDERER.

"Calm down, Vlad. This is a very influential newspaper. It's read all over the world, and it'll be picked up by other news outlets. Believe me, it'll be big. I just hope you're prepared for the blow-back. There'll be a lot of that, even from Putin apologists here in the States."

"At least no one here will beat me to death and throw me in a ditch," replied Vlad, his voice embittered by the memory of discovering his father's body in Bittevskiy Park. The horror of that night seemed at once long ago and only yesterday.

Holmes grasped the significance of Vlad's rejoinder. It was almost physically painful to see such a young man so consumed by hatred. As gently as he could, he said, "No, Vlad. That's not likely to happen here.

Vlad controlled the anger that scorched and darkened his soul. The inescapable guilt for betraying his father's secret to Olga Polyanskaya was a cilice that pricked his conscience daily. It filled his thoughts with an oppressive blackness that colored even his joy at the impending revelation of one of the Kremlin's darkest secrets. Maybe he was no longer capable of happiness.

Chapter 52

The old man led an unsteady Olga, clutching one of his heavy terrycloth robes around her, into the living room where two strangers studied her with unconcealed curiosity. The man was barrel-chested and sturdy with black hair and piercing blue eyes. There was the shadow of a beard on his face. He was not dressed for the mountains, and his trouser legs and shoes were wet from the snow.

The woman was taller and older than Olga, with auburn hair and hazel eyes, wearing jeans and a sweater. She was quite attractive, but her demeanor was businesslike, and she wore a badge and pistol on her belt. Under the woman's steady gaze Olga was acutely aware of her own disheveled appearance. She must be the very image of guilt.

After an uncomfortable silence, the old man performed introductions. Olga's discomfort increased now that she actually faced the man from the FBI and the woman identified as a police officer. Why a police officer? Surely they meant to arrest her.

"Why don't you all take a seat by the fire," said the old man. With a meaningful look at Krystal and Ferguson, he added, "You need to get acquainted and explain why you're here." The first order of business was to build rapport with the subject of the interrogation.

He led Olga to the sofa, and the policewoman sat next to her. The old man and the FBI agent pulled up some chairs. Olga pulled to robe closer and sank her chin onto her chest.

Krystal had a plethora of experience dealing

with crime victims, and if she had ever seen a victim, this young woman was one. In the gentlest voice she could muster, she took Olga's hand in her own and said, "Olga, may I call you Olga? We're here to help you. We understand that you've been through a terrible experience, and all we want to do now is hear your story."

The policewoman's hand was warm on her own, and Olga resisted the urge to pull away. In her experience the police assumed a person was guilty and all their questions were intended only to prove that guilt. There was no threat in this woman's voice, but it could be a trick.

"Do you understand English?" Krystal asked.

Olga nodded mutely.

"Good. Can you tell us what happened, how and why you turned up here? We'd like to know about the two men, as well."

Mention of the Chechens brought back the horrors of her kidnapping and the terror of the night before. She could not prevent the fat tears that rolled down her cheeks. But she still said nothing.

Krystal turned to their host. "Do you know how to make a hot toddy? I think it would be a good thing."

The old man busied himself with honey, lemon, hot water, and a generous slug of whiskey. Olga accepted the steaming mug in both hands and sipped the sweet contents that began immediately to spread warmth throughout her body. Finally she was able to speak in a barely audible voice. "You're going to arrest me, aren't you?"

Given what Strachey's account of the girl's story, Krystal understood her fear. "No one is here to arrest you," she said. "You must believe me. If anything, you are a victim, and our only intention is to help you in any way possible. But we have to understand everything that happened. It's the only way we can protect you."

They expected her to say something. She *had* to say something, but what could she say without incriminating herself?

"Why don't we start with how you came to be here?" asked the policewoman. Did those men kidnap you?"

Yes, she had been taken by force. That was no crime. She could safely talk about that.

"Yes." The words in English came slowly. "They came to my apartment at night saying they were from the Embassy. When I opened the door they grabbed me. They tied my hands and gagged and blindfolded me, and carried me to their truck. When they removed the blindfold, I was in a dark room in that old house. When they left me alone, I managed to free myself and crawl out the window. I didn't know where I was or which way to go, so I just set off blindly toward the forest. After a while I saw a light and followed it here."

"Where is your apartment?" asked the policewoman.

"In Arlington, near the Clarendon Metro station." She immediately regretted mentioning the Metro.

Krystal and Ferguson locked eyes. The conversation was moving in the right direction.

"Why do you think these men kidnapped you?" It was Ferguson who asked the question.

"I ... I don't know." How could she tell them that this was the way the FSB handled unreliable people?

"That's not what you told our host last night, is

it?" There was an edge to Ferguson's voice now, and Krystal gave him a warning glance.

"Well," said Krystal, "whatever the reason, they're no longer a threat. Your apartment is in Arlington, and I work for the Arlington Police. You were kidnapped, and that makes it also a matter for Special Agent Ferguson here. We mean you no harm. We're only here to help."

When Olga said nothing, Krystal continued, "Last night you told our friend here that you work at the Russian-American Study Group in Washington. Would you like us to call them now?"

Call Zaretskiy? He undoubtedly would notify Karpov at the embassy. Her heart sank as the realization hit her that she could not go back. She could never go back. Karpov was FSB, and so was Gleb Solntsev. She no longer had friends in the FSB. Something broke inside, and like a piece of jetsam in a raging sea she was swept under alternating hot and cold waves until she drowned in blackness.

"She's fainted," said Krystal.

Ferguson carried Olga to the bedroom, and Krystal made sure she was comfortable before leaving her to rest.

"She's finally realized she has nothing to go back to in Russia," said the old man. "I've seen it before. She couldn't cope with it, so she just shut down."

"But she told you the whole story last night," objected Ferguson.

"She was in shock and wasn't thinking about what she was saying. Eventually, she'll make peace with the situation, but right now it's like she's being dragged over hot coals and the pain is too much to bear." The old man smiled crookedly at Krystal, "That was a very clever question, Lieutenant."

"I didn't expect her to faint," said Krystal.

"There are two frozen dead guys outside," said Ferguson. "And you shot 'em. Kidnappers or not, it doesn't look like you gave 'em much of a chance."

"That's how you stay alive, son."

"Nevertheless, there has to be an investigation to sort all this out. I think a good place to start is to have a forensics team go over that old farmhouse down the mountain."

"Let's not get ahead of ourselves," said Krystal. "We have to call Whitehall first."

"What about the JTTF and Homeland?"

"Hey, Nick, you're the FBI guy here, remember? Anything that happens from here on should be Whitehall's decision."

He couldn't argue with her and wondered if anyone could.

Chapter 53

At seven AM, Gleb Solntsev was stirred out of sleep by the telephone. The caller was Assistant Administrative Director of the office of the President of Russia, Oleg Verbin. No one of that rank had ever called so early before, and it did not bode well.

"Yes, Oleg Mikhailovich, I'm listening." Solntsev struggled to erase the sleep from his voice.

"I want to hear what *you* have to say." Verbin's voice was rough. "How do you explain all this?"

"What are you talking about?" His lungs were squeezed by a nauseating chill.

"Fuck me, but he doesn't know!" exclaimed Verbin, loading his words with the entire weight of Solntsev's fall from grace. "Well, now you'll find out what it means to wake up famous. While you slept you became the main subject of conversation in the States. The *Washington Post* published an article devoted entirely to you."

"*The Washington Post?*"

"Yes, exactly. They say it was you who organized the apartment bombings in Moscow fifteen years ago and that you've created a destructive cult in the guise of a youth organization that has a secret team of 'special operatives' for 'wet work,' hooliganism, beatings, and murders. They speculate that you ordered your 'death squad' to kill the journalist Sergey Illarionov because he planned to reveal the truth about you. Do you want to hear more?"

He didn't reply. The premonition of a moment ago was replaced by a terrible thought, even a certainty. That damned punk! It could only be him.

But how could he have made it to America and gained access to a publication of such importance? How could they have believed such a worthless youngster?

"The article concludes by asking if it is possible that the President of the country knew nothing about the actions of a member of his own administration. By morning the article was being discussed on CNN by their talking heads and politicians," added Verbin.

Was there a hint of malevolence in his boss's voice? But that would be only logical – if there was a scandal, Verbin would be threatened no less than he. His head was spinning. *The Washington Post.* CNN. A fifteen-year-old crime. Illarionov's murder. What a nightmare.

This couldn't just have happened. There had to be a lot of money behind such a huge maneuver – that's the way it works in Russia. Big media information campaigns against individuals are mounted only on direct orders from "on high." Huge sums are paid out of the federal budget, and "journalists" base everything on a Kremlin script. Solntsev couldn't think of any other way it would work. Who in Washington would launch a campaign of persecution against a mid-level Russian official? Could it be some powerful enemy here who did business with the West? But who? Even worse, had the President made some sort of deal with the damned Yankees, and decided to sacrifice him, Solntsev, like so much small change? If it was like that, he was finished.

"There was a young man." He had to be careful, try to dig a little deeper to discover how high up and from which quarter he should expect the most trouble. "Just a kid who should now be dead. It's not my fault that he got away. It was up to someone else, real specialists, and it's them you should be sorting out. The boy had a recording, the evidence of another man who accused me of the Moscow explosions. But that man was a criminal, a prisoner already in jail, and he's no longer among the living. His word means nothing ..."

"Whatever his word means, you'll have to explain it." Verbin delivered his message with calculated brutality. "They'll be waiting for you today at eleven AM at *Ilinka*[13]. We'll listen to your explanations and suggestions about how to cope with the situation. And don't dare be late – immediately after the meeting I'll be sending a report to the Kremlin."

"I understand."

Verbin closed the connection.

What time was it? A quarter to eight. There was still time to drop by the Lubyanka. It was only a short distance from there to *Ilinka*. Lisitsyn habitually arrived early, sometimes at dawn, but just in case he made a call.

"Nikolay Davydovich? It's Gleb."

"Yes?" There was nothing that could be read in the general's voice. *He knows everything already.* "May I come see you right now?"

"Come ahead."

Solntsev lived in a pre-revolutionary house at the intersection of *Petrovka* Street and *Kuznetskiy Most*. The windows overlooked a pedestrian street that was lined on both sides in summer with café tables

---

[13] *Главное управление специальных программ Президента Российской Федерации* – General Directorate of Special Programs of the President of the Russian Federation is located at Staraya Square, 2/14, Ulitsa Ilinka in Moscow.

adorned with umbrellas. Down the center was a line of old-fashioned street lamps and orderly beds of flowers. But in the gray pre-dawn the familiar street offered no comfort. He decided to walk to the Lubyanka. He turned up the collar of his winter coat and nearly ran to the intersection with *Petrovka* before entering the wider *Kuznetskiy Most*.

He had always loved old Moscow. The city was as much a part of him as he of it. He loved the columns and stucco cornices of her low-rise buildings – squat and massive, with strong walls and high ceilings. He loved her dark, twisting alleys that opened suddenly into broad avenues. His entire life, and his work, too, had been like that: twisting, shadowy, hidden from prying eyes by the massive masonry of thick walls that finally opened to reveal the spacious and brightly lit thoroughfare leading to Olympian glory. Although, truth be told, the sort of fame that visited him now he wouldn't wish on anybody.

He turned into *Neglinnaya*, a wider and more heavily inhabited street than *Kuznetskiy Most*, and hurried past GUM. There was much that was unclear. How had Vlad Illarionov succeeded without connections, money, influential protectors? Solntsev didn't doubt that someone else was behind it, but he had no idea who it might be.

Panic was unnatural to him. Fear had the power to paralyze the mind and will, to confuse. He'd been trained never to lose the capacity to think clearly and logically in high stress situations. He should be able to find a way out of any situation. But now his very ignorance of what was really happening interfered with his analytical ability, and despite everything such powerlessness gave birth to irrational fear.

He entered *Teatralniy Proyezd*, a broad, majestic avenue that gave onto Lubyanka Square. FSB Headquarters was already visible ahead, but this time, the yellow façade promised no surcease.

Lisitsyn was waiting for him, and when Gleb entered his office, the old man's face did not radiate its accustomed welcome, not in the slightest. The general was absolutely opaque. He simply rose from his desk with an unblinking stare.

There was no invitation to sit. Gleb returned his mentor's gaze. "How could this have happened?"

Instead of answering, Lisitsyn asked, "You've already seen it?"

"No. Not yet. There was no time. I came here immediately. I'm to report to the Administration in a couple of hours."

"I'm aware." Lisitsyn's voice was quiet, and he extended a newspaper clipping. "Here, read it."

Gleb took a seat and read quickly through the clipping, his mood turning darker with every word. "How could this have happened?" he repeated. "I mean, how did he get away from your people alive? How did he get to the States? Who the hell helped him? Why me? Why now?"

Lisitsyn drummed his fingers on the polished surface of the desk before speaking. "Do you think it's a political plot of some kind? I don't think so. Over the past few years you've been too distracted by politics. You thought only about power. You forgot what we taught you and everything to which you intended to devote your life. In the real world not everything is determined by backstage intrigues. This," he pointed at the clipping, "may be the work of an intelligence organization. You didn't even think of that, did you? You may have forgotten about its existence, but that doesn't make it go away. Your little 'punk' may well have contacted the CIA – that would be typical of money-hungry traitors like him. He associated with trash his entire life. If the Americans are behind this, it would explain everything."

"Maybe." Gleb didn't hide his relief. The worst danger, that he had been betrayed by his own people, faded in the face of the dread CIA. There was likely no Kremlin plot against him. "So that means it's not my fault. Your people were supposed to take care of Illarionov's kid. They let him get away. I did my part."

"It's not a matter of guilt." Lisitsyn said in a tone that made Gleb raise his head in alarm.

"Gleb," began the general forcefully, "you were always my favorite student, and you know how much I value you. I always thought you learned your lessons well. When you joined our service, when you took your oath, even while you were still in the Academy you knew the rules. Our work demands complete selflessness for the good of the Motherland, including readiness to sacrifice your life for her sake. There is no place for pointing fingers or speculating on guilt. We taught you from the beginning that in espionage work and counter-espionage anything can happen."

He went silent again as Gleb grimaced with irritation. What was the use of all this pompous flummery?

Lisitsyn continued, "Once, the GRU had a wonderful illegal officer, Captain Marya Dobrova, pseudonym Maisie. Her case officer was one of the worst traitors in our history, Dmitriy Polyakov. One of his first treasonous acts was to betray Maisie to the Americans. FBI agents visited her at her hotel and tried to recruit her. And what do you think she did? She leapt from a window and killed herself. She didn't ask who was guilty, although she was in no way responsible for the compromise."

"Nikolay Davydovich, drop the pathos. What's your point?"

"The point, my dear Gleb, is that if necessary you must accept all the guilt. Admit it was on your own initiative to organize the apartment bombings. You did it to strengthen the role of the FSB inside the Russian system. You must say the Kremlin knew absolutely nothing about your actions then and nothing about your "Svoi" death squad now. You must be prepared to be arrested, be subject to a public trial followed by one of the penal colonies. But don't be alarmed – of course, no one will demand that you sit out your entire sentence. After a few years, when things have calmed down, you'll be quietly set free to live out your life in peace and prosperity. We'll give you a new name and appearance. We'll never forget your sacrifice."

Gleb was on his feet, shouting. "Arrest? A penal colony? Public opprobrium?" He couldn't believe what he was hearing. "Nikolay Davydovich, I'm no longer a junior lieutenant ready to dive under a tank with a grenade. I'm ... an official of the Presidential Administration. I'm responsible for youth work and must be an example for them. What you propose would sink not only me but everything I've created."

"You're a Chekist, Gleb." The appellation of which Gleb had been so proud now returned to haunt him. "You gave an oath and swore to be loyal to this country to the very end. You wore the epaulets. And now the country demands this sacrifice for the common good and stability. Did you think that serving the Motherland only meant going to receptions at the Kremlin Palace? No, Gleb, your brother officers serve under much worse circumstances than you. Besides, I'm not demanding anything extraordinary. Yes, your reputation will be ruined, and you can forget about a political career, but these are small things. In no time you will be free and rich. And we will get our revenge. I give my word as an officer that we'll track down young Illarionov, even in the States. We have reliable and capable people to do this from one of the East European countries. They never lived in Russia, so there can be no connection to you or us. You'll just have to be a little patient."

"No, I won't be patient." Gleb couldn't hold back the words as his emotions exploded. "I didn't serve the country for so many years for this – to have my life ruined because *your* people couldn't take care of a twenty-something kid. If the omnipresent CIA magically appeared from somewhere, no one from your great organization was capable of stopping them. I'll never take the blame for everybody, Nikolay Davydovich. Never! Of course, I would never mention *Himself*," he raised a finger toward the ceiling. "But if they come after me, if they resort to an arrest, I'll name every high-ranking general that was in charge of the operation – the whole bunch, right to the top."

He was panting with rage now. "Don't you understand how much I've accomplished, how much more I could do? I'm better at this than anyone else. I'm not a simple functionary to my people. I'm their god! They would follow me through fire and water. I can do whatever I like with them – send them to fight in the Donbas or kill liberals in courtyards. Only I can do this. Explain that upstairs. Find someone else, some decrepit colonel who's outlived his usefulness and put it all on his head."

"You were named in the article," intoned the general. "A new Cold War already has begun. The West wants blood – *your* blood. I'm sorry it turned out this way."

"I won't do it. I won't take the blame for everything. I'm no mere pawn to be sacrificed. When I took that job I was promised protection. If they come after me, I swear I'll name everybody."

He turned on his heel and stormed out of the office, slamming the door behind him.

The old general spoke sadly to the empty room. "I'm sorry, Gleb, very sorry. You've understood nothing I taught you. It's a shame things have come to this, but you leave me no choice, my boy. I hope you know that I spoke truthfully when I promised to avenge you ..."

The telephone receiver felt like a heavy weight when he lifted it.

Chapter 54

They were all there, gathered around the conference table in Enoch Whitehall's office. Krystal Murphy, Nick Ferguson, Bob Strachey, and the President's National Security Advisor Duane Claiborne. Whitehall had provided formal non-disclosure agreements for Krystal and Strachey to sign. These agreements, known as NDA's, were *de rigeur* for employees of Washington's three letter agencies. Everyone in the room but she and Strachey had up to date NDA's. Their purpose was to bind them to strict secrecy, and to violate them was a criminal offense.

The formalities complete, Whitehall said, "We are part of an exceedingly small group who know the truth behind the Clarendon Metro outrage. Although Mr. Strachey currently holds no official government position, his knowledge of the truth is why he is here.

"The drama that took place in Shenandoah County and everything that led up to it are well-documented, thanks to the fine work of Krystal and Nick in debriefing Olga Polyanskaya. It was not an easy interview for either side, but the young lady finally realized that she had no choice other than to cooperate. As you know, Polyanskaya will be placed in the witness protection program and relocated within the United States under a new identity. She is under severe psychological strain, and we'll see that she gets the proper help. The U.S. Marshals Service will keep a close eye on her.

"Our forensic specialists discovered ample evidence in the Shenandoah farmhouse that the two deceased men were involved in the Metro bombing, including traces of explosive and bomb-making materials. This makes it possible for us to inform the public that the Metro investigation has been concluded and that the attack was the work of renegade Chechen Islamists, much like the Boston Marathon tragedy."

Krystal wasn't sure she had heard correctly, and her look of consternation caught Whitehall's attention. He continued, "The concept of 'need to know' is new to some of you, but it is an important part of national security. Despite what the media think, there are some things best kept secret, and at times it is better to hide the truth from the public. This is such an instance. Yes, Polyanskaya related her experience, both in Russia and here in Washington with the FSB. The account of her conversation with Valeriy Eduardovich Karpov was chilling and laid responsibility for the bombing directly on the Kremlin's doorstep. But in reality, her testimony is second-hand, what would be called 'hearsay' in a court of law. Given Karpov's diplomatic immunity, the certainty that Moscow would never divest him of it, and the deaths of the two perpetrators, there is nothing we could legally do. But the important thing to keep in mind is that if word that Moscow was behind the bombing were to be made public, it would amount to a *casus belli*, and the Administration would find itself in a ticklish situation."

Whitehall turned to Claiborne for confirmation.

"We have the means to let the Kremlin know that we are aware of what really happened," said the White House advisor. "It's a club we can hold over their heads. We'll also be expelling Karpov and refusing to permit the Russians to replace him. Given that he oversaw a debacle, we suspect that Karpov will not be received kindly at home. If he should ask for asylum here, we will see that he is carried kicking and screaming on board a Russian flight to Moscow. We have no use for him."

The atmosphere was more rarified than anything Krystal had ever experienced. This was how the real business of Washington was done, and she wasn't sure she ever wanted another glimpse. Her black and white world abhorred gray, and this was as gray as it gets. Across the table from her Whitehall was grayness personified. How many more dark secrets did he hold?

*****

Ethan Holmes called Vlad Illarionov to another meeting at the *Washington Post*. The reporter was smiling broadly. "Vlad, I don't know exactly what's going on, but the White House called the editor this morning and praised your piece on the Moscow bombings. Given the Administration's efforts to make peace with the Kremlin, this is somewhat surprising. The National Security Advisor himself told us that the White House would very much like to see a string of similar stories about the situation in Russia. We'd like to give that assignment to you."

Vlad was at a loss. "But I'm only here on a temporary visa. I'm not allowed to have a real job ..."

Holmes was still smiling. "That's the other thing I don't understand, but it appears you have a friend somewhere in high places. They said that if you asked, you would be granted political asylum immediately."

Chapter 55

Gleb Solntsev was hunched over his desk at the office on *Sretenka* Street. He had issued his ultimatum, and now he would gather his troops. They would present a solid front, guided by his iron will. There was nothing his enemies could do about it. He knew too much about their dirty laundry to dare.

He raised his head as Pasha led Kostya and Volodya through the door. No one would get to him through these three. He walked around the desk to greet them. The personal touch never failed.

But instead of taking his extended hand, Pasha grabbed him and swung him around trapping his arms at his side. There was a yellow gleam in the big man's eyes that Solntsev belatedly recognized as the first blow landed.

THE END

Michael R. Davidson was raised in the Mid-West. Heeding President Kennedy's call for more young Americans to learn Russian he studied the language, and military service took him to the White House where he served as translator for the Moscow-Washington "Hotline." His language abilities attracted the attention of the Central Intelligence Agency, and following his military service Mr. Davidson spent the next 28 years as a Clandestine Services officer. Seventeen of those years were spent abroad in a variety of sensitive posts working against the Soviet Union and the Warsaw Pact. In the private sector he worked as a business owner and security and economic development consultant before devoting full time to his writing.

Kseniya Kirillova is a Russian journalist who focuses on analyzing Russian society, political processes in modern Russia and the Russian-Ukrainian conflict. She writes for Radio Liberty and other outlets and is an expert of the Center for Army, Conversion, and Disarmament Studies and the Free Russia Foundation.

Also by Michael R. Davidson

The RESURRECTION Series

Did the Cold War end or did the KGB find a way to retain its power and dominate the new Russian Federation? "Harry's Rules" is an espionage thriller set against the backdrop of post-Soviet Russia in the early 1990's.

Who killed President John F. Kennedy? A long buried secret that could change the course of history draws murder to a quiet Washington suburb. Only an exiled CIA officer can solve a mystery that both the White House and the Kremlin will protect at all costs.

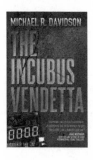

Revenge is said to be a dish best served cold. A suicide bomber and a serial killer are the instruments chosen by a deposed Russian president.

But his targets are anything but helpless.

Find them all at: www.michaelrdavidson.com
All books also available at Amazon.com

THE CALIPHATE SERIES

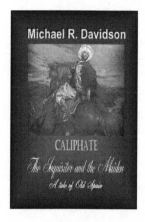

THE INQUISITOR AND THE MAIDEN - Disillusioned by Spain's falling fortunes in the 30-Years-War, Eduardo Macías returns home. His reputation as a valorous soldier wins him the position of Captain of the Santa Hermandad, a Spanish force charged with protecting the people and maintaining the law. He is forced to accept a mission by officials of the Holy Inquisition to investigate a charge of heresy against a nobleman with royal ties. What he discovers places Eduardo at odds with the Inquisition, and he must decide between honor and excommunication.

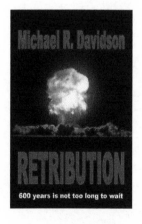

RETRIBUTION – The saga that began in 1492 continues into the turbulent present. An ancient enemy threatens the world with nuclear terror, and CIA officer Robert Strachey and his friend Spanish Police inspector Alberto Macías find themselves in a race against time to avert a holocaust.

Find them all at: www.michaelrdavidson.com
All books also available at Amazon.com

KRYSTAL - **Sassy** Detective Krystal Murphy who appeared in INCUBUS and THE INCUBUS VENDETTA at last gets her own novel.

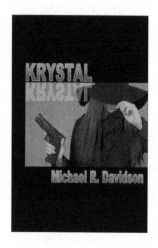

A controversial Miami judge is murdered in a Washington hotel room. Homicide detective Krystal Murphy identifies an ideal suspect, a person with motive and opportunity. Following the suspect's trail to Miami, she is confronted by an unspeakable tragedy that leaves her prime suspect dead. Convinced her initial instincts were wrong and driven by guilt, she teams with a Miami detective to continue the investigation. But she encounters unexpected opposition from her own superiors who want only to call the case closed. While coping with her own personal tragedy and under great pressure from her superiors, Krystal doggedly pursues the case with the help a new ally and perhaps more than just a friend, the Miami detective. When more people associated with the case begin turning up dead, Krystal finds herself in a race against time before she herself becomes the next victim of an increasingly desperate killer.

Find them all at: www.michaelrdavidson.com
All books also available at Amazon.com

Made in the USA
Middletown, DE
14 December 2016